Relentless Love

HEATHER GREER

Faith, Hope, and Love Series - Book One

Scrivenings
PRESS LLC

Published by Scrivenings Press LLC
15 Lucky Lane
Morrilton, Arkansas 72110
https://ScriveningsPress.com

Printed in the United States of America

Paperback ISBN 978-1-64917-007-1

eBook ISBN 978-1-64917-008-8

Library of Congress Control Number: 2020939901

Cover by Diane Turpin, www.dianeturpindesigns.com

(Note: This book was previously published by Mantle Rock Publishing LLC and was re-published when MRP was acquired by Scrivenings Press LLC in 2020.)

All characters are fictional, and any resemblance to real people, either factional or historical, is purely coincidental.

For Grandma Forby who faithfully shared God's love with family, friends, and strangers alike. May we all be as dedicated to living out His love in our everyday lives.

"And now abide faith, hope, love, these three; but the greatest of these is love." 1 Corinthians 13:13

Becky!
May you know and experience God's great love for you every day!
Heather Greer

Acknowledgments

I always want to give God thanks for allowing me to minister to others through something I love doing. His choice to use His people, even with their failures and flaws, to reach out to others is one more blessing in a long list of blessings He gives to His children.

Thank you to my family. You're always in my corner, cheering me on.

Thank you to those who help me grow as a writer including the Mantle Rock Publishing and Scrivenings Press teams, everyone in the Carbondale Christian Writer's Group, and the Once Upon A Page girls.

And special thanks to Jason who patiently answered every question I had, no matter how simple they might have seemed, about proper riding etiquette and terminology.

Chapter One

"He'd be as happy as a flea in a doghouse if you'd just let him stay with me."

Frustration rose as the familiar argument resurfaced for what seemed like the hundredth time in the last two months. Katie Blake silently counted to ten before addressing her father. "Sammy needs time with other children, and he'll be happy there. There's no need to worry."

Her elderly father paced back and forth across the living room coming to rest at the fireplace. He pounded his fist down on the mantle. "I'm not worried. But this is his home. And he's only three years old."

She couldn't have stopped the eye roll if she wanted to. She only hoped he didn't see it. "I'm sending him to K3, not boarding school."

"But you don't have to do that. I can take care of my grandson while you're out doing whatever it is you think you've got to do. Think of all the money you'd save."

"I'm not concerned about the money. Austin took care of us."

Cal shook a boney finger at her. "Then why are you putting

Sammy in one of those daycare things? You're his mother. He can stay with you now and socialize in kindergarten."

She ran a hand through her auburn curls, winding one between her fingers. She had her reasons. None of them were finalized though, and she refused to get into them with her dad until they were. "You know why. Sammy will be three this weekend. Austin's been gone for almost three and a half years. My only focus in all this time has been Sammy. I love being that little boy's mom. He means everything to me. But it's time I branch out a little. I've thought about this for a long time, and I've prayed about it too. I have peace this is what God wants."

His already stooped shoulders sagged further. "Fine. But what am I supposed to do while you and Sammy are away every day?"

He looked so lost Katie had to blink back tears. The thought of giving in and staying home nagged. In her heart, she knew she couldn't. Cal moved around fine for someone in his late eighties, but Sammy was an energetic little boy. There was no way her father could keep up with him all day, every day. Besides, the fog that surrounded his mind at various times came with more frequency these days. While she didn't feel it was anything out of the ordinary for someone his age, it didn't lend itself to taking care of a small child day in and day out.

She dropped onto the couch. Resting her forearms on her legs she looked up at the man who'd been her rock since the day she was born. He'd lost the only woman he'd ever loved when her mom died right before Sammy was born. Not long after, she and Sammy moved back to her childhood home. They needed each other after so much loss. She and Sammy became his world. It was no wonder he was struggling with the change.

"I don't know, Dad. All I know for sure is I have to do this. It'll be good for Sammy. And it will be good for me. We'll make sure it's good for you too. I don't know how yet, but please, please don't fight me on this anymore."

Doubt flared in his eyes. Katie tensed, sucking in a breath. Finally, his head lowered in a nod of acquiescence. "Fine. Sammy will have his school. And you'll be free to chase after whatever it is you're chasing after. Don't you worry about your old dad. I'll make it just fine. We all will."

An hour later, taking Sammy's small hand in hers, the doubts Katie had kept locked away rushed to the surface. She watched him take in the colorful daycare building with big, pale green eyes that looked like his daddy's. She put her shoulders back and forced a smile. "Doesn't this look fun?"

His little hand tugged back when she stepped toward the entrance. She glanced down to find his bottom lip tucked between tiny teeth. She knelt beside him and waited for him to look at her. "You okay, buddy?"

"I want you, Mommy. Can I go with you?"

Her heart ached. She'd never pushed him into anything like this before. She'd kept him close and been with him every day of his life. It was probably part of the reason he could verbalize his displeasure almost as clearly as an adult. He'd spent almost all his time around adults. Could she do this any easier than he could? He was all she had left of Austin. Could she let that go for eight hours every day?

She inhaled the cold February air, feeling it like a thousand needles pricking her lungs. Despite the discomfort, it left her more focused and determined. She could do this. She needed to do this. There wouldn't be a better time.

"We talked about this. You'll be starting school like a big boy while I do big people things like work."

"I can work too. I'll be a big helper."

His earnest expression was adorable on its own. But with his puffy blue winter coat zipped up under his chin and the hood framing his face he looked like a frozen Stay Puft marshmallow man. She fought the giggle trying to escape. Her son was serious. She needed to be as well.

3

"I know you're a great helper Sammy. But at school, you'll get to play and make new friends. It'll be fun. How about we pray for God to bring you a new friend?"

His strawberry blond head nodded, though his eyes were wide and his lips puckered.

"God, please help Sammy find a new friend today. He knows You're with him all the time, but he'd like someone to play with too. Amen." She smiled at her son. "Now, are you ready to go find that new friend?"

He looked less than convinced. There was no helping it. Katie led them into the school and down the hall to Miss Connie's class. Spying the colorful walls and shelves of toys and books, Sammy's wary expression became a little less guarded. Before the teacher could make her way across the room to greet them, a jumper-wearing little girl hopped from her spot in the block area to stand in front of Sammy. Her curly blonde pigtails bounced with each movement.

She used one index finger to push up the glasses that slid down her button nose before extending it toward Sammy. "Hi. Who are you?"

Sammy glanced down at the pudgy finger pressed into his chest. "Sammy."

"Let's play blocks, Sammy."

Katie watched in amazement as the nameless little girl captured her son's attention and led him to the blocks. Together they flopped onto their knees and began building.

She moved to help him remove his coat. Without taking his attention from the blocks he stacked, Sammy slipped his arms from the sleeves. "I'll be back later to pick you up. I love you, Sammy."

"Bye."

She hung his coat under the hook on the wall with his name written above it on a cut-out dinosaur. She needed to leave but couldn't make her feet obey her brain. He hadn't even looked at her when he said good-bye. And he hadn't expressed his love for her. Maybe she should stay a little longer.

"It gets easier every day."

Katie found Miss Connie observing her. The lady, who had a benign fifties look, meant well. She even seemed to have a good handle on her classroom, if the well-stocked, cheery room was any indication. But Katie didn't need reassurance that Sammy would do well. "I think he's doing okay. He already seems to have made a friend."

She smiled. "Oh, yes, Sammy's going to be fine. But I wasn't referring to Sammy. I was talking about you. Letting go for the first time can be hard on mothers."

Maybe Miss Connie was more astute than she gave her credit for. Why shouldn't she be wary of leaving her son? He'd been by her side since the day he was born. But Erin and Paul were waiting with the realtor she'd contacted. She'd found the perfect space to become the home of the Christian bookstore she was going to open, and she valued their opinions of the site. She flicked a glance at the teacher still standing beside her. "I think I'll just go make sure he's settled and then take off."

Miss Connie's hand touched her forearm as she shook her head. "It's better if you don't. Look at him." She waited until Katie followed her directions. "You've already said good-bye. He's playing without another thought about you leaving. If you interrupt now, chances are good he'll get upset. And he'll do it because he senses you're upset. Trust me. Sammy is going to make it through this day splendidly, and you will too."

Katie looked from her son to the teacher and back again. He did appear settled. She didn't want to jeopardize his mood. She shrugged as if there wasn't a tug-of-war going on in her mind. "You're right. I'll see you and Sammy at five."

～

KATIE WAITED until the door closed behind the realtor. She spun around with her arms stretched wide and a smile on her face. "So what do you think? It's perfect. Right?"

Her arms fell to her sides. Paul looked at Erin without shifting his face away from Katie. Katie glanced at Erin who seemed fascinated with the pattern of the carpet. A tight feeling landed squarely in her middle. Erin always had something positive to say. Excitement over each new idea oozed from her pores. Now she had nothing to say? She couldn't even look at Katie?

Katie refused to ease the silent burden her friends carried. They obviously had something to say, and they felt like Katie wouldn't want to hear it. Otherwise why the worried faces and refusal to speak?

Paul shifted from one foot to the other. He cleared his throat and made eye contact. Katie lifted her eyebrows and waited.

"You're heart isn't in it."

Frowning, Katie stared at Paul. "What do you mean my heart's not in it? It's a book store. It's the dream I went to school to follow. How can my heart not be in it?"

Paul opened his mouth but closed it again when Erin laid her hand on his forearm. Katie moved her attention from him to his wife, her best friend. "I know you don't want to hear this, but it's true. We understand you went to school to open a bookstore, and you did. Pages was a great success. It's still a success with Paul owning it. But that doesn't mean it's what you're supposed to do now."

Katie eyed the space around them. She could picture where each shelf would go and which books would fill those shelves. It didn't take a lot of imagination for her to picture a children's section decorated like the garden of Eden with animals of every type gracing the walls. Designing the layout for the store came naturally to her. Carbondale lacked a Christian bookstore, and bookstores were her area of expertise.

Katie looked back at her friends. Concern filled their expressions. They were sharing the truth as they saw it. But why did they see it this way? "I'm not rushing into anything. Erin, you know I've considered this since I sold Pages. I probably would have done it a long time ago if..."

She shrugged the ending to her statement. It had been three years, but it didn't get easier. How did one nonchalantly throw their husband's death into a conversation? Maybe it would be different if he'd suffered some disease instead of being stabbed by an addict he'd been trying to help, if it hadn't been so unexpected.

Erin tucked her bottom lip between her teeth. A sure sign she was struggling with her emotions. Katie looked away before she lost control of her own. "Besides, I need to work."

"No, you don't." Paul's voice was quiet but sure. "I know what you made from the sale of Pages. That doesn't include the monthly payments you receive from the sale of the bakery. You own your jeep, and your dad's place is paid for. I know there are living expenses to consider, but think about the time commitment to owning your store. You remember what those first years were like with Pages, don't you?"

Memories flooded her mind. Long, frustrating days watching every financial detail, hoping for the best. Coming home carrying every concern in the muscles of her neck and shoulders. Those early years hadn't been fun, but they'd been worth it when Pages finally took off. Would that be true now? She didn't have a little one waiting at home then. Could she put everything she needed to into the store and still be both mom and dad to Sammy?

She lifted a hand to her hair and wound a curl around her finger without thought as she glanced around the space again. The realtor would be back soon to lock up. She left Paul and Erin by the glass display case that doubled as a checkout counter back when the space housed a cosmetics store. It would be the perfect location and size for the bookstore she'd been considering. How come the thought didn't leave her giddy with excitement? Were her friends right about her heart not being in it? Did it matter?

She knew the bookstore business. Even with the hits brick and mortar stores, especially locally owned ones, took due to online shopping and e-books, she was certain she could make a go of it. Pages was still operating in the black. And Carbondale didn't have a Christian bookstore. None of the surrounding towns did either. Hers would be the only one.

Paul was right though. She remembered all the hard work and the roller coaster ride of emotions it took for Pages to be a success. She'd lived and breathed the store back then. It was her passion. Could she do it all again if the passion had passed?

Erin's voice broke through her internal monologue. "Katie? Are you okay?"

She looked over her shoulder at them and forced a small smile. "I'm fine. I just need some time to think. You two go ahead. I'll wait for the realtor. You've got Erin's family to spend time with while you're here. Since I'll be monopolizing your time on Saturday with Sammy's party, you'd better give them their time today and tomorrow."

Paul cocked his head toward the door. "Come on, Erin. Let's get out of Katie's hair."

Erin watched her. Katie could read the discomfort on her face. She forced a faint smile. "Really. I'm good."

Paul took Erin's hand. She hesitated before following. "We'll see you Saturday. Call if you need us before then."

Katie waved them away with more gusto than she felt. "Will do. Now get outta here."

KATIE ENGAGED in the necessary small talk with the realtor only until the key turned in the lock. With an assurance she would get in touch to give her final answer about whether or not she wanted to make an offer on the store, Katie made her way to her jeep. The loop of thoughts she'd been wrestling with since her talk with Erin and Paul turned in on itself. She was left with a tangle of partial ideas that no longer made sense. She had to get somewhere quiet to think.

She could go home, walk to the waterfall where she did her best thinking. But if her dad saw her, he would know something was wrong. He didn't need worry about her adding to his own issues. She pulled from the parking lot and headed south on Giant City road. She pushed every thought from her head and drove to the park on autopilot.

Katie turned into a familiar parking spot at the base of Stonefort Trail. Her hand froze on the door handle. She'd not hiked up Stonefort Trail or any other trail in Giant City State Park since Austin's death. The cliff overlooking a picturesque clearing had been his waterfall spot. He'd shared it with her. He'd proposed to her in that spot. Katie swallowed the ache closing her throat. She couldn't do it. She couldn't be in this place without Austin by her side.

Katie closed her eyes against the sting of tears. Where could she go to find the quiet which would allow her to sort out her jumbled thoughts and calm her spirit? Without a destination, Katie drove through the park, down Carbondale's backroads, and back into town before making a last-minute turn down the street leading to the local university's lake. A cold February weekday afternoon would mean relatively few college students or Carbondale residents using the paths of Campus Lake. If she stayed on the south end where it was wooded, she could find the calm she sought and the privacy to sort through her tangled thoughts.

The parking lot was empty when Katie arrived. She headed down the wooded path until she found a bench. If it weren't for the fact that the lake, path, and bench were all part of the college campus, a solitary bench in the woods would have reminded her of the lamp-post in the Chronicles of Narnia. It was slightly out of place but welcome in her present frame of mind.

She dropped onto the cold, hard seat and stared at the lake through openings in the trees. With her back to the path, Katie let the feeling of solitude wash over her. She inhaled the cold air coughing briefly as it entered her lungs. Better not to do that.

The questions tumbled through her mind. Could she devote herself to a new store when Sammy was all she had? Did she want to if she could? If she didn't stick to this plan what was left for her? She considered her options, desperate to find an answer. She couldn't start over with a new bookstore. It wasn't feasible with single parenting. Besides, Paul and Erin were right. She didn't have a passion for it like she once did. Her head dropped to her hands as she realized a larger truth. She couldn't think of one thing, outside of Sammy, that succeeded in sparking a passionate flame inside her.

"Oh, God, what am I going to do?" She whispered the desperate prayer. Her plea didn't bring a message written in the sky just for her. She knew it wouldn't, but she kind of hoped. She'd often thought it might be nice if God worked that way.

"Kate?"

She started at the unexpected voice. She didn't need to turn around to know Nathan Phillips stood behind her. He was the only one who got away with calling her Kate. Turning on the bench to allow herself to see the trail behind her confirmed her deduction. Nathan stood, holding the lead of a massive husky. At least Katie thought it was him. He looked like Nathan except for the track pants and tennis shoes that replaced the boots and blue jeans making up his trademark look. The athletic gear wouldn't look odd on anyone else, but on Nathan, it didn't feel like it belonged.

Brows lowered over his bright blue eyes. "Are you okay?"

She couldn't muster anything resembling a smile. "Yeah."

His furry friend tugged on the leash. Nathan tightened his hold. "Your dog is beautiful."

He moved from the path, leading them both closer to the bench. "I won't argue that, but Jackson isn't my dog. I'm just walking him while his owner is out of town."

Katie repositioned herself as Nathan sat beside her. She fidgeted under his scrutiny. "You know, Kate, it's been ages since you and Tonya spent every afternoon together at our house."

Katie grinned thinking about those days with Nathan's younger sister. They'd been best friends up until Tonya's family moved during their high school years. "It wasn't every day. At least not at your house. We spent plenty of days at my house too. How's Tonya doing these days?"

His shoulders lifted. "She's doing okay. She's married to an accountant and raising their twin boys. But that's not why I brought up the good old days. You and I were around each other enough in those days for me to get to know you as well as I know my sister. I admit it's been a while. You may have changed as much as I have through the years, but I can still tell something's not quite right. You wouldn't be sitting here on a bench in the most secluded part of the lake trail if it was all hunky-dory."

"Did you just say hunky-dory?"

He tipped his head. "Yeah, I did. But you're not changing the subject. What's up, Kate?"

Just as he knew her enough to know there was a problem, Katie knew him well enough to know he wouldn't let this go. She wound a stray curl around her finger as she thought about how to answer. "My friends just handed me a piece of truth I wasn't prepared to deal with."

"Bad news?"

She shook her head. "Not bad. Just different. Did you know I owned a book store in Bloomington?"

"I'd heard it through the grapevine."

"I sold it when I moved here. But the bookstore business is

what I know. At one time I thought God wanted me to open a new store here in Carbondale, only it would be a Christian bookstore."

"And now?"

She shrugged. "I went to check out a potential space. Paul and Erin went with me. You remember Paul and Erin?"

She waited for his silent nod. "Well, I expected them to be excited for me. It's the perfect spot. Only they weren't. They told me my heart wasn't in it anymore. Maybe they're right. It takes a lot of time and energy to run a store, especially a new one. I'm a mom now. I have to think about Sammy's needs."

Jackson whined. Without looking away from her, Nathan's hand dropped to rub his head. "It sounds to me like you've got your answer."

"But what am I supposed to do with myself? I can't not work for the rest of my life."

"If what you've been doing is taking care of you and Sammy, and you know you're not supposed to do the store thing, I'd say keep doing what you've been doing. Pray about it. Wait until you know what God wants you to do."

"But I need to work."

"Why?"

"I just do alright? People work. It's not like I'm suggesting going to the moon or something."

She watched one eyebrow lift at her outburst. "So it's not about money then."

"You're infuriating. You know that right? You always were. I've always been Little Kate. Your baby sister's annoying friend. But I'm not a kid anymore. I know what I need to do, and that happens to be working. I'm not even sure why I'm discussing this with you."

He nodded slowly before standing. He paused at the edge of the bench. "I'm sorry I made you feel that way. You've never been my sister's annoying friend. I hope you get everything worked out. I'll be praying for you. See ya around, Kate."

She didn't move or acknowledge his leaving. She listened until his steps faded from her hearing. He hadn't said anything untrue, but it struck a nerve. Paul and Erin hadn't understood her need, but Nathan seemed to get it. She couldn't quite figure out why that bothered her.

She spent the next hour praying through her tumultuous emotions. Between desperate prayers, she took out her phone and opened the Bible app installed on it. First, she would read, then pray, then read, and then pray again. When she finally felt the peace of God settle in her heart and mind, she knew her time of reflection was complete. She smiled as she stood to go pick up Sammy. Maybe God had given her a handwritten message, but instead of being scrawled across the blue sky it came in the form of Nathan Phillips.

Chapter Two

K atie retrieved her phone from her dad. He'd scrolled through all of the pictures of games and decorations she needed for the party. He'd even shown them to Sammy, who nearly burst with excitement at the thought of his party. But her father hadn't stopped peppering her with questions.

She set Sammy's child-sized plate in front of him. "Tell you what, you can go with me tomorrow. We'll drop Sammy off at school and go get everything we need. That way you'll have something to do and can help me figure out exactly what I need for Saturday."

"What's Saturday?"

Katie frowned as she watched him scoop a helping of mashed potatoes onto his plate. What was happening? They were discussing the party. He was looking at pictures of games. Did he not realize it was taking place on Saturday?

Sammy stuffed a chicken nugget in his mouth. "Papa, you know. Saturday is my party. I'm three."

Understanding lit his eyes. He winked at his grandson across the table. "Of course it is. I was just seeing if you remembered."

Katie wished she could believe it, but she refused to say

anything. She would not borrow trouble. There'd been enough of that in their lives. They were due a little sunshine and laughter. Besides, Sammy thought it was a great game. Regardless of the reason, her son would always remember playing like this with his grandpa.

After cleaning up the last of the dinner mess and hanging the towels to dry from Sammy's bath time, Katie stood outside his room listening to him recount the adventures of his first day of school to his grandpa. She smiled at his re-telling of the little girl with the blocks. Sammy had already regaled her with his stories on their way home that evening. She sighed knowing she'd made the right choice. She only half-listened this time, focusing instead on the peaceful picture her son and dad created as she watched them. She hated to interrupt, but it was getting late.

"It's about time for prayers and dreams. Who do you want to say your prayers with you tonight?"

"Hmmm." His eyes were serious as he looked back and forth between them. He pointed a little finger at her dad. "Papa."

She crossed the room and planted a kiss on his cheek. "Okay." She turned to her father. "We were in the story of Joseph in his kids' Bible." She looked back at Sammy. "But no talking him into extra stories. It's time for bed. Got it, mister?"

His nod was sharp dislodging a strawberry blonde curl to fall across his forehead. "Got it."

"Love you for forever and a day."

"Love you forever and a day, Mommy."

She placed her hand on her dad's shoulder. When he looked up at her she reiterated her instructions. "No extra stories. Just Joseph, prayers, and bed."

She knew the innocence in his eyes was false. He would do whatever his grandson asked once she left the room. "Of course. One story, prayers, and bed. You go ahead. We've got this under control."

She paused at the door. "If I'm not downstairs when you get there, I've gone for a walk."

"Just bundle up. It's cold enough to make Santa shiver out there. You don't want to end up with pneumonia."

~

"Unlock the door so I can get in."

Katie frowned. "Did you forget something?"

Her father shook his head. "No, but I need you to unlock the door if we're going to go get Sammy."

She motioned to the craft supply store. "We've got to get the stuff for Sammy's party before we go get him."

He looked at the store and back to the car. Had she asked him to do too much? After dropping off Sammy at school, their day of shopping had begun. He'd taken off on his own at one of the stores claiming a secret mission. She'd worried her way through her shopping, but her dad waited for her at the checkout counter with a cat that ate the canary grin and talk of a special surprise for Sammy. With one store done and one to go, she decided to stop at a drive-through shop to get her oil changed. It seemed she never remembered until she was overdue. The craft store was supposed to be their last stop. She had a list a mile long of supplies she needed for the party games and decorations.

Should she skip it and come back later? While her dad had always stayed busy during her childhood, he'd gotten used to spending quiet days at home in recent years. Maybe the increase in activity wore him out and led to his confusion. Would one last store cause him too much stress? She didn't have extra time to make a return trip.

"This is the last stop, Dad. I promise. We'll get the things on my list and head over to pick up Sammy. It won't take long."

His brows knit together. "Of course we've got to get your list taken care of. We've got to have those things for my grandson's party. Let's stop wasting time and get this done."

He turned from her and marched toward the store as if none of the previous conversations had happened. Katie stared after him. He had to be exhausted. It was the only reasonable explanation for the conversation to yo-yo that fast. Katie grabbed her purse out of the front seat and shut her door before taking long strides to catch up with her dad.

"I DON'T NEED plastic table cloths."

Katie watched her dad remove the offending items from her cart and put them on the nearest shelf. She grabbed them from where he put them and dropped them back into her cart. "You don't need them, but I do."

"I'm not buying plastic table cloths when I don't need them."

"I understand that. You're not buying them. I am. I need them for Sammy's birthday party."

Her explanation seemed to clear the fog from his mind. They continued down the aisle with the red, green, and yellow table cloths safely contained in the cart. Katie mentally checked them off her list and picked up a helium tank and balloon kit from a nearby bottom shelf before heading to find poster board and paint.

Katie blew out a frustrated breath. For a man who was exhausted and complaining about wanting to go home, her father was wasting enough time looking at every little item on the shelves. While choosing the paints she needed, she'd had to convince him he didn't need paint of his own. Then, he'd wandered away while she found the rest of the items she needed to make the games for the party.

She looked down each aisle as she moved in the direction

she'd seen him go. She found him looking at model cars. "What did you find, Dad?"

"I used to love these things when I was a boy. Maybe Sammy and I could do one together. Or he could do one, and I could do my own. Do you think he'd like to?"

Would her son like to make a wonderful memory with his grandpa? She smiled. "Yeah, I think he'd enjoy that. How about I pick out one that will be easy enough for him while you find one for yourself?"

She'd never been into making models. She'd done quite a few puzzles, but putting together model cars had never appealed to her. Had her dad missed having a son to do that kind of thing with? She was glad he now had Sammy and that her son was blessed to have a man to spend time with. She found a simple click together type model meant for children a year or two older than Sammy, but she was sure he could handle it. Her father picked one off the shelf at the same time.

"If you'd like me to, I'll wrap this for Sammy and you can give it to him for his birthday."

"I'd like that. When is his birthday again?"

Katie took the box from him, and along with hers, dropped it into the cart. "His party is this Saturday in the fellowship hall at Orchard Hills Church, remember?"

"Am I going to that?"

She pushed the cart toward the front of the store. It was time for them to check out and pick up Sammy. "Of course, you are. You're Sammy's best buddy. You have to be there. Now, let's get out of here and go get him from school."

Chapter Three

The caterpillar cupcake body wriggled across the cake board. Katie smiled as she stuck the number three candle into one of the cupcakes and lit it. Across the church's fellowship hall Erin shut off the lights over where Sammy waited less than patiently, knees folded under him on his chair, bouncing up and down. Carefully, she picked up the cake board and carried it over to Sammy while the guests sang "Happy Birthday."

Katie scooted the little hand away as it reached out. "You don't want to do that, Sammy. Let's blow out the candle first. Ready? One. Two. Three. Make a wish."

His chest puffed up with the giant breath he inhaled before releasing its full force on the single flame. At least he'd learned how to blow the air out without covering the cupcakes in toddler spit. She'd call that a win considering his failure to do so on his second birthday. The crowd cheered and clapped. Sammy beamed. The love they had for her small son warmed her.

She plucked a cupcake from the end of the hungry caterpillar, removed the wrapper, and set it on a colorful napkin in front of Sammy. The rest she carried to the counter, placing them between a caterpillar made of apple slices and a rainbow-colored tray of fruit. She placed a few halved grapes and banana slices on a green paper dessert plate and delivered them to her son.

"I want to thank everyone for coming today and for honoring our wishes to limit your gifts to a children's book which we will donate to the struggling families that visit the Bread of Life Meal Ministry. Your gifts will be a great encouragement to the children we see come through the line. Now, if you've signed our copy of *The Very Hungry Caterpillar* for Sammy, feel free to enjoy a cupcake and the rest of the food."

As children rushed forward to fill their plates and adults followed at a more reasonable rate, Katie made her way back to the kitchenette to get a damp cloth for Sammy's frosting covered hands. Erin stood behind the counter helping children fill their plates and pouring punch for everyone. Katie's dad stood beside her putting ice cubes into the cups.

"So, young lady, how do you know my Katie and Sammy?"

Katie sighed but Erin didn't miss a beat. "Katie and I are best friends. We met when she moved back to Carbondale a few years ago. I don't live here now, but I wouldn't miss Sammy's birthday. He's a special little boy."

Her father's grin told Katie her friend's words were well chosen. "That he is. My little Sammy's going to amaze us all one day."

"I can believe it."

Katie moved past them to clean up the subject of their discussion before freeing him to play. He ran to the other side of the room where Katie had set up games. He was fascinated by the cardboard caterpillar face she'd made. She was happy it was a hit but started toward him as she realized his interest was putting him in the line of fire for the children trying to toss the fake fruit into the caterpillar's mouth. She stopped as Jake and Tommy moved out of line to coax him out of the way. The twins, who Katie knew from the days she taught Sunday school class at Orchard Hills, were older so they had to stoop to his level to help him take a turn tossing a foam apple at the caterpillar. The thud as it smacked into the caterpillar's eye instead of finding the hole caused Sammy to giggle. It didn't matter that he'd missed it. All her time putting together the simple game was worth it.

"I miss those giggles up in Bloomington. Sometimes it's almost enough to make me want to move back."

Katie turned to Erin. "Nice to know where I rank. You don't consider moving back for your best friend, but one giggle from my son and you're ready to pack up."

Erin threw an arm around her shoulders and laid her head against one, which was a feat in itself considering their height difference. The ends of her straight blonde hair tickled Katie's bare arm, but she wouldn't think of moving. She saw her friend rarely enough since Erin and Paul tied the knot and moved four hours away. She was glad they were doing well, but Katie wasn't the social butterfly Erin was, and she hadn't found someone to fill the void. The unsatisfied craving to have a friend close by was more than enough to let Erin invade her personal space for a little while.

"To be honest, Paul and I have talked about relocating. But neither of us feels like it's what God is leading us to do right now. You can't believe how much we miss you guys though."

Katie just smiled. She knew Erin's words were true, and she would never discount the sentiment. But they had each other. Katie was alone since Austin was killed and her mother died shortly after that. She was happy her two friends had found each other, but they'd married and moved only six months after Sammy was born. In the two and a half years Katie had adjusted to this new way of life, but there were times she desperately wished she had a friend to share her days with.

She wanted to tell Erin she'd better move back down before having children of her own, but the wistful look on Erin's face stopped her. Erin had confided in her about their desire to get pregnant about six months into their marriage. As of yet, it hadn't happened. Erin seemed to handle it with the same grace she handled most things, but Katie knew her friend feared she might never be able to have children.

They watched Sammy playing with the other kids. A few from Sammy's preschool class had made it. However, most were older, like Tommy and Jake, and from Katie's old Sunday school class. As she looked around the room at the mix of people from the church she grew up in and the new church she attended with Erin's grandma, Gigi B, the dull ache was pushed back a little further. She may not have a close friend living in Carbondale to confide in, but the room was full of people who loved her and Sammy. How could she allow even a moment of melancholy with all of them sharing in this special day?

She scanned the room one more time as she realized her dad was not in the group. "Did you see where Dad went?"

Erin shook her head and looked around the room. "When I left him, he was speaking with Gigi B. Is everything okay?"

Katie frowned. "I'm sure it is."

"You don't sound sure. Do we need to go look for him?"

The tightness constricting her chest told her they should look. A desire to be reasonable warred with it. Anxiety had nearly secured its victory when her dad walked through the double doors leading into the fellowship hall. The bands around her chest eased. "No. There he is. But I probably should go check on him. Can you keep an eye on Sammy?"

"I'll keep both eyes on him if that helps."

Katie shook her head as Erin giggled at her tired joke. Erin took her job as Sammy's godmother seriously, and Katie knew she would keep him out of trouble while she checked on her dad. She wound her way through tables, chairs, and a sea of kids to reach her dad where he sat sipping a cup of punch and chatting with Gigi B. God had given her family a blessing the day He brought Gigi B into their lives. She was always there for Katie, and she adored her role of adopted grandma to Sammy. It made it easier on special days, like this one when Austin's parents couldn't make the trip in from Arizona.

"Well, hey there, lady. It's quite the party for your little man today. Thank you for inviting me."

Katie took the seat across from her, next to her father. "Did you think I'd have a party and not invite you? Especially a party for Sammy? You're like a grandma to him."

A dramatic huff filled the air. "Like a grandma? We've been over this. Grandmas are dull and old. I'm a Gigi, and that's a whole other ball game. I'm not sitting around knitting and living vicariously through the lives of those on the soaps." Gigi B turned and laid a hand on her father's arm. "Don't get me wrong. I've nothing against the ladies having their daily stories, though some of what's on them is nothing but trash, who's in whose bed and all that. But I aspire to be a little livelier than that. Won't catch me getting old. No sir. I aim to live every day I'm given. How about you?"

Her dad's gaze bounced between her and Gigi B. Wide eyes gave him a bewildered look. "I suppose if I'm going to live there's not any other option. Is there?"

Gigi B chuckled and patted the hand that held his cup. "Quite right, Cal. Quite right. Now, if you two will excuse me, I'm going to go see the guest of honor for some sugar. Those cupcakes can't compare." She stood but addressed her father before moving off. "You let me know how that boy does. I can't have him slacking on the job. Of course, I've never known him to be lazy. He's a hard and willing worker."

He nodded. "Sure will. Thanks for the recommendation."

Katie watched Gigi B sashay across the room and scoop up her son for a kiss. "What's she talking about? What recommendation?"

A twinkle shone in his eyes. "Don't you worry about that none. Me and Gigi B have things under control. It's just a little surprise for my favorite grandson's birthday."

Katie waited for him to divulge more information, but instead, he simply rose from his seat and went to get a refill on his punch. She had no choice but to wait for answers.

KATIE SWIPED the suds from the table and dipped the rag into the bucket again. Wringing it out better this time, she continued to wipe frosting and crumbs from the tables. She looked up briefly when movement at the side door caught her attention. Erin shut the door and joined her, fishing around in the sudsy water for her rag.

"Gigi B has your dad and Sammy. She's taking them straight home. But that reminds me, how did your dad handle selling the old station wagon? I can't imagine he likes being reliant on others to get around."

"Remind me to tell Gigi B thanks for taking them. I know dad was worn out. Sammy could use a nap too. Not having to stay while we clean is a real blessing for them and me. As for the car, he's doing okay with it. At least most days he does. I'd prayed about how to get rid of it without a fight, and when the alternator went out, it gave me the perfect opportunity. All I had to do was talk about how much money it would save if we only had one vehicle and how much it would cost to keep fixing up such an old car. He was ready to sell it then."

Erin paused mid-swipe. "I take it Cal is getting worse?"

"In some ways. He always knows me and Sammy, but everyone else comes and goes. Gigi B is wonderful with him. She just rolls with whatever he calls her and keeps talking like nothing is out of the ordinary. He's getting a little forgetful too. He can't ever find things, even though they're in the same place they've always been. He gets turned around a lot. It wasn't safe for him to drive anymore, but that's a battle at times. He doesn't want to lose his independence."

"You think it's the normal stuff that goes with getting old?"

Katie shrugged. "I have no idea. I'd like to think so, but then I see people like Gigi B. Unless I miss my guess, she's as sharp as she's always been."

Erin rolled her eyes and pressed the back of her hand to her forehead. "Heaven help us all if she ever starts to lose her mind. She's hard enough to keep up with now when she's perfectly lucid."

Katie laughed. Erin's dramatics had a way of making even the most difficult situations appear less dark. Besides, the mental picture of Gigi B flitting from room to room in her stylish wedge sandals with the draped ends of one of her colorful tunics flying behind her as she looked for a hat that happened to be sitting atop her head was too outrageous. No, she couldn't imagine what life would be like for everyone in proximity if that wonderful woman ever started losing her grip on reality. It was hard enough to keep tabs on someone with a less exuberant personality like her father. And whether the elderly person was more like her father or full of flair like Gigi B, it was painful for their loved ones wondering how long it would be before things progressed further.

Katie started as a wadded up dish rag flew in front of her from the other end of the table. She grimaced when it landed in the bucket of water splashing it all over her hand and the area she was wiping. She hadn't realized she'd gotten lost in her thoughts. Looking from Erin with her sheepish grin to the rest of the room, Katie realized the last of the tables were now clean. She mopped up the puddle created by Erin's three-point shot and went to dump the water down the sink.

Katie grabbed her purse and flipped off the lights. Erin stood at the exit with the door open waiting for her.

"I know Paul and I aren't here all the time, but you know if you need something, all you have to do is call, right?"

Katie went against her nature and pulled Erin into a quick hug. "I know. Thank you."

"There's nothing to thank me for. You're my best friend, and I love you. Now, I'd better go find Paul. We'll see you tomorrow at church before we head back to Bloomington. Gigi B would have my hide if I came down for a visit and didn't go to church with her."

Katie watched Erin pull onto the blacktop in the direction that would take her home. She was glad her friend made the trip. She could always count on Erin to be there for her, but she couldn't help feeling it wasn't the same. No matter how many friends she had, she had the feeling there would always be an ache for what she'd had with Austin. Love and loneliness continued to see-saw her emotions on the drive home.

Chapter Four

Whose truck was in the driveway next to Gigi B's eco-friendly hybrid? It was familiar, but Katie couldn't quite place it. She parked out of the way in the spot previously reserved for her dad's old station wagon. The pounding of a hammer coming from the side yard encouraged her to investigate.

Her father's comments about Sammy's birthday surprise were cleared up as she took in the pieces of a wooden play structure coming together not far from the weeping willow she played under as a child. But who was putting it together? Certainly not her father. As much as he'd once loved building things, he wasn't able to do even the simplest of construction projects anymore. Besides, hadn't he mentioned someone else coming over to work on the surprise when he and Gigi B had their super-secret conversation?

Katie caught sight of jeans and boots between some of the boards on the far side of the project. Though the builder's face was hidden behind a yellow plastic slide, she had a sneaking suspicion about the mystery man's identity. A knot formed in her stomach as the slide slid into place giving away the builder's identity. She owed him an apology, but she wasn't prepared to do it so soon. *God, give me the strength to humble myself and do what needs to be done. I was unfair to him, and I need to make it right.*

She waved as he caught sight of her. "Why am I not surprised to see you're the one they drafted to carry out this surprise?"

Nathan adjusted the slide. "I was hoping your cleanup would take a little more time. I didn't get started as soon as I would've liked. I'd hoped to have this done before you got home."

Katie set her purse down on one of the bricks lining her mother's old flower gardens. "You've accomplished quite a lot in a little bit of time. Imagine how quick it will go now that you have help."

He removed his faded ball cap and ran a hand through his short, light brown hair. His fingers left the damp hair raised in messy spikes. "While I wouldn't mind the help, you've got the little one to take care of."

"I'll run inside first to make sure Sammy's okay with my dad. It's supposed to be nap time, if dad and Gigi B were successful getting him to lie down after the truckloads of sugar he ingested at his birthday party. As long as he's asleep, I'll be back to help. Think of it as my way of apologizing for the other day at the lake."

He readjusted his cap. "Nothing to apologize for."

"That's kind of you to say, but not at all true. It wasn't about you."

"I know that."

"But I took it out on you, and I'm sorry. You didn't deserve that, and I shouldn't have responded that way. Now, I'm going to check on Sammy and Dad. Be back in a minute."

Without waiting for his answer, she scooped up her purse and went to find her dad. He and Gigi B were "shootin' the breeze" over a couple of glasses of iced tea.

Gigi B took her glass to the sink and rinsed it out. "Been good visiting with you, Cal, but now that your girl is here, I need to find my own way home." She turned to Katie. "Sammy is down for his nap. It took a while, but he fell asleep about fifteen minutes ago. I'll see you tomorrow at church? Erin's going to be there."

"I'll be there. Thank you for letting Dad and Sammy ride home with you while I cleaned up. Dad, since Sammy's asleep would you mind if I went out to help Nathan with the birthday surprise? Between the two of us, we might have it ready for him by the time he wakes up."

"That suits me just fine. I'm a little too old to get out there myself. I'll let you know when Sammy wakes."

Katie followed Gigi out the door and waved good-bye before making her way back to the construction site. "What do you need me to do?"

"Why don't you hold this in place while I bolt it to the rest of the structure?"

Katie moved to take the green roof panel from him and held it steady as he attached it. She was impressed by the amount of work he'd accomplished on his own. It couldn't have been easy. She knew her dad wanted the playhouse to be a surprise for her as much as Sammy but arranging for Nathan to do it all on his own was far from fair.

She moved to hold the second roof piece while he secured it. "You've done a lot of hard work today, and I'm pretty sure that pair of loveable old people probably talked you into doing it all pro bono. Am I right?"

"It isn't fittin' to discuss such matters as what one gets paid for a job. My mama taught me better than that. Besides, I didn't get the little guy anything for his birthday. Consider it my gift too."

She raised an eyebrow. "You got him a gift but you didn't even get a piece of cake or a glass of punch?"

He patted his flat abdomen with his free hand. "Why, Kate, do you think I get this stunning physique eating cake and sipping punch? No, ma'am. It's hard work, plain and simple. I don't need any birthday cake."

"Well, you might not need any birthday cake, but you do need to eat dinner. And tonight, it's going to be my treat."

He eyed her. "Nope. I don't need to weasel a dinner invitation from you. I'm doing this because I want to and your father asked me to. Your thanks is enough for me."

She turned from him and picked up one of the swings. Reaching up, she slid the chain over the metal hook hanging from the wooden beam. "I'd really appreciate it if you'd let me do this. I don't feel like I have to, but I want to. Please."

THE QUIET WAY she tacked the please at the end of her request broke through Nathan's resistance. It was true. He agreed to build the playhouse because it was the right thing to do. He didn't do it for thanks or dinners or anything else. He did it to be neighborly. But taking him out to dinner seemed to mean a lot to Kate. He'd wager she'd turned her attention to hanging the swing to downplay how important it was to her. He figured she thought it would help her save face if he said no. He wouldn't though. Besides, she was easy enough to be around, and he did need to eat.

"Fine. We can get some dinner, and I'll even let you beat up on my manly pride by letting you pay like you want to."

Kate guffawed. "Manly pride? I don't think it's going to injure your manly pride to have me buy your dinner. I seem to recall you take your eating very seriously."

"I'll have you know eating is serious business to every teenage boy out there. I was not an exception. I was the rule.

Boys that age have a lot of growing to do. Just wait until Sammy reaches the teen years."

He scooped up stray cardboard packaging from the ground and tossed it onto the pile of garbage he'd collected while building. He glanced at Kate whose pursed lips and raised brows telegraphed her imaginary boredom with his reasoning.

"Yes, miss know-it-all? Is there some part of my argument you'd like to refute?"

Her curls danced as she shook her head. "Not at all. You're right. I know I'm in for a growth spurt in my grocery bills once Sammy gets that age. But that doesn't completely negate the fact that some boys go above and beyond in the eating department. And I seem to remember someone putting down nearly a whole pizza by himself every Friday night at the Phillip's family movie night."

He struck a pose, waving a hand down the length of his body. "I'll give you that one. But can you honestly tell me all the eating I did back then did anything to hurt me now?"

Pink tinted her cheeks for a moment before she busied herself picking up the remaining garbage. Why would she be embarrassed about that? He adjusted his ball cap. In the years since high school when she'd been best friends with his little sister, he'd forgotten how confusing she could be at times. One minute they'd be easy going and playful. The next she would clam up and find excuses to leave the room. It looked like some things weren't going to change any time soon.

They finished the task in silence. With the garbage dumped into a metal barrel by the shop, Nathan safely lit the contents on fire. The majority was cardboard that wouldn't take long to burn. Conscious of the dinner they were to share, he carefully kept his distance from the smoke. Of course, constructing the playhouse had him sweating like a pig. He should probably work in a shower if he wanted her to have any appetite at all.

"If you don't mind, while that burns I'm going to check on Dad and Sammy."

"No problem. And since I've so generously agreed to placate you by letting you take me to dinner tonight, I've got one request."

"What's that?"

He pinched his t-shirt between two fingers and fanned it out from his chest. "I need to go home and shower before we go out. Is it a deal?"

She sniffed the air and wrinkled her nose. "I definitely don't have any problems with that."

He laughed as she turned and walked toward the house. He yelled after her. "I'll be back by five if that works for you?"

She didn't turn, but her words carried to him anyway. "Sounds perfect."

Chapter Five

Nathan stood on the front stoop waiting for someone to answer his knock. He brushed a piece of lint from his black t-shirt. Maybe he should have worn the blue plaid button-up. He hadn't wanted her to feel like he was dressing up for her but at least pairing those with his dark blue Wranglers and black cowboy boots he wouldn't stand the chance of looking like the lint trap in his dryer by the end of the evening. Why did he even care? It wasn't like this was a date or anything. She just wanted to take him out for dinner to say thanks. The door swung open. No more time for second-guessing.

"Evenin', Kate."

"You're right on time."

"I always try to be. My mama taught me it wasn't polite to keep people waiting on me."

"I'll go get Sammy and tell Dad we're leaving. "

He watched her go. How was it that she hadn't dressed up any more than he had but she looked like she could have stepped from the pages of a magazine? Her purple top was one of those long flowing things that hung down lower on the sides than the front and back. Kate wore it over a pair of black jeans that hugged the length of her legs all the way down to a short pair of boots that were more decorative than practical. He'd never understood the style, but for reasons he didn't want to examine, Nathan found he appreciated the finished look.

"Ready?" Kate reappeared with Sammy on her hip. "We can take my jeep if you want. That way we don't have to mess with switching his car seat."

He held the door and waved her through. "Whatever you think is best. Either one will get us where we're going. But I don't mind driving if you're not up to it."

"No. You worked hard on the playhouse all afternoon. The least I can do is drive and pay for your dinner."

Nathan moved in front of her to open the back door. Kate smiled her appreciation as she lifted Sammy from her hip and buckled him into his car seat. His brows puckered as he stared Nathan down. Nathan lifted his hand to wave and smiled. He was rewarded with a frown.

Kate looked back and forth between them. "I probably should have introduced you two. I know you've met, but it's been a while. He tends to forget people he doesn't see on a regular basis."

Nathan smiled again, hoping to put the toddler at ease. "Hi, Sammy. My name's Nathan."

His efforts were rewarded with a continued glare. Nathan could only imagine what he was thinking and was mildly relieved the boy didn't seem to talk much. He was sure the little guy would tell him to go away without hesitation, but Nathan hoped to rectify that.

"Sammy, look at Mommy."

The child shifted his gaze without turning his head.

"Nathan is Mommy's friend. He helped grandpa build your birthday surprise. Remember, you played on the slide after your nap today?"

"My playhouse?"

"Yes, your playhouse and your new slide. Nathan made that slide and the swings and even the little clubhouse underneath it. Do you remember how much fun it was? You need to tell him thank you."

The look that had relaxed as his mother spoke to him turned back into a frown as attention was once again brought to Nathan. He fought the urge to laugh at the seriousness of Sammy's glare. He was sure if he did, it would earn an equally harsh look from Kate. Even without kids of his own, Nathan could recognize a teachable moment.

"Sammy."

The child muttered something under his breath that might have been thank you, but there was no way to prove it.

"You're welcome. I hope you have lots of fun playing on it."

Sammy looked back to his mother who rewarded him with a smile. "Good job. Are you ready to go eat?"

"We can get chicken nuggets?"

"I'm sure wherever we go there will be chicken nuggets. " She turned her attention to Nathan after shutting the door. "I hope you don't mind. He's a pretty good eater, but when we go out, he loves his chicken nuggets. But don't worry. We don't have to go to a fast food place. Any restaurant with chicken nuggets is good."

Nathan buckled his seatbelt. "Any place you want to go is fine. When a little tyke wants chicken nuggets, he should have them. Besides, fast food or not, I'm sure they have something to fill the empty spot."

KATIE CONSIDERED the man sitting beside her as she drove toward the west side of town. There weren't a lot of choices, but maybe he'd like Denny's a little better than the plethora of fast food options. No matter what he said, she wouldn't thank him with a minuscule burger patty and stale French fries. A quick glance in the rearview mirror told her that Nathan's attempts at earning Sammy's trust were starting to work. At least, Sammy was no longer shooting daggers at him.

Other than at church, Sammy hadn't met a lot of people. If not for starting preschool, the guest list at his party would have primarily been adults and the kids from her old Sunday school class that he didn't even know. It had been her, her dad, and Sammy for the last three years. It was hard, but she hoped his school would change that. Not being a joiner herself, she understood the struggle. The idea of dinner with Nathan had come to her unexpectedly, and she'd offered it before her mind had a chance to reject it. At least it gave her and Sammy a way to get out of the house so her dad could have some alone time.

She felt Nathan watching her and quickly glanced at him. He had an expectant look on his face. Oh no, she'd zoned out completely. "I'm sorry. What did you say?"

He grinned but didn't comment on her failure to pay attention. "I asked how you like going to Faith Chapel. Gigi B mentioned you started going there with her and Erin after Austin died." His cringe was immediate. "I'm sorry. I shouldn't have brought that up. "

Katie shrugged as she flipped on her blinker. "No. It's okay. You knew him too. And it's part of our lives. I appreciate your sensitivity to it though. I've not always been at a healthy place emotionally to talk about it, but it's getting better."

Nathan mercifully picked up the first thread of his questioning. "How do you like Faith Chapel? I've heard their pastor a few times, and he seems pretty solid."

Katie pulled into the parking lot. "I like it. They took me in immediately. I like worshiping with people who I can consider family. Of course, I can probably thank Gigi B for that. I don't think she'd have let them treat me any other way. "

"She definitely has a way about her. I guess we can be thankful she uses her powers for good."

Katie laughed. "I've never heard truer words."

"Are we here? Do they have nuggets?"

Katie turned off the car and faced her son in the back seat. "Yes and yes. We're getting your nuggets." She looked back at Nathan. "We'd better get in there, or we're going to have a mutiny on our hands. And with a three-year-old, you don't want to see what that looks like."

His grin creased the five o'clock shadow covering his cheeks. "I thought it was the terrible twos."

"I'm not sure. Sammy's a pretty good boy most of the time. But when he does have a meltdown, it's a doozy."

"We don't want that. Come on. Let's get in there and get this boy his chicken nuggets."

Katie walked across the parking lot holding Sammy's hand. As they neared the door, Nathan stepped ahead of them to hold it open.

"Thank you. You know there was a time when I thought it was insulting to have a man open a door for me."

His head tilted to the side as he frowned, but he didn't say anything. Obviously, he didn't understand. Truth be told she didn't either anymore. That woman was long gone, and she was better for it.

It wasn't until after the hostess showed them to a booth and brought a booster seat for Sammy that Nathan pursued the matter. "Your dad strikes me as the kind to hold doors for your mama. What made you think it was an insult?"

Katie rubbed her lips together as she thought. "It was a man. I always believed Jacob was older and wiser than me. The first time I teased him about not opening a door for me, he was offended. He told me he understood women were not inferior and there was no reason a capable woman would ever need a man to open a door for her. If I believed I needed a man for such menial things, I didn't have enough faith in who I was as a woman."

"And now? I'm getting the feeling you don't think that way anymore. What changed your mind?"

Katie smiled with the memory. "Austin. He opened doors without even considering it. Doing those kinds of things was part of who he was. I remember him telling me it wasn't about whether or not I could open a door for myself. It was about the fact that I shouldn't have to. He wanted me to know I was that special to him."

Katie glanced at her son using the trio of colors the hostess had given him to scribble on the kids' menu. "I want Sammy to be that kind of man one day. But sometimes I wonder how I'm going to instill the lessons in him that should come from his father. How does a mother teach her son to become a man?"

She glanced down in surprise as Nathan's strong hand covered hers, stilling her fingers from twisting her napkin into shreds. Their gazes met when she lifted her head.

"You tell him what you just told me. You teach him about the man his father was."

Silent understanding passed between them until he jerked his hand away in an awkward gesture. The parking lot must have been extremely interesting from the way he refused to look away from the window. Katie left him alone with his thoughts as she fussed with Sammy next to her. He couldn't comprehend how beautiful and encouraging his words were to her aching heart. She doubted her ability to teach her son, but Nathan was right. There was still a lot for Austin to show Sammy about being a man.

"Are y'all ready to order?"

Their waitress broke the uneasy silence that had descended. Katie looked to Nathan who nodded. She smiled at the waitress and placed the orders for her and Sammy before Nathan rattled off his and handed the waitress his menu. Katie wracked her brain for a new line of conversation as she watched the waitress drop off their order and move to the drink station. She settled on the most obvious thing she could come up with.

"I know you volunteer at the nursing home, but what do you do for a living?"

Before he could answer, the waitress returned with their drinks. Nathan took his sweet tea from the waitress and thanked her before returning to the question. "After high school, me and some buddies of mine got together and bought a barn."

Katie frowned. "You bought a barn? You're a farmer?"

Nathan's eyes crinkled as he laughed. "No. We're definitely not farmers. Though there's nothing wrong with making a living that way. Lots of folks around here do, even though it's a tough life. But our barn is a horse barn. We train cutting horses and the riders. We even have one woman that teaches barrel racing."

"I'm not sure I follow. You train horses so people can ride them?"

"Not exactly. Although there is breaking involved some-times. It depends on how much the horse has been trained before it comes to us."

Nathan took his plate from the waitress and waited for Katie to do the same.

"Would you like to say grace, please?"

Nathan nodded and waited until Katie convinced Sammy to put his chicken nugget back on the plate and fold his hands to begin the prayer. His ease with speaking to their heavenly Father washed over her like the warm sun on a cool spring morning. She loved it when her father prayed like God was his best friend. Austin had prayed that way too. Maybe if she continued surrounding Sammy with men who prayed that way, he would learn to do the same.

After the amen, Nathan picked up the original thread of conversation. "Cutting horses are specially trained. Traditionally they were used on ranches to help move cattle out of the herd.

There are still some ranches that use them like that. Most of them are out west though."

Katie stopped with a fry halfway to her mouth. "If people don't use them, why are you training them?"

"People use them, just not as frequently as they once did for actual ranching. We train them for competition."

"Like rodeos?"

"Have you ever been to a rodeo?"

Katie couldn't help her arched brow.

Nathan chuckled. "Okay. So, no. We'll have to remedy that sometime."

Katie opened her mouth to respond, but Nathan's raised hand stopped her before she could speak. "One day we'll revisit this conversation. But back to the question. No. Cutting horses have their own competitions. Rodeos have different events. Both grew out of the need for skilled cowboys for ranching and round-ups. Both pay respect to the way things used to be for cowboys with friendly competition."

"Are you telling me cowboys had to ride wild bulls?"

His sly smile lent a childlike quality to features she normally considered more rugged.

"Maybe not that, but even cowboys have to have fun. But what about you? You said bookstores are what you know, but you sounded like you'd decided against opening one in Carbondale when we talked the other day."

Katie shifted uncomfortably. "When I sold Pages, my bookstore in Bloomington, to Paul I assumed I would open one here in Carbondale. But it didn't happen. Austin and I were just starting out. I didn't have to rush things because he had the bakery. After he died, I guess I was the owner of By Sweet Design. It never felt like it, and I never wanted it. That bakery was Austin's dream, and without him, I couldn't bear to keep it. I sold it to Lucy who'd been managing it since before Austin and I were even a couple. Now, the money from my store is in savings, and the monthly payment from the bakery is what I live on. Really I don't have to work at all."

He swirled his straw through his sweet tea. "But you're not content with that?"

No. She wasn't, but before she could answer a splash of soda demanded her attention. She was surprised to find a French fry swimming with her ice cubes. If she could have been mistaken about the culprit's identity, the giggles emanating from the little one beside her would have put an end to the doubts.

"Splash."

Katie wiped the soda from the table and fished the soggy potato from her glass. She put on her "mommy's serious" look and turned to her son. "Yes, the soda splashed. But food is for eating. We don't throw our food. You made a yucky mess."

"Sorry."

"No more throwing food?"

His eyes grew wide, and he shook his head. "No throwing food."

She pulled him close and planted a kiss on his silky, strawberry blond curls. "Good. Now finish your nuggets."

The plate was pushed across the table with surprising force. "No more nuggets."

Katie knew dinner time was over for Sammy. She glanced at Nathan's plate and then her own. Both were empty. Hopefully, Nathan wouldn't mind cutting their conversation short. The projectile French fry proved her son had reached his limit. Too much boredom without anything to play with lent itself to creative methods of entertainment. The fact that he'd been so well behaved through the rest of the meal was a minor miracle in itself.

Seeming to sense the need, the waitress brought the check. Though his shoulders were stiff and his lips pressed tightly together, Nathan refrained from saying anything as she moved the check to her side of the table and laid her debit card on top. Katie smiled at the discomfort her insistence to pay for their meals brought. It was nice to know men like him still existed. The waitress scooped up the check and her card with a promise to return momentarily. Within minutes, they were out the door and on the way back to Katie's house. The conversation was light and made short work of the road between the restaurant and her house.

"Is that your dad?"

Katie looked where Nathan pointed as they pulled into her usual parking spot. It couldn't be her dad. Why would he be wandering in the old pasture at this time of the evening? She stared at the figure shadowed with twilight. The slight hunch to the shoulders and the slow, methodical gait to his steps told her it was indeed her father. But why?

She looked from the field to where Sammy slept in his car seat. She needed to check on her dad, but she couldn't leave Sammy, even if he was safely buckled in his seat. If he woke, he might be afraid. And she didn't relish the idea of leaving her dad in the field while she took Sammy to his room.

"Kate?"

He waited until she looked at him. "Take Sammy inside. I'll get your father."

"But..."

"No buts. You need to take care of your son. Cal knows me. I'll make sure he's okay."

"He can't stay out there. Not by himself. He may seem like he can, but he can't."

It was the second time that day she'd drawn comfort from the warmth of his hand covering hers. "I understand. I've volunteered at the nursing home for years. I'm not blind to what's going on. I'll make sure your dad follows me back to the house, and I'll do it without damaging his pride. You can trust me."

For reasons she couldn't explain, Katie did trust him. No longer reluctant, she got out of the jeep, got her son, and walked to the house without a backward glance. After changing Sammy into overnight training pants and tucking him into his bed, Katie went to his window overlooking the fields beyond the barn. Two dark figures walked side by side toward the house. A catch in her breathing stole her attention. Tightness stretched across her chest.

Katie recognized the signs. She hadn't experienced a panic attack in ages, since long before she and Austin had married. Unrestrained fear had ruled her days and kept her body captive to its whims. She couldn't go back to that. *Father God, protect my heart and mind. No matter what the future holds, help me remember You are there with me. You are with my father. If we're walking into the fire, Lord, walk right beside me and keep me safe. Thank You, Father.*

Focused on the message that had taken so long to filter into her heart and become part of who she was now, Katie found her pulse slowing and her breaths coming with ease. The bands around her chest loosened, and she smiled. It never ceased to amaze her how completely God changed her ability to deal with the panic when it tried to insert itself into her life.

She didn't know for sure a storm was brewing for her and her father, but she needed the ability to think with clarity if it was. Even if her dad wasn't getting worse, if everything stayed as it was for them, there were enough challenges in the day to day to keep her on her toes.

Voices carried up the stairs. Katie turned off her son's light and went to join them.

"No, sir. It was a pleasure putting it together for you and Sammy."

"It was a good surprise. Did my Katydid tell you he played on it from the time he woke from his nap until right before you arrived?"

Katie came behind him and put a hand on his shoulder. "Of

course I did. It was his best birthday surprise. He is one happy camper and completely worn out this evening."

She placed a kiss on his cheek and took a seat at the kitchen table next to him. He stood almost immediately. "He's not the only one. My evening walk's got me tuckered out too. I think I'm going to turn in. Thanks for the company, Nathan. It was nice of you to humor an old man with a few minutes of friendly conversation."

Nathan nodded. "I wasn't humoring anybody. A visit with you is always welcome. You have a good night now and get some rest."

Katie waited until her father had finished his nightly rituals and settled into his room before venturing further with Nathan. Careful to keep her voice quiet, she asked the question on her mind since she got out of her jeep. "What was dad doing out in the field alone?"

Nathan glanced behind her into the shadow of the living room. "He said he wanted to go for a walk. With all the ruckus of the party, he wanted to spend some time in the quiet. He couldn't think of a more peaceful quiet than out in the field under the stars."

Katie's own penchant for finding her calm in nature had come from her father. She knew that. But all the little things had taken a toll on her over the months since she'd moved in. Seeing him out there hit a raw nerve.

"I don't want to overstep, but he seemed fine. Just a little melancholy. Lonely maybe."

Katie's head shot up, her defenses raised. "Lonely? Do you think dad's lonely? That's the whole reason we moved in here after Austin died. So we'd have each other. Are you saying I'm not spending enough time with him?"

Nathan raised his hands in front of him much like a criminal when confronted by the cops on television. "I'm not saying anything like that. You and Sammy are wonderful for him. But,

Kate, how long were your parents married? Think of all those years together, side by side through everything. And now she's gone."

He paused. Thinking he was finished Katie started to speak but refrained at the look on his face. There was more he wanted to say. But he was wrestling with whether he should. She could see the war in his blue eyes which had grown stormy with his indecision.

He took a deep breath. "You of all people should understand his loneliness. You and Austin only had each other for a short time, but unless I miss my guess there's not a day that's gone by that you don't ache to see him again. That's your dad's loneliness too."

NATHAN WATCHED her hands cover her mouth as tears escaped their lashed prison. He swallowed, waiting for her to tell him to leave. He probably deserved it. He wouldn't feel bad for showing her the truth, but it was too much to watch his words break her in this way. Every muscle in his body tensed with the desire to comfort her. But she wasn't his to comfort. They'd barely re-established their friendship.

He sat in indecision until she looked up at him. The hurt emanating from those green eyes seemed to plead to him to ease her pain. He ran a hand through his hair as he stood and turned away from her. What should he do? What could he do? The muffled sobs told him her head had dropped back into her hands. He bit his lip battling within himself. He had to do something. He went to her, took her hands in his, and drew her up beside him. Her head fell to his shoulder as she continued to cry.

One arm slipped around her shoulders while the other cradled her head. He wanted to say something. He wanted to calm the emotion he'd loosed with his words. He searched for

47

the right words, anything that might soothe, but there was nothing. All he could do was hold her. Reason told him Kate's tears were good for her. She'd carried more than her share of pain over the last few years. She deserved her time to cry. Knowing it didn't keep the feeling of helplessness from spreading through him.

He couldn't guess how long they stood holding each other before he felt the gasping breaths that came with a return of emotional control. He reluctantly dropped his hand from where it had been buried in her hair. From the way it shone like fire in light of the setting sun, he knew it would be soft but it had felt like silk between his fingers. She lifted her head to look at him. The green of her eyes was as rich as an evergreen at Christmas, darkened with her emotion and shining from her tears. His hand fell from her back as he stepped away. He forced a thin smile.

"Better?" Please don't let her hear the strain. Please don't let her question.

A slight nod. Her cheeks were flushed, but he couldn't tell if it was from crying or embarrassment at having broken down in front of him. Her eyes might have told him, but they were the last place he was going to look. His own would be too apt to give him away.

"Good. You know what, you've had a long day. Why don't I get out of here and let you get some rest? You sure you're okay? 'Cause if you're not, I'll stay."

Don't let her ask me to stay. He sought out her eyes only to look away quicker than pulling his hand away from a hot stove. He didn't want to hurt her any more than he already had.

"I'm fine. You go on home. I think I'll just go up to bed."

Her voice was soft, but he'd take the lifeline she offered. He nodded his good-bye and headed to his truck. At the end of the driveway, he stomped the brake and shoved the truck into park. His hand smacked the steering wheel. How could he have let this happen? All he wanted to do was be there for her, to help a friend through a difficult time. That's all he was doing. It was a fluke, and it didn't mean anything. It couldn't mean anything. For heaven's sake, she was upset over the loss of her husband. The whole conversation was saturated with emotion. Kate was an emotional person, and he wasn't used to dealing with that. That's all it was. He was sure of it.

He put the truck in gear and pulled out of the driveway. Tomorrow the whole situation would look foolish. Everything would be back to normal by the time he saw her again because it didn't mean anything. No matter what it seemed like at the moment, he was positive he didn't really want to kiss Kate.

Chapter Six

K atie stood unmoving long after Nathan left. Her tears left her drained and unable to process the evening's events. She started up the stairs to her room but thought better of it. Instead, she filled the bathtub and slipped into the hot water to soothe away the cares of the day. How could she have let Nathan hold her like that? She'd been so caught off guard by his statement the tears overtook her without warning.

Thinking of her pain was difficult enough. Celebrating Sammy's birthday should be a purely happy affair. So should Christmases and the day he took his first steps or said his first word. None of those should be tinged with loss, but they were. Every time they were. She had friends to share them with. She had her father and Sammy. But at the end of those days, when she lay alone in her queen size bed, the truth came out. Austin wasn't there with her like he was supposed to be. They couldn't laugh over their toddler's antics. He couldn't build his son's playhouse.

Nathan's words drew the truth from her. She was lonely. That reality would have been enough to reduce her to tears, but he hadn't let it stop there. He'd shown her the pain her father was in too. Her daddy had always been the strong one. He'd been steady as long as she could remember. Thinking of him being lonely was too much. It took more strength than she had left.

That's why she'd leaned on Nathan. Never in all the years she spent as best friends with his sister did she consider that one day he'd be her friend as well. They'd always teased each other and harmlessly flirted as teenagers do without any real feelings behind their actions. Even when she'd harbored a crush on him, she knew their antics would never lead anywhere. And they hadn't, not to anything but a superficial friendship based on proximity. Not once had they indulged in meaningful conversation or spent time together like they had today. And never would she have guessed he would one day be there to offer her comfort with such solid strength. Or that she would turn to him for it in the first place. But when she found herself empty, that's exactly what she'd done.

And it had made him uncomfortable. She could see it in his eyes when she looked up at him. The quick frown as he stepped away from her confirmed it. The way he wouldn't make eye contact except for the briefest of moments before excusing himself told her he didn't want that place in her life. She'd left him no choice. He couldn't leave her in that state when she started crying. What was that phrase he was always reminding her? His mama had raised him better than that.

Katie sunk under the water with a groan. As she came back up for air and wiped the water from her face, she considered how she could salvage the situation. However frivolous their past friendship had been, Nathan had shown himself a true friend more than once since Austin's death. She knew the value of that kind of friendship and didn't want to lose it over an emotional breakdown. She'd have to show him she was capable of spending time with him without getting caught up in emotional situations. She could do it. Now she simply had to come up with a plan.

KATIE HAD BEGUN to doubt Gigi B's directions when the gate to the ranch finally came in view on the backroad between Carbondale and Goreville. She was pretty sure the area would still be considered Carbondale, but she wouldn't swear to it. The last time she'd been anywhere near here she'd wrecked her jeep after hitting a deer. Figuring out her exact location had been far from her mind.

Of course, Gigi B's directions weren't the only thing she doubted. The idea to surprise Nathan at his ranch had come to her almost immediately. She'd talked herself out of it by the next morning and back into it by Monday. Now it had been almost a week and Katie had called Gigi B for directions and taken off before her mind could change again. If she didn't pay attention to the road in front of her, it wouldn't matter. She'd be in a ditch needing to be saved once again. That was not going to happen.

The narrow gravel drive wove through trees not yet awake from their winter naps. Katie could imagine the canopy of shade they would provide in the summer and the kaleidoscope of color that would form overhead in fall. Beautiful. Even in its bare state, the path couldn't be described any other way. After what had to be a mile or more the cover of trees gave way to wide open fields. She scanned the scene before her. At the end of the drive to her right stood a single-story cedar-sided ranch house with three dormer windows spaced to break the monotony of the long roof. It's covered porch running the length of the home and large windows gave the rustic house a comfortable, homey feel.

Stretching out from the house was a simply styled yard leading straight into the pastures. Beyond the house and to the left a massive cream-colored pole barn stood vigil. It lacked the charm of her dad's old-fashioned red barn, but clean lines and its size made it impressive nonetheless. The metal roof, a shade darker than the home's cedar siding, complemented the rest of the design and gave it just enough personality to be pleasing to the eye.

In a corral not far from the barn a rider sat astride a golden brown horse with black mane and tail. With the approach of her jeep, the rider had reined the horse to a halt and sat watching the drive. Nathan. Probably wondering why she was there. As far as he knew, she didn't know where to find the place.

As she drew near to the corral, the man on the horse moved to the fence and dismounted. Standing apart from the horse, Katie realized her mistake. There was no way the guy was Nathan. He fell short of Nathan's six feet by at least a couple inches, though he was still taller than Katie.

"Hi. Mr.?"

"Just Chris, ma'am."

"I'm sorry to interrupt, Chris, but is this Nathan Phillips' place?"

His voice was smooth and slow when he answered. "Yes, ma'am, it is. Nathan's over in the barn. You can go on over there if ya want. Main door's open."

She looked to the door he indicated then back at him. "Thank you."

He nodded. "No trouble at all."

With the conversation ended, he hoisted himself back into the saddle and rode back into the center of the corral. Katie made her way to the barn. As she stood in the doorway she couldn't believe the difference a modern barn made. Her father's barn, even when it wasn't in shambles, was always dark and close. The light filling this one left no room for the shadowy places that filled her with dread as a child. Stalls lined both walls. The bottom half of each was solid, but the top halves were barred. The stalls in her dad's old barn were mostly open with planks of wood and gates holding the animals in their places. The difference was incredible.

Shuffling sounds at the far end of the barn caught her attention. A stall door stood open. A wheelbarrow stood outside it piled with refuse.

"Hello?"

Whinnies and movement came from several stalls, but the head that popped out of the one in the back was the one she was looking for.

"Kate? What are you doin' out here?" Nathan emerged from the stall to dump a shovelful of waste and hay into the wheelbarrow. He set the shovel against the wall and picked up the handles of the wheelbarrow.

Katie shifted her weight from one foot to the other. Maybe Nathan wouldn't appreciate an interruption to his day. She should have thought of that before her impromptu trip to the middle of nowhere. Honestly, she had no clue what a day in the life of a horse trainer looked like. "I got directions from Gigi B. I hope you don't mind."

He pushed the wheelbarrow past her and out the door leaving her to follow or stand in the doorway by herself. She followed.

"Well, that answers how you got here. But it still doesn't answer why."

Was he mad that she'd come or just frustrated at the interruption? Katie wished she knew him well enough to understand his tones. "I guess to make up for Saturday night."

He dumped the contents of the wheelbarrow into a pile of refuse. Katie scrunched her nose. He grinned at her discomfort and shook his head. "You get used to it. What're you making up for?"

Katie lifted a shoulder unsure of her answer. "I guess that I got so rattled at the end of the night. I was trying to tell you thank you for building Sammy's playhouse, but I ended up breaking down on you. I'm not usually like that. I wanted to show you we can be friends without you worrying about having to pick up my broken pieces every time we're together."

Nathan deposited the wheelbarrow into a small room in the

barn and retrieved the shovel to go with it. His hand stilled on
the door after he shut it. Katie mindlessly twisted a strand of hair
around her finger. Why was it just now dawning on her that he
might not want to take that chance?

"Don't ever apologize to me for hurting. You've had more
than your share of trouble in the last little bit. You don't have to
prove your strength to me. I see it. But you don't have to go
worryin' about needing a shoulder to lean on either."

He saw her strength. That's what he said, and it meant more
than she could give words to. She'd felt weak for so long.
"Thank you."

He was silent as he appraised her for the space of several
seconds. She was moved by his words. Would he see that as the
weakness she'd just assured him wasn't there all the time? Her
chin lifted. She refused to fidget under his gaze. One side of his
lips pulled up bringing out the dimple under his scruff.

"Let me go wash up real quick. It's about time for me to take
a break anyway. Do you have time for lunch or do you need to
get home to Sammy? Or better yet, why don't we go pick up the
little guy and have a picnic together. I'll follow you out to your
place, and no one will have to bring me back when we're done."

Katie smiled. "That sounds perfect."

Chapter Seven

Katie didn't notice anything amiss until Nathan's truck pulled up behind her. Confusion set in as she watched his face drain of color. His eyes were wide as they focused somewhere behind her. Turning to see what had his attention, Katie noticed smoke filling the screened-in front porch. Fear spiraled through her seizing her muscles. Fire. Her dad. Sammy. Sammy!

Thinking of her son loosed her from the paralyzing grip of fear. Katie ran for the house only steps behind Nathan. Before plunging into the smoky depths, he hastily removed his denim shirt and held it over his mouth and nose. As she choked on a mouthful of acrid smoke, Katie wished she could do the same. Trying to breathe as shallowly as possible, she stayed in step behind him into the kitchen. It took only seconds to assess the situation.

Flames spurted from a cast-iron skillet on the stove. A stray spark landed on the dishtowel hanging from the oven door. Fairly contained at this point, Katie knew the fire needed put out immediately or it would soon rage out of control. Her mind said to put out the fire, but her heart screamed to find her family. She stood frozen with indecision.

Nathan turned at that moment. She knew her eyes would betray her frantic thoughts, but she had no other choice. His sureness broke through her hesitation. He waved her away. "I've got this! You get Sammy and your dad out of this smoke!"

She watched him throw the towel to the floor and stomp out the growing flame. She turned and ran from the room and up the stairs. Breathing was easier, but not by much. Stairs were no match for the tendrils of smoke filling the house. A few more minutes and the stench would find its way into every nook and cranny of their home.

Katie went straight to Sammy's bed only to find it empty. Where was her child? She raced back down the stairs and through the living room to her father's room only to find it empty as well. *Dear God, let me find my family, please!*

Memories of fire prevention lessons from childhood flooded her mind. Stealing much-needed oxygen, smoke was as deadly as an unrestrained fire. Smoke took lives. Would her father remember this and keep himself and her son under the smoke? Had it already rendered them unconscious somewhere in the house?

"Dad? Sammy?"

A coughing fit seized her as her panicked cry caused her to inhale more smoke than her lungs could handle. Before she had the smoke expelled from her lungs and her cough under control, Katie felt a strong hand grasp her wrist.

"I've got the fire out and the windows open. You get out of here. I'll search for Cal and Sammy."

"No, I ..." Another coughing fit commenced.

Nathan grasped her shoulders. He turned her and propelled her toward the door. "I'm not arguing with you about this. Now get out into the fresh air. I'll check the rest of the house."

Katie knew he was right. She couldn't keep looking with the burning in her chest. Even now her head was beginning to swim. She nodded. "Please find them. This smoke. It can't be good."

She gulped the fresh air as she stepped away from the front door. With the windows open, smoke was quickly dispersing into the wide-open sky where it couldn't do any more damage. Katie couldn't make herself go more than a few steps from the house. It was far enough to find clean air to purge the poison from her lungs but close enough she could return to search on a moment's notice. She wanted to be near when Nathan brought Sammy and her father to her. Seconds felt like hours as she stood there watching.

"'Gin. 'Gin, Papa."

Sammy's giggling voice found its way around the house to Katie. Tears sprang to her eyes as she realized her son and father were safe on the other side of the house. On her way to them, Katie stepped to the open front door and yelled into the empty room. "Nathan! It's okay, Nathan! They're out here!"

"Thank God!" His voice came from somewhere upstairs.

Unable to wait for him, Katie rounded the corner of the house. Sammy sat in the toddler swing of his playhouse while her father stood behind him pushing him again and again as he'd requested. The relief was sweeter than the fresh air she'd taken in to clear her lungs. Tears flowed down her cheeks, and she fought the desire to sob hysterically. Sammy wouldn't understand. She doubted her father would either.

"Mama! I'm high!"

She swiped the tears from her cheek sure she was leaving sooty trails in their place. "I see, Sammy. Papa's swinging you high, isn't he?"

"To the sky."

Katie crossed her arms in front of her to still the shaking overtaking her body. Her father and Sammy were oblivious, and now that she knew they were safe there was no reason to panic them. If she could only convince her legs not to give out on her everything would be alright.

"Lean back if you need to." His deep, quiet voice spoke behind her resonating with calm.

The thought of leaning back into Nathan for strength while her body purged itself of the extra adrenaline sounded wonderful. But she had to be strong. She had to show him friendship with her didn't mean forever picking up the pieces of her life. With steadiness she would've thought impossible, Katie stepped away from him and the support he offered. She moved to the swing that had inhabited the grassy area by her mother's flower gardens since Katie moved back home after Austin's death.

"I'm okay now that I know they're safe."

Nathan didn't wait for an invitation before joining her on the swing. She looked sideways at him. Grime from the smoke-filled kitchen was streaked across his forehead. She smiled.

"You know it's not every friend that will run into a burning building with you. Thank you."

He leaned forward resting his arms on his knees, hands clasped together, as he watched the pair at the playhouse. "I'm not that great a friend. The house wasn't actually on fire. Just the pan on the stove and that kitchen towel. Which, by the way, I hope wasn't a favorite." He crinkled his nose in a grimace. "I failed to save it."

She nudged his shoulder. "I think I'll live without it. We have others. But seriously, you didn't know it was contained. Don't sell yourself short."

He shook his head. "It's not a big deal. It's just how my mama raised me."

"You say that a lot. And while I can't argue that your mom did an excellent job raising you, I think it's more than that."

"Ya do, do ya?"

"Yes, I do. How we're raised goes a long way in who we become, but it's more than training that sent you into that house. It's who you are at your core. It's the way you were raised, your faith, and just you all wrapped up into one. Thank you isn't enough."

He looked everywhere but her. "I guess you'll just have to owe me another burger then."

She laughed.

He jerked his head toward the house. "I think we caught things early enough that once the smoke clears out everything will be fine. Might have to do some laundry to get it out of curtains and such. But other than maybe right above the stove, I don't think there's any lasting damage. I do want you to promise me one thing though."

"What's that?"

"Get yourself some new batteries in your smoke detectors. Not one of them went off today. Don't let it happen again."

"Deal."

Chapter Eight

"God was surely watching out for your daddy and your little boy."

Gigi B had a knack for stating the obvious while still cutting to the quick. Katie cleared the tightness from her throat. She'd considered all the possible outcomes, and she hadn't ceased to praise God for protecting her loved ones. "I know."

The elderly woman sat in the pew next to her while the rest of the congregation filtered out the doors of the church. "And it seems someone else was watching out for you too."

"Huh?"

Her eyes rolled in time with her exasperated sigh. "You didn't run into that house all by your lonesome, now did you?"

"Oh, Nathan."

Her elderly voice mocked in a sing-song tone. "Oh, Nathan. Yes, Nathan. That man is proving himself a worthy friend. Of course, I never doubted that for a minute. That boy's been raised right."

Katie shook her head. How many times would she have to hear that? Seemed like everyone thought Nathan Phillips was raised right. Of course, after so many times of coming to her aid, she wasn't going to argue. "Yes, he is that. Back in high school I never would've thought it."

Wrinkles deepened as Gigi B's eyes narrowed into a hawkish stare. "Is it more than that?"

Katie hoped her look was as incredulous as she was aiming for. Gigi B did not need encouragement. "No. Nathan's friendship is all I need. Me and Sammy and Dad have a good thing going."

"Hmm. I guess so. Speaking of your good thing, did you find out what happened?"

Katie shrugged. "As near as I can tell, he made Sammy some lunch and then took him outside to play before his nap. Only he forgot to turn off the stove and the grease caught on fire."

"Do you think it was a one-time thing?"

"Mama!"

Sammy threw himself into her lap. A teenage girl followed close behind. "He couldn't wait any longer. He's been dying to see his mommy since the other kids started getting picked up."

Katie glanced around the now empty sanctuary. "I'm so sorry, Cadence. I didn't realize we'd been talking so long."

"It's no biggie. Sammy is a great little boy. I'll see you next week okay, Sammy?"

"'Kay."

The toddler launched himself at Gigi B with speed Katie feared would knock her out of her seat. Instead, she threw her arms around him with as much abandon as he did her. Katie smiled at the exchange. Sammy would never know his real grandmother, but with Gigi B around he would never lack one.

"Sammy, what do you say we take Gigi B out to lunch today?" She looked at the woman cuddling her wiggly son. "There's a fellowship meal at dad's church today. So, we're on our own and would be honored if you'd join us. Our treat."

Gigi B looked Sammy in the face. "What do you think of that plan? Should we all go to lunch together?"

"I'm hungry."

She pulled him in tight, kissing his silky curls. "It's settled then. Why don't we take my car, and I'll drop you back here on the way home. No sense in wasting gas when we're going to the same place."

Katie knew the futility of arguing when Gigi B had a plan. "Let me grab Sammy's car seat, and we'll be ready to go."

AN HOUR later Katie watched Gigi B pull out of the church parking lot where she dropped her off after their lunch at the Chinese buffet. Sammy had kept them in stitches pretending his noodles were worms to slurp off his plate. But once he started on his cup of ice cream, Gigi B had broached the subject of her father once again.

It wasn't the possibility of her son listening that made her reluctant to talk about the fire. Fear didn't play a part in it either, at least not fear of what could have happened. No, she was aware that her hesitance came from the sinking suspicion that all was not right in her father's world. While episodes seemed to happen more frequently, they were still silly things that amounted to forgetting to turn off a curling iron after use. Everyone forgot things like that sometimes. Why did it have to mean something bigger when it came to her dad?

Katie drove toward home with Sammy nodding off in his car seat. The quiet gave her time to reflect. Her stomach was unsettled at what she might find when she arrived home. Dad had gone with his pastor's family, but he should be home by now. The phantom scent of smoke assailed her. Would she arrive to find another disaster in the making? And if there wasn't truth to Gigi B's concerns, why did that thought threaten to strike fear into her heart?

Chapter Nine

"So this is where they're hiding all the cute boys. Wish someone had told me a few decades ago."

Nathan looked up from where he squatted on the floor tightening the screw in the door hinge. He couldn't help the goofy grin that followed her over the top compliment. "Well good afternoon to you, too, Gigi B. Don't take this the wrong way, but I doubt back then you had trouble finding the cute boys as you call them. In fact, unless I'm missin' my guess, they probably came out of the woodwork any time you were around."

She swatted his shoulder, but she couldn't hide her grin. "Go on with you now. It wasn't like that at all. What are you doing here on a fine Sunday afternoon? Didn't miss church this morning did you?"

Dropping the screwdriver he'd been using into his canvas tool bag, he stood and stretched the kinks out of his long legs. "No, ma'am. As much as the nursing home can use my volunteer time, I'm not going to miss services to do it. I need that time of worship with other believers. Sets me right for the week. But there were a few repairs I didn't get to yesterday. I may not make it back this week, and I wanted to get them done in case."

"Good man. Got your priorities straight. When you get done with everything would you have a minute for a cup of coffee at the canteen?"

Nathan winked at her. "For you? I'll set aside two minutes."

A faint tint of pink crept across her wrinkled cheek. "You are shameless dear boy. But don't let that stop you. I get precious few compliments these days. I'll take them when I can get them. I'm going to go pray with Mr. Jeffers while you finish up. I'll meet you in about ten minutes?"

He tilted his head in agreement. He watched her purposeful stride down the hall to Mr. Jeffers's room before picking up his tool bag. He had just enough time to fix the blinds on Miss Paula's window before meeting Gigi B.

Nathan growled under his breath. The mini-blinds were twisted up worse than he'd first thought. He wasn't sure how the frail ninety-year-old woman sitting in the rocker in the corner always managed to make such a mess of them, but he wished she'd let him take them down. As many times as he'd come to fix them, he was beginning to wonder if she did it on purpose to have a visitor for a few minutes. The last piece finally slid back into place without twisted strings.

"There you go, Miss Paula. All fixed. Is there anything else you need while I'm here?"

Frail fingers fidgeted on her afghan covered lap. Thin lips pursed momentarily before parting only to close without uttering a sound. There was something, but she didn't want to say anything. She was probably worried she was asking too much of him. They had the same argument every time she needed help.

"I was hoping there was something else I could do for you. You know me. Always lookin' for a new project, even if it's a small one."

Her features relaxed. "If you're looking for something to do, I do have one more small task."

"Name it."

She motioned to the tiny bathroom on the wall adjacent to the one with the window. "The light above my vanity went out, and I couldn't see to put on my face this morning. It's just too dark in there without it. But they put that light so high a little old lady like myself can't ever hope to reach it. Could you replace it for me?"

"I can get your light changed for you. But I want to know one thing first."

"What's that?"

"Who are you putting on your face for? Is it that new widower that moved into B Hall a couple of weeks ago? I thought I saw you and Miss Violet watching him pretty close when he moved in."

She huffed but couldn't hide the sparkle in her eyes. "You impertinent thing! You just get in there and change that lightbulb. Land sakes, you've got to be worse than the busiest busybody in the place."

He grinned at her obvious deflection. It took only moments to fish a new lightbulb out of the cabinet and replace the old one. He stepped back out to find the elderly woman pretending to glare at him.

"Now, Miss Paula, I didn't mean any harm. I was just joshin' you. Forgive me?"

Her stare stayed trained on him. The clock on the wall made the only sound in the room for the space of several ticks. "Of course I'll forgive you. The Good Book says I should, and I always try to do what it tells me to do."

He smiled. "I find that works best for me too. And I thank you kindly for forgiving my hastily spoken words. I've got to meet Gigi B down at the canteen now. I'll see you next time I'm here."

Gigi B was waiting with two foam cups in front of her at one of several round, white plastic tables scattered around the room.

He rushed to sit down. "Sorry I made you wait. Miss Paula's blinds were giving me a fit."

"Never did like those things. They always prove to be a lot of trouble for a little bit of shade."

"My thoughts exactly. But I don't think you wanted to meet to discuss mini-blinds. And I'm fairly certain we're not fixin' to have a friendly, light-hearted chat either."

She licked her lips and watched the foam cup between her hands like the creamy depths held the answers to all the questions of the universe. He'd never known Gigi B to hedge around when she had something she wanted to talk about. This couldn't be good.

She looked at him. "Tell me about the fire. What happened?"

The fire? At Kate's house? "When Kate and I got back to her house I noticed smoke filling up their sun porch. We didn't know where Cal and Sammy were, and we didn't waste any time getting in there to find them. Saw quick enough that the fire was contained to a frying pan. I worked to put it out while Kate went to search for her boy. Turns out they'd gone outside to play after lunch. They didn't even know there was a problem until there wasn't."

"Katie seems to think it was nothing more than a simple matter of forgetting like we're all want to do. What do you think?"

Careful. "What does it matter what I think?"

She speared him with a look. He fidgeted under it no matter how he tried to sit still. How could such a little old thing make him feel six years old again? Still, he didn't want to have this discussion. It wasn't his place to decide what was going on with Kate and her father. And he didn't want to jeopardize their growing friendship.

"I don't know what you want to hear, Gigi B. Did he forget? Sure he did. Has he been forgetful as of late? I guess so. But I'm not the one to judge if it's normal or not. That would be Kate's place, and she seems to think everything is fine."

"How long have you been coming here?"

Nathan frowned at the change in topics. He tallied the time in his head. "I guess I've been volunteering here for about seven years. Why?"

She stood and picked up her empty cup. "Walk with me a minute, will you?"

He nodded and scooped his cup off the table. "Lead the way."

Gigi B led him around the circuit of rooms. With the hallways making a giant circle, there weren't a lot of places for residents to get lost. Eventually, they'd make it back to their rooms. As she walked a couple of steps in front of him, Nathan couldn't help thinking the bright spot of color that accompanied the elderly woman everywhere she went didn't seem to belong in a place like this. Of course, maybe that was what made her need to be there most, at least for her weekly visits.

He lengthened his stride to get beside her. "What're ya thinking?"

A sweeping motion of her hand drew his attention to the rooms lining either side of the hall. "Look at this place. You've spent time with enough of the men and women here to understand the problems of growing old. You've seen the ones like Tess who've still got all their faculties for the most part. You've seen more than your share of ones like Bert down the hall that doesn't know his wife or daughter anymore. You know the difference between the usual forgetfulness of aging and the signs of dementia and Alzheimer's. I'm not asking you to be a doctor. I just want to know what you've observed."

She wasn't going to let this go. And Gigi B couldn't be confused with any of the nursing home residents. Her mind was as sharp as it had been when she was in her twenties. He'd have to bite the bullet and have this conversation, like it or not. "Well,

I guess if you're going to rope me into having this talk, I'd have to say I'm not sure. Back when Kate moved home, I noticed the forgetfulness. But it didn't seem to be an unusual amount for his age."

"And now?"

He shook his head. "It's coming more often. He's getting turned around, forgetting the day, and struggling for names and words that should be commonplace. It's more frequent, but I can't say for sure. Kate seems to think it's all within normal limits."

Their circuit complete, Nathan followed Gigi B to the couches that served as a welcoming center near the front door of the facility. She sat. He followed suit.

"Katie isn't in the best position to judge at the moment."

"What do you mean?"

"Katie's lost a lot the past couple of years. I don't think she believes she can handle another. Besides, she's a daddy's girl. Admitting there's a problem isn't going to be easy for her."

He could feel the truth settle inside. "So what can we do?"

Gigi B stood and looped her purse over her shoulder. "Let's just keep an eye on things for now. When the opportunity comes up, we can broach the subject with Katie. Maybe one of these times she'll be ready to hear it. Until then we can pray God opens her eyes and keeps every last one of them safe."

Nathan sat replaying their conversation long after Gigi B said her good-byes. He left the nursing home praying for Kate and her family. If they were right, the path ahead of Kate wasn't going to be an easy one.

Chapter Ten

"Where did Austin get to?"

Katie paused with the butter covered knife hovering over the slice of toast. She didn't hear what she thought she heard. She turned to face her dad. "What did you say?"

"I asked where Austin got to. I haven't seen him all day. Wanted to thank him again for his help with Sammy's playhouse and see if he was ready for another job."

Nathan. He was asking about Nathan. Not Austin. "Nathan doesn't live here, Dad. He's going to meet me and Sammy here when I get done in town this afternoon though. You'll see him then."

If he noticed the name change, he didn't let it show. Katie wished she could do the same. It had been three weeks since her talk with Gigi B, and since then every little thing her dad did stuck out like a rose in a bouquet of weeds. She finished buttering the toast and put it down in front of Sammy sitting next to the table in his booster seat.

"Sure. Sure. I can wait. I wanted to get some work done in the shop today anyway. Somebody's always needing something made, but I can't complain. It's the gift God gave me, and He wants me to use it to minister to others."

Katie felt sick. "Yes, it is."

Though he spent plenty of time doing for others in his shop while she was growing up, her dad hadn't been able to use his skills to help family and friends for years. Was the past overtaking the present like Gigi B seemed to think? Katie shook off the thought.

Still, it couldn't hurt to be careful. "Don't worry about fixing yourself lunch today. There's a bowl of spaghetti in the fridge that's just enough for one person. It needs to be used today, and I'd appreciate it if you warmed it in the microwave whenever you're ready to eat."

If it was a favor he could do for her, Katie was sure her father would agree. There wasn't any need to disturb him with the thought that he shouldn't use the stove.

He nodded. "Of course, Katydid. Whatever helps."

He finished his coffee and rinsed the cup in the sink before heading toward his room. "I'll see you two later. I'm going to go read my Bible for a while before I get to work."

Katie waited until he was out of the room before she wiped Sammy's hands and cleaned up their breakfast dishes. She bundled him into his coat and slid into her own before moving to turn off the kitchen light. She paused catching sight of the stove. It wasn't his fault. People forgot things like that all the time. It wasn't a sign of something bigger going on. Still, she couldn't ignore her growing unease. She quickly pulled each nob from the stove and dropped them into her purse.

She turned from the stove to find Sammy watching her. She smiled. "Let's get going before we miss storytime at the library."

With the promise of stories ahead, Sammy raced out the front door and to the jeep. Katie followed behind with a prayer that all would be well when they returned.

"I'm sorry, but there isn't going to be a story time today. In fact, it's going to be put on hold for a while."

Katie saw fatigue on the face of the woman behind the counter. "Do you mind my asking why?"

The woman sighed as she pushed her glasses further up her long nose. "Marie, our story lady, went and eloped this morning. Not so much as a day's notice. And they're moving too. Worst part of it is that she's our children's department activity coordinator. I'd read to the kids myself seeing as how we've not had time to make other arrangements, but I don't have much patience for the littles as she always called them."

An idea came to Katie and took hold. It felt like the answer to the prayer she'd been praying since deciding that opening a book store was not God's plan for her. She said a quick, silent plea to her heavenly Father to keep her mouth shut if it wasn't from Him and then dove in headfirst. "How about I make you a deal? I owned my own bookstore for years, and we hosted children's activities and reading regularly. I did the readings myself unless we had a special guest. I'm looking for a part-time job, and books have always been a huge part of my life. I'd love to be your children's department activity coordinator. I'll conduct your reading today, and you can consider it a trial run. If you like what you hear, I get the job. If not, I keep looking. Deal?"

The woman's eyes darted to the children's section where a group of children waited less than patiently with their parents. Katie could see the battle inside. She could let Katie lead story time, or she could contend with a mob of disappointed littles. Another sigh. "It's a deal. Of course, you would have to pass a background check to continue working with the children." Her tone suggested she believed that alone could be the deal-breaker.

Katie smiled as sweetly as she could. "I wouldn't have it any other way."

As she chose a book and assumed her spot in the reading chair, Katie was aware of her possible employer watching her every move. She forced the woman's shrewd look from her mind and instead focused on the eager faces of the children, with Sammy front and center. The mothers around the room varied. Most sat around the outer edge of the children, a human barrier providing the boundaries of the group. Some sat heads down focused on the screens in their laps. The offerings of phones and tablets were more interesting than the book their children were about to hear. Others read books of their own, and a few even moved from the group to peruse the shelves for new stories to begin. They must have been secure in the knowledge that their precious offspring were well supervised. But there were a few that sat with as much interest showing on their faces as the children at their feet.

Katie took a deep breath. Today's book was one of Sammy's favorites. She knew the story well and could find its rhythm without trying as she read. "Once upon a time on an old farm on the top of a great, green hill there lived twin lambs."

Movement at the edge of the group caught Katie's attention as she read. Without missing a word, she glanced toward the newcomers. A little boy with a head full of straight black hair sat with his large, chocolate-colored eyes transfixed on her. One pudgy hand was up to his mouth where his thumb was held securely. The other was nestled in the petite hand of a woman, no a girl, who had the same eyes and straight black hair. Hers was pulled into a low ponytail that draped over her shoulder.

Something about the pair created a gentle nudge in Katie's spirit. She made a mental note to seek them out after the reading. For now, she had to give the book the attention it deserved if she wanted the opportunity to keep reading to these children in the future. And though her decision had felt impulsive, Katie found she did want to see it continue.

"The end." She scanned the room's smiling faces before

continuing. "I hope you liked today's story and come back next week for a new one. Moms, you can check out this book or any of our other children's books. Reading to your child now will help build strong readers as they grow. I hope to see you all next week!"

Katie collected Sammy from the front row and began making her way through the crowd of children pairing up with their parents. She wanted to make contact with the woman and child who'd caught her attention. She spotted them moving toward the door, but before she could reach them the woman from the front desk stood in front of her.

"You didn't disappoint, Mrs.?"

Katie's shoulders dropped as the pair she sought opened the door and stepped outside. Oh well. Maybe next time, if the librarian's pleasant tone meant anything. She held out her free hand. "Blake. I'm Katie Blake, and this is Sammy."

A forced smile and quick nod in his direction told Katie all she needed to know. It was no wonder the small library needed a children's activity coordinator. The head librarian didn't seem to enjoy being in the company of the littles. That suited Katie just fine. She needed a part-time job, and this one seemed perfect for her.

"I'm Mildred Fitzgerald. I know it's spur of the moment, but can you tell me what you'd like to see done with the children's program?"

Katie didn't have to think about it. Her years of experience with children and love of children's books rushed in. "Sammy and I have come to story hour a few times, and he loves the readings. But I'd like to see more interaction between the children and the books we read. Simple, frugal crafts or activities tying into the theme of the book would be wonderful. It could be something as simple as a coloring page or singing a song. And to encourage parents to continue reading with the children in their homes, I'd also add a listing of similar books and easy follow-up activities they can do with their children. I know several semi-local authors as well. I'd love to showcase them on occasion. But these are all rudimentary ideas I've not had the opportunity to flesh out completely, you understand?"

Mildred nodded her grayed head and pushed her glasses further up her nose before answering. "Yes. I understand completely. Now, the position is only twelve to fifteen hours a week, and we can only afford the minimum wage. However, if you're interested, I could meet with you tomorrow around nine to discuss particulars when you don't have your little one with you. Would this work for you?"

"It sounds perfect to me. I'll see you tomorrow at nine. It was a pleasure meeting you, Mrs. Fitzgerald."

"Please, call me Mildred. Until tomorrow then." She waved and was off to the circulation desk without a backward glance.

Katie smiled down at Sammy. "Well, it looks like Mommy got a job. What do you think about that?"

"Picnic now?"

Katie giggled as she led them out the door. "Yes, Sammy. We'll go meet Nathan for our picnic now. You've been very patient. Thank you."

Her praise was rewarded with a skip in his step as they made their way across the parking lot to the jeep. She felt a little like frolicking herself. She hadn't gone looking and had barely begun praying about a job, but that hadn't stopped God from working it out for her. *Thank you, Father. You know what I need before I do.*

KATE'S EYES were bright and her hands motioned throughout her re-telling of the job opportunity with the library. Nathan couldn't help smiling at her excitement. "It sounds like God dropped it in your lap."

Her curls bounced with the nod of her head. "I'm not sure

I've ever seen anything work out so perfectly. And it's part-time too. Which is great for me. I don't want a lot of hours, but I feel like I need to do something. I mean, we've talked about it before. It's not about the money, but I need to be working, you know? And now I can and still have plenty of time with Sammy and Dad. And children's books are the best. So it's kind of a win-win."

Impressive. A whole monologue delivered in a single breath. "I'm glad it's working out for you. I know it was botherin' you the other day. It's good to see you find some direction."

She opened her mouth.

"Mommy! Mommy come slide with me, please!" Sammy called to her from the nearby playground equipment he'd been climbing over while they talked.

She excused herself from the metal bench and moved toward Sammy. Nathan let out a contented breath. Though they still needed light coats, the sunshine had created a great day for a picnic. Not the usual picnic season, Sammy hadn't had a lot of other kids to play with, but he seemed fine with that. He'd entertained himself on the jungle gym, and that had given Nathan time to talk with Kate. She was more than excited about her new job, and he was happy for her. If not for a slight catch in his spirit, it would have been a perfect afternoon. As it was, Nathan pushed the uneasiness away as he considered how nice it would be to have days like this more often.

Kate gestured toward him, and Sammy waved frantically before plopping down on the slide and giggling all the way down. Nathan waved back with a smile. Yes. He could get used to days like this.

He'd known she was back in town over three years ago before Gigi B had even drafted him to help Kate move from the home she'd shared with her husband into the home she'd grown up in after his death. Though they were close enough to claim each other as friends, she'd been his sister's friend through their childhoods. It hadn't occurred to him to reach out to her. Besides, she'd been married at the time.

In the years that had passed since then, he'd seen her now and again. He'd run into her at the store or filling up his truck. Gigi B kept him apprised of the important goings-on when they'd run into each other in the halls at the nursing home. But it seemed like here recently, Kate was becoming more of a fixture in his life again. Only this time his little sister wasn't there to act as the glue to their friendship. It would have to survive on its own.

As Nathan watched Sammy take Kate's hand to lead her to the swings, he couldn't deny the hope growing inside for his friendship with Kate to go beyond mere survival. To be a bright spot for both of them for years to come. The duo was quickly becoming an important part of his life. He didn't want to think about going back to simply acknowledging their existence while having no contact.

He watched Kate lift Sammy into one of the secured toddler swings and push him as high as he knew she dared. He smiled at her protectiveness and left his place of observing on the bench to join them at the swings.

"I never thought I'd see the day when Little Kate wasn't the biggest daredevil on the playground."

She eyed him as she continued to softly push the swing. "I'm not sure what you mean."

"We spent plenty of time on the tire swing in my back yard when we were kids. Tonya tended to be careful, but you? You practically flew. All it took was a little challenge."

Her eyebrow raised. "Challenge? Is that what you called it? I seem to remember it as more of a taunting. Ruthless taunting."

Her voice sounded slightly more emphatic than usual. He grinned. He still had it. "It wasn't taunting. Maybe a little bit of a dare. I'll grant you that, but you didn't ever fail. Didn't matter what it was. You always took the dare."

Her cheeks colored pink. So she remembered. Through all the years of friendship with his sister, Kate always rose to the challenge when he baited her. There was only one dare she'd never taken, and Nathan couldn't help wondering what she thought about it now. There was no way he was going to ask. He had more important business at hand.

"So are you going to take it now?"

Her eyes widened until white practically swallowed up their usual vibrant green. Her voice was tight and high. "What?"

He forced an innocence he knew was less than genuine. "Are you going to loosen up and let Sammy there fly a little higher?"

Her shoulders sagged as the breath rushed from her lungs. "He could get hurt."

"Or he could have the best time ever in a swing designed to keep him safe. He can fly without fear. I dare you."

Her spine straightened. She looked from him to Sammy. "I suppose he might like to go a little higher. But I'm doing it so Sammy can feel what it's like to fly, at least for a child, not because you dared me."

It took all his control to maintain his innocent look. "I'm glad you cleared that up. I'd hate to think I still had the means to get you to do anything just with one well-placed dare."

She looked away from him to Sammy. Her cheeks glowed. Nathan smiled and returned to the bench, stretching his legs out in front of him as he sat. He was right. This friendship was going to be good for both of them.

WHAT WAS she getting herself into with Nathan? One simple statement was all it took to put more blush on her cheeks than a million cosmetic counter make-overs. Surely he didn't remember that dare? It was years ago, and he hadn't meant it. That was the whole reason she'd been able to resist.

Without turning her head in his direction, Katie nonchalantly transferred her gaze to where Nathan sat sprawled out on the bench. She narrowed her eyes. She could see the dimples under the light scruff on his cheeks though his lips held only a slight curve. His blue eyes fairly sparkled. Both were a sure sign he was fighting his good humor at her expense. The nerve of the man. He knew exactly what he was doing, and he was proud of it. That smug look said it all.

It was just as potent now as when he'd given the same look to her the day she turned seventeen. He'd come home from college for summer break. His family needed him to help pack up their lives into the moving van that would take them out of Katie's life. Anxious to spend as much time as possible with her best friend before she left for good, Katie spent nearly every day until they moved at the Phillips's house packing up boxes and memories.

"Can you find Nathan and see if he wants Mom and Dad to take this stuff or if he wants to take it back to his dorm room?"

Tonya's request had been innocent. Nothing, not even hindsight, would ever convince Katie of anything to the contrary. She would have gagged if she'd known what transpired that day in the barn when Katie found Nathan or how much Katie had wanted to take him up on his dare.

The conversation began simply enough. She'd asked, and Nathan had given his answer. His belongings would travel the miles to his parents' new home. It was when she turned to go that she heard, or thought she heard, Nathan suggest something so outrageous she froze. No. He wouldn't have said that. She turned to face him. He looked completely at ease.

"What did you say?"

"I said it's a shame that you've become so kissable right when we're leaving forever."

Her mouth dropped open. Yep. That's what she thought he'd said. But what on earth would prompt such a statement?

He rolled his eyes as he laughed. "Now don't go lookin' so shocked, Little Kate. You and I both know there's a spark between us. There always has been, but the timing's never been right."

She continued to stare, unable to limit her mind to one coherent thought instead of a hurricane of them spinning so fast she couldn't keep up. Sure she'd flirted with him once she'd started seeing guys as more than just buddies. Why wouldn't she? He was gorgeous. Who wouldn't have a little crush on him? And sometimes he seemed to flirt back, but then he'd remind her she was only a kid and tell her what pests she and his sister could be. She only saw it as flirting because that's what she wanted to see. He'd just seen her as a sister. How could he say these things? And now, when he was getting ready to move? Was it a joke? It had to be more joking. Nathan was good at that.

"So how 'bout it?"

She cleared her throat. "How about what?"

One side of his mouth raised. "How about we admit that spark, and I give you a birthday kiss?"

"What?" Her voice sounded squeaky to her own ears. He couldn't be serious. The thought brought reality crashing down and restored her ability to think. "Knock it off, Nathan. You know you don't mean it."

He stepped closer. She breathed in the scent of the men's shower gel she'd seen on the bathroom sink earlier. She couldn't think straight with him staring at her like that.

"Don't I?" One eyebrow lifted as his look took on a mischievous tone. "Tell you what. If it makes it easier for you, I dare you."

She blinked. "Dare me? To what? Kiss you?"

Dimples appeared as he smiled. He lifted one hand to her cheek and rubbed his thumb across her jaw. "I dare you to kiss me. One kiss for your birthday, or maybe just to say bye before we move."

That grin was enough to turn her legs against her. If only he meant it. She'd kiss him, and he'd go back to college in a of couple weeks and forget all about this nonsense. He would find a college girl, and Kate would be stuck at home wishing for him to come back to see where their relationship could go. She stiffened and stepped back. He'd not said anything about wanting a relationship. He just wanted a kiss. It wasn't real. He might find her pretty now, but he didn't like her. But she could easily like him if she didn't already. One kiss wouldn't mean much to him, but it could devastate her.

She stepped away. This was one dare she wouldn't take.

"Higher, Mommy. Higher."

Sammy's voice ripped her attention from the past into the present. She pushed him higher enjoying the giggles that erupted. Enough of the past. She wasn't a starry-eyed teen anymore. Her life didn't have enough room in it to drag up memories from the past. And she wasn't going to entertain thoughts about why that particular memory and the self-satisfied grin on Nathan's handsome face caused a tiny flutter in her middle.

Chapter Eleven

"I'm going to take Sammy to school and head over to the library for a few hours. If you need me, I'll have my cell phone."

Her father folded the newspaper and laid it on the kitchen table in front of him. "Fine. Fine. I'll stay here and get some work done."

Katie fought her sigh. She wasn't sure what work he had in mind. Maybe she could give him some direction. "That'd be great, Dad. I know the flower beds could use a good weeding if you've got the time."

He shrugged, lips barely pursed as his head bobbed slowly. "I might just do that. Sharon is pretty particular about her flowers, but it'd sure be a nice gesture."

A nice gesture? For whom? It almost sounded like he thought Mom would appreciate the effort. "It would be nice, and I would appreciate it. But you don't have to be worried about doing it the way Mom would've done it. You just do it the way you want to do it."

He harrumphed. "You don't know your mother very well. She'd have my hide if it wasn't up to her specifications."

A knot formed in her stomach. There was no way to spin it and make it better. "Dad, you know Mom's gone right?"

"Of course, I know she's gone. You think I'm daft or something?"

She hated to push further, but he could still be misunderstanding her. "I don't think that. I just ..." She just what? How could she broach the subject without hurting or humiliating her father? "It's just that I miss her sometimes. Remembering how she liked the flower beds is a nice memory to think about since she died."

She saw a flicker of understanding in his brown eyes. She hated that she also saw a bit of the light fade to be replaced with pain. Now that reality was sinking in, she had to do something to return some joy before she left.

"I'm not quite ready to leave yet. I don't suppose you could take Sammy out to swing for a minute while I finish up?"

His face relaxed as he straightened his stooped shoulders. "Of course I'll take him out. Sammy! Come on in here. We'll get your coat on and swing a bit before you go to school."

Her son ran from the living room and launched himself at his grandfather who caught him in a giant bear hug. "I 'ready got my coat, Papa."

His wrinkled hand mussed the toddler's hair. "Why yes, you do. Let me get mine on, and we'll both be set."

Sammy followed him onto the screened porch and out the door. Katie moved to the kitchen window where she could watch unobserved. Her father lifted Sammy into the swing and began gently pushing him. Watching the joy on both their faces brought her a measure of peace. Her father would be fine. His confusion had lifted quickly, and his time with Sammy was brightening his spirits. Besides, she would only be gone for a couple of hours. He was getting older, but her dad was still the man she'd always counted on. He'd have a fit if she intimated anything different.

Katie retrieved her purse from the kitchen counter and

headed out the door. Sammy had school to get to, and she had her job. Her dad? Well, he could use some time to himself without her and her busy toddler underfoot.

KATIE TOOK a peek at the time as she flipped her phone into the vibrate setting. Five minutes until nine. She'd planned to arrive at the library a little earlier, but Sammy had been clingy when she'd dropped him off at school. Still, she was better than right on time. The pointed look Mildred Fitzgerald gave her as she pushed her glasses up the bridge of her nose convinced Katie the woman was not impressed with her display of mere punctuality. As Katie stashed her purse in the breakroom, she couldn't help wondering how early she would have to be to gain Mildred's approval. Probably more than she'd ever be able to manage. Oh well. She would do her best and be on time. It wasn't part of her job to suck the sour from a grumpy life.

"Good morning, Mildred. Would you like to hammer out the details of the position before I get started or would you rather wait until after story time today?"

She made a show of lifting her wrist to look at the watch sitting there. A slight pursing of her lips before she spoke. "I guess we should wait until story time is finished. I assume you don't have a story picked out for today's reading yet and the children will start arriving momentarily."

Katie nodded. "You know best. I'll go get set up and be back just as soon as we're done."

"Very well."

Katie bit her lip to hold in the giggle as she made her way to the children's section. The woman was so serious. Katie knew she was going to enjoy her new job, but her boss was not going to add rainbows and sunshine to her day. Rainbows and sunshine. She could add a group reading time for older kids and start with *The Wonderful Wizard of Oz*. Each week they could read a chapter or two and discuss it as an adult book club would. She'd have to remember to pitch the idea to Mildred during their meeting.

Children started wandering into the reading area as Katie pulled a fun rhyming book about a little llama off the shelf. The kids would love it. Sammy always did. As they had done the previous day, the children huddled near the place where Katie would sit. Parents made a ring around the outer edge, those that stayed anyway. She waited as long as she could for stragglers without running everyone else late before beginning the story, complete with voices and dramatic facial expressions.

Katie scanned the crowd as she read. Several were familiar faces, with just as many new ones scattered throughout. There, near the back edge of the group sat the mother and son from the day before. She watched a grin grow around the thumb he kept securely in place between his lips. It was an identical image to the day before except for the smile which replaced the wariness she'd noticed during the prior reading.

This time they wouldn't get away. Almost in perfect time with her "the end", Katie stood and made her way through the group. She intercepted the pair as they were turning to leave.

Katie managed to maneuver herself into position to introduce herself. "Hi. I'm Katie. I noticed you came to story time yesterday, and I'd hoped you would be back so I could introduce myself."

"Hello." The voice was soft. "I'm Anna, and this is my son, Gabriel, but I call him Gabe most of the time."

Katie squatted in front of the boy. "Hello Gabe. I'm Katie. How old are you?"

Two pudgy fingers lifted on his free hand. His thumb stayed firmly in his mouth. His brown eyes were curious. Why wouldn't they be? He didn't know her.

"You're two, huh? That's just a little bit younger than my son, Sammy. I'm sure he'd like to meet you sometime."

A familiar voice spoke from behind her. "Are you about ready to begin our meeting? It looks like things are wrapping up here."

Katie stood, turning to face Mildred as she did so. "Of course. I haven't forgotten. I even have an idea or two to run by you that I didn't have before coming in today. Let me just say good-bye to Anna and Gabe so we can get started."

She turned to find Anna and Gabe had already dismissed themselves from the conversation and were heading out the door. She sighed as she followed Mildred into the break room, which also served as the office they would use for their discussion. At least she had names now. Even if it took a hundred story times, Katie was determined to find out more about the pair. Something about them just wouldn't let her go.

Anna and Gabe were still on her mind when she left the meeting with Mildred two hours later. Mildred hadn't loosened up any throughout their conversation, but she'd been open to Katie's ideas. That's what mattered, and it freed her thoughts to return to the young mother and son.

"Why them?" She prayed. "Why have they taken hold of me like this?"

She got in her car and laid her head against the seat rest waiting for an answer. With her eyes shut and silence enveloping her, Katie jumped as the boisterous song announcing a call from Erin came through. Answers would have to wait. She fished the phone from her purse.

"Hey, Erin."

Her throat tightened at the sniffle on the other end of the line. "Erin? What's wrong?"

Her friend's voice was subdued. "Why doesn't God think I'd make a good mother?"

Katie felt relieved even while a rock settled in her stomach.

Erin and Paul had been trying to get pregnant almost from the time they married. She'd been so sure the intrauterine insemination procedure was the answer to their problems. Apparently, it hadn't worked for them. "I'm so sorry. I don't even know what to say, but I do know God doesn't think you'd make a bad mom."

"Then why can't I get pregnant?"

There were so many things she could say, and none of them would be a good enough answer. Erin's heart was breaking again. Over twenty-four months of the same heartbreak took its toll. Anything she said would sound trite no matter how true it was. "I don't know. But I'm here as long as you need me."

Her breaths shuddered. "I feel like such a failure. I can't even get my body to cooperate with the thing it's supposed to be created to do."

Katie fought her own tears. "Oh, sweetie, that is so not true. I know it doesn't feel like it, but this is not a reflection of you as a woman. You are not a failure. You are a wonderful wife to Paul, and he loves you with everything in him. You are an awesome friend. The best there is. You're funny, smart, beautiful, giving, and loving. And I know none of that matters to you right now, but I want you to know it deep in your soul. You're a blessing to everyone who meets you, and I love you so much."

Erin sniffed. "Yeah." She cleared her throat. "I am pretty awesome. You're lucky to have me as a friend."

It lacked conviction, but it meant Erin was regaining control of her emotions for the moment. "You better believe it. Who else would've stuck by my side, putting up with all my less than stellar quirks, all these years? You deserve a medal."

A breath of a laugh. "I do. You outrun your fairy godmother and your guardian angel regularly. But you can't get away from me."

"I wouldn't want it any other way."

"Can you do me a favor?"

"Anything."

"Pray for me. I've still got to tell Paul."

"You've got it. All day and all night."

"Thanks, Katie. I'd better go splash some water on my face before Paul gets home for lunch."

Katie sat in her car for several minutes after the call ended. You couldn't find more loving people than Erin and Paul. And all they wanted to do was share that love with a child. It didn't seem right that a child was the one thing that seemed out of their reach. "God, You must have a reason. I just wish we knew what it was."

She didn't know what to pray. That a baby would eventually be theirs? That their hearts would find peace with what appeared to be an answer in the negative to that very prayer? That God would show them His plan for them? Katie wasn't sure what the correct direction was so instead she prayed, "Your will be done. Help them to see and want Your will above all else. And please, let them know You love them."

Chapter Twelve

How had she let him talk her into this? Katie watched from the fence as Nathan led two horses out of the barn and began to saddle them. A trail ride? She'd never ridden a day in her life. Truth be told, horses always made her nervous. They were beautiful, but they were so big. Now she was preparing to ride one.

When Nathan met her at the grocery store a couple of weeks ago, she was still distracted with Erin's predicament. Nathan asked, but it wasn't her story to tell. She'd honored her friend's trust and left it that she simply had a lot on her mind. He'd looked at her with such compassion as he offered "the perfect solution". She hadn't thought to turn him down at the time, and she'd found herself in the corral being led like a child. She'd enjoyed it more than she thought she would, but she hadn't realized she'd graduate to a trail ride so soon.

When he suggested she come back the next week, she hadn't refused. It was too late now. The horses were ready, and Nathan had come to stand in front of her. She prayed she wouldn't humiliate herself, but she was afraid her prayer came a little too late.

She refused to fidget under his scrutiny. She'd carefully chosen the faded boot-cut jeans and plain V-neck black t-shirt layered with a plaid button-up in hues of green. Finishing the look with a pair of brown slouched cowboy boots, Katie knew she wasn't a cowgirl by any stretch of the imagination. But she'd pass for a leisurely trail ride.

A crooked smirk told her Nathan understood how hard she'd tried. Oh, well. She'd hoped for effortless. But she couldn't help being less than an authentic cowgirl. The perfect look wouldn't distract him from her inexperience anyway.

He raised his hand to the crown of his cowboy hat lifting it from his head. "You just need one more thing to look the part."

He dropped the hat onto her head with a wink. Even with the added volume of her curls, the hat fit loose. She flicked the brim up away from her eyes. Nathan laughed. Katie tried to ignore the warmth the deep, smooth tone of his happiness sent through her. She didn't need those kinds of distractions in her life. Things were going well, and feelings like that only led to heartache.

He turned from her to grab his worn baseball cap from a peg on the wall behind him. "It'll do for now. But you know we're gonna have to fix that one of these days."

He loosened the reins of both horses from the post they'd been tethered to and led them to the edge of the field. Katie followed. He must trust his horse implicitly. He let go of the reins without securing them before turning to Katie.

"Do you need help up?"

She shook her head. "Nah. I've got this."

As she moved to the horse's side, she realized how high the stirrup sat. Oh, please, don't let me embarrass myself. She took a deep breath before lifting her left foot to the stirrup and grabbing hold of the saddle horn to bounce herself up into the saddle. Her breath released in a rush as her free leg swung over the horse's back on the first try.

She tried to muster a look of confidence before chancing a

glance at Nathan. He didn't look impressed. Of course, working with riders every day, why would he be impressed that she could get on the horse by herself? In his world, even older children could manage that. But at least she hadn't fallen or pulled a muscle.

He gave her the reins and swung up onto his horse with such a fluid motion that he looked born to it. He took the reins where they crossed into his left hand, clicking to the horse as he lightly squeezed its sides with his legs. Katie mimicked what she saw him do with her horse, releasing a relieved breath when the animal moved to follow. Side by side they made their way down a worn trail at an easy walk.

"Relax. Buck can sense your discomfort."

Katie shifted her attention to Nathan briefly before looking forward again. How did he know she was uncomfortable? He hadn't even looked her direction. He just rode along with one hand on the reins and the other on his thigh like he didn't have a care in the world.

"Easy for you to say. You do this every day. I've never ridden before."

He shook his head without looking at her. "Still can't believe that. A southern Illinois girl worth her salt should've ridden a horse. Tonya and I have been ridin' since we could walk, maybe even before. How is it that she never got you on a horse? Relax your reins just a bit. All it takes is a light touch of the reins on either side of his neck to tell him where to go. Too tight and you're gonna confuse him."

She draped the reins a bit more, unaware she'd tightened her hold and trying to remember Nathan's instructions from when he led her around the corral the previous week. Maybe if she focused on his questions she'd relax a bit more. "They always looked so big. Mom and Dad never kept any. And I guess it just never came up with Tonya. We always did other things together."

"You don't have to worry about Buck. I've had him forever,

and he's about as sure and calm a horse as you're gonna find. Nothing spooks him, and he's gentle enough I'd let a baby on him."

A wry twist turned her lips at the less than flattering comparison, but she didn't voice her opinion. After all, when it came to riding she was little better than a baby. One day maybe she'd find something she knew about that eluded Nathan, and she'd return the favor.

They rode in silence for a bit allowing Katie the opportunity to take in their surroundings. Between her growing comfort on the horse and the sunshine soaking into the fabric of her shirt spreading spring warmth through her body, Katie felt her shoulders relaxing. The rhythm of the horse's movements under her added to the peacefulness of the wide trail they followed through the budding trees. Katie breathed the fresh air deep into her lungs. Winter had kept her inside breathing stale, dry air for far too long.

She chanced a quick glance in Nathan's direction. His gaze was trained on the horizon. He sat confident, completely relaxed. He moved with the horse like they were the same. Katie was caught by the idea that there was something extremely attractive about a man who could sit a horse as Nathan did. She turned her attention back to the path, hoping the warmth in her cheeks didn't translate into tell-tale pink. What on earth had gotten into her?

They rounded a bend in the path to find a clearing bordered by a shallow creek. Nathan pulled back gently on the reins. "Whoa."

Katie followed his example, stilling her own horse's movements. She watched him dismount before leading his horse to what looked like a small section of wooden fencing. Someone had crafted a hitching post at the edge of the clearing? Who thought to do something like that? Well, Nathan, obviously. And why wouldn't he? His whole livelihood was wrapped up in horses.

She watched the object of her thoughts move in her direction. Once he secured her horse, she lowered herself to the ground. She was glad he'd turned from her to walk Buck to the hitching post as she took her first steps. Even the short ride had stiffened her untrained muscles. With his back to her, Katie took the opportunity to stretch out the kinks before he joined her again.

She watched Nathan fiddling with a pack she hadn't noticed at the back of his horse's saddle. He pulled a woven blanket from the open saddlebag.

He jerked his head toward the creek. "Don't just stand there gawking. Come on."

He spread the blanket out at the edge of the creek before motioning for her to sit. After she'd settled, he sat beside her with his legs stretched out in front of him and his arms extended behind him to prop himself up. Katie chose instead to fold her legs underneath her with her hands in her lap. The silence surrounding them could have been awkward, but Katie only sensed peace.

"I put in that hitching post not long after I bought this place. I'd meandered down here on my first visit to the property and knew I'd be coming to the clearing regularly. Through the years, it's where I come to think or pray or escape all the noise and busyness of life."

Katie grinned seeing a different creek in her mind. "I know what you mean. Ever since I was a little girl, the creek behind my house has been my special place. There's a little waterfall that empties into a still pool. As a kid, it was just deep enough to cool off in. It wouldn't be deep enough for that now, but that wasn't why I loved that place. I preferred sitting on the rocks with my legs dangling over the waterfall. Something was relaxing about letting the water run over my bare feet. When my mom and I got into it, which was often, I'd go there to think.

After a bit, my dad would join me and help me talk it out before leaving me to sit alone soaking in the silence."

She cleared her throat of the emotion threatening her ability to speak. How long had it been since her father had been able to join her at the creek? When did the man who'd always been her rock become someone who seemed to be slowly forgetting her completely?

NATHAN SENSED Kate's rising emotion. He couldn't imagine what it was like trying to raise a toddler on your own while learning to deal with the declining mental capacity of your parent. Kate and her dad had always been close. That had been evident even growing up, and it didn't appear the relationship had waned in her adult years. It had to be heartbreaking.

He sat up and crossed his legs underneath him freeing his hands. One of Kate's hands moved from her lap with her reminiscing and was weaving a strand of hair through her fingers. Further proof her emotions were churning under the surface. He reached out and took her hand in his, sheltering it under his palm on the blanket before looking back to the creek.

He saw her look at him from out of the corner of his eye. He kept his gaze trained on the scene before him. He wanted to comfort her, to help her know she wasn't alone. It was why he'd taken her hand. But would she accept the comfort he offered?

He fought the urge to meet her gaze. He knew the moment she looked back to the creek. He felt the tenseness leave her, and he rubbed his thumb over the back of her hand. He couldn't tell if it was the softness and warmth of the skin under his touch or whether he got a glimpse of something deeper, but Nathan sensed softness in Kate.

No, that wasn't right. It wasn't softness. It was fragility. That didn't make sense either. Kate was one of the strongest people he'd ever met. To live through the loss she'd faced and come out on the other side with her faith intact was no small feat. But what reason told him was overshadowed by this new revelation. Kate Blake was fragile, and he would have to handle their friendship with care.

He turned to her, but her eyes stayed fixed on the creek. As much as he'd complained about her and Tonya growing up, she was the one friend of his sister that he didn't mind being around. As they'd gotten into the teen years, he'd begun to look forward to it. He never delved into the reason why. He simply enjoyed their innocent flirting. Then, when things got a little too real he'd pull back into the big brother, little sister mode until the spark passed.

Sitting in his spot with her, Nathan found himself wondering at the sanity of his teenage self. Kate was cute as a teenager. Now? He wasn't sure she'd be considered gorgeous by society standards. She wasn't perfectly made up like all the movie stars. She was more than just cute though. She was a girl-next-door kind of beautiful with a heart to match it. Of course, he couldn't tell her any of this. All he could do was enjoy the warmth of her hand nestled under his.

Kate wasn't ready for more than friendship, and she might never be. She'd given her heart completely to Austin, and Nathan wasn't sure she'd gotten it back with his passing. He had to change the way he thought of her. Even if it meant breaking his own heart, he refused to do anything that might bring more pain to hers. She needed a friend, and that is exactly what he would be for her.

He looked back to the scene in front of them. "You seem more relaxed than you did a couple of weeks ago. Things going better?"

Her shoulders lifted with a sigh. "Did you ever want something so much that every day without it broke your heart a little more, but you felt powerless to change circumstances?"

His heart tried to pause inside his chest. He willed it to keep beating. "Sure."

"It's not my story to tell. So, I can't give details, but I have friends going through something like that. I want to help them, but there's nothing I can do to change anything. There's nothing anyone can do, short of God Himself."

His muscles relaxed. This he could deal with. "I get it. You hurt for them. But you're on the right track too. God knows what's goin' on. He knows what's down the road for everybody involved, and He's the one you need to give it to."

He was rewarded with a smile. "You know, when we were kids I thought you were nothing more than another dumb boy. But you've gone and gotten yourself some wisdom as you got older."

The laugh burst from deep in his chest without warning. Kate stared at him with wide eyes looking as innocent as a newborn foal. Too bad he knew better.

She leaned her shoulder into his. "Just kidding. You've always been wise. You just hid it better back then."

His lips twisted into a half smile. "Thanks. I think."

When she didn't move to restore the distance between them, Nathan knew he had to or completely lose the battle to keep things friends only. He nudged her back to sitting up straight. "We'd probably better be getting back. I've still got to muck out stalls."

There. You couldn't get less romantic than horse manure. It worked like a charm to force his mind away from the unwelcome thoughts. He pushed himself up from the ground and reached a hand out to Kate. She folded the blanket while he got the horses. In minutes they were back on the trail.

Kate was the first to break the comfortable silence. "You know who'd love this?" She didn't wait for him to guess. "Sammy. Of course, he's probably a little young yet."

Nathan lifted the bill of his cap slightly before returning it to its previous position. "Not by a long shot. I was on the back of a horse before I could walk. Sammy's a little behind in my book."

She looked at him from the corner of her eye. "Still. They're really big. That could be scary for a little guy like him, don't you think?"

"Naw. I'd probably take him on Buck there. He'd sit in front of me, and I'd be in control the whole time. He'd be as snug as they come. Not to mention, I'd give him a riding helmet just in case the unforeseen were to happen."

She rolled her eyes. "It's the unforeseen I'm worried about."

"Tsk. Tsk. Little Kate, don't you know you can't live your life in fear? And you definitely can't do that to Sammy. The boy's gotta live."

She ignored the commentary on how she needed to live her life, focusing instead on the way out of the nickname he'd given her so many years ago. "I'll make you a deal. No more Little Kate, and you can take Sammy out for a ride."

He nudged his horse closer and stuck out a hand. "You've got yourself a deal, Kate."

The way she eyed his extended hand told him all he needed to know. She wasn't crazy about the way he'd stressed her name at the end, but he'd left off the little exactly as she'd asked. He moved his hand closer. She briefly touched hers to his before returning it to the reins. They had a deal, and he would hold her to it.

Chapter Thirteen

"No one has been here. Just me, you, and Sammy."

Her father paced the kitchen in frustration. He spun to face her and jabbed a finger in the direction of the refrigerator. "Then, just how did that get there?"

Katie didn't look. She'd seen the postcard secured under a magnet when she'd first come into the kitchen. It was a reminder of an upcoming appointment with the air conditioning people for a check of their system. "It came in the mail two days ago, Dad. You took it and put it on the fridge so you wouldn't forget the appointment."

"I did no such thing. I'm telling you, someone was in this house. I can't even think what they might have wanted, but they were here."

Breathe in deep. Breathe out the frustration. There was no reasoning with him when he got like this, and it seemed to happen more often as of late. "I don't know. I guess they wanted to make sure you were home for your appointment next week."

The conversation needed to end. Katie picked up her cell phone and the basket of wet clothes from the table. "I'm going to go outside now and hang up these clothes. I'll be back in just a minute. If Sammy wakes up, please come and get me."

He regarded her in silence. She wished he wasn't so given to pouting after these episodes, but there was more hope that the sun would stop shining. She hefted the basket higher onto her hip and headed outside. What was she going to do?

The basket sat forgotten on the ground while she contemplated who she could call. If she didn't give vent to the storm churning inside, she might take it out on her dad and that was not going to happen. He couldn't help the changes he was going through. She could call Erin. She should call Erin, but as mad as her best friend would be, Katie knew she couldn't dump this stuff on her. Erin was dealing with a pretty heavy load herself.

She scrolled through her slim list of contacts. One name stood out and before she could rethink it, she hit the call icon.

"Hello, Katie. To what do I owe this call on such a beautiful day?"

"Hi, Gigi B."

"Land's sake, girlie! What's wrong?"

"I didn't say anything was wrong. All I said was hi."

Silence. "Really? You're going to try to pull that with me. Don't you know any better? It isn't what you said. It's how you said it. Now, would you like to keep on this line of talk or do you want to get to the real reason you called? I will ask you again. What's wrong?"

Katie pulled a shirt from the basket and pinned it to the clothesline. "It's my dad. I know he can't help it, but it's so frustrating at times. Today he's convinced someone came into our house uninvited and put a postcard on our fridge. Like an intruder would break in to remind us of an air conditioning appointment. I try to set him straight, but there's no use. If he's got it stuck in his head that something happened, nothing I say will change his mind."

Katie continued to hang clothes with the phone pinned to her ear with her shoulder. Gigi B didn't answer immediately. Either she was thinking something through or hesitant to say what was on her mind. That rarely happened, but when it did, Katie knew to watch out. She tried to steel herself for whatever might come next. It could be anything, really. How did one prepare for anything? Might as well dive in headfirst.

"I know you enough to know silence doesn't mean you don't know what you're thinking. Go ahead. What've you got?"

"Katie child, I want you to listen and listen all the way through before you say anything. Try not to overthink or react emotionally to what I have to say. I guarantee you won't want to hear it, but it's got to be said. Can we agree to that?"

A sick feeling settled in her stomach. This was not going to go well. "I'll try. It's the best I can do."

"Honey, it's the best any of us can do. Maybe the good Lord gave us two ears and only one mouth to remind us which we need to use more and which we need to use a little less. I know this situation with your daddy isn't easy for you. You've been through more in your short time than a lot of women will face in their lifetimes. But I think we both know you're heading into another storm."

She fought the urge to argue. She'd promised after all. "Tell me why."

"Why you're going into one or why I think this is an oncoming storm?"

"What makes you think this is going to be a stormy situation?"

"You've seen the signs as well as I have. The forgetfulness may have begun innocently enough, looking for misplaced keys and glasses and such, but it's more than that now. Your dad has to be introduced to people he's known for forever. He forgets why he's come into a room or whether he was even coming or going. He sees evidence of things he can't remember doing, and for his mind to make sense of it, he creates the idea of other people doing those things. It doesn't matter, that, as you said, no one would come into your house to post an appointment notice. His mind doesn't even see that as outrageous. His past and present are starting to merge more than the occasional slip of calling someone by someone else's name. I could go on. But you and I both know where this is headed. You've known it for a while, or you wouldn't avoid leaving Sammy alone with him or arranging for other people to take him places."

Katie swallowed back the tears clogging her throat. She swiped her fingertips under her eye to catch a stray tear that broke through her defenses. "So you're saying you think Dad has Alzheimer's?"

"I didn't, but you picked up where I was going without any problem. I do think it's time for him to see someone so you know for sure and can figure out what to do going forward."

She cleared her throat. "Well, I asked. You're just telling me what you see. But as you just pointed out, you're not a professional in these matters. I shouldn't have called. It was just a little hiccup in our day, and I was frustrated. I got tired of everything. Thanks for listening. I need to get back to it."

"Katie..."

"Talk to you later, Gigi B."

Katie hit end as she sunk to the grass. Without an audience, she let angry tears fall freely. How could Gigi B say those things? Didn't she see how hard Katie was trying to keep it all together? She'd been through a lot, but so had her dad. Even Nathan had pointed it out. So he was forgetful. Was that really so bad considering everything they'd faced in the last few years? And he was getting older. Older people got confused all the time. Gigi B was wrong, and she could keep her opinion to herself from now on.

Katie took a bracing breath and rose from the ground. She swiped up the empty laundry basket determined to show Gigi B and anyone else who might think those horrible things about her dad how wrong they were. There was nothing wrong with her father that every elderly person didn't face.

"I'm back from hanging out the laundry."

His voice came from the living room. "Okay, Katydid. Be sure to let your mother know. I think she may have another chore or two for you."

He didn't mean it. He spoke without thinking. Everything is okay. Katie played these thoughts on the loop while she went upstairs to check on Sammy. If she reminded herself often enough, she might succeed in warding off the dread creeping into her heart.

Chapter Fourteen

Nathan made faces at Sammy in the review mirror while Kate finished fastening him into his car seat. The toddler's giggle was infectious. His smile widened at the sound.

Kate climbed into the front of the extended cab. "Thank you for letting me and Sammy tag along with you to church today."

He waved to the passengers of the small car that Kate's dad had just gotten in. "No problem. Glad to have ya. It's awfully nice of the preacher and his wife to pick up your dad each week and take him with them."

Kate's grin seemed forced. "They're great people. Dad wanted to keep going to Orchard Hills after mom died, but I couldn't make myself after losing Austin. It just wasn't the same."

"I get it. It must have been nice to find a new church home with Erin and Gigi B. I've visited there a couple of times. The preacher's really down to earth. Solid teaching."

Kate shifted in her seat. "I've enjoyed him."

He watched her from the corner of his eye. "They have something special goin' on that they canceled services today?"

An almost imperceptible pause. "No. They're having services."

He waited. His unasked question hung heavy in the air. He looked in the mirror. Sammy played with an assortment of plastic animals he pulled from a metal lunchbox embossed with a superhero, oblivious to the tension around him.

"I just wanted something different today."

She sounded light-hearted enough, but Nathan knew her better than that. It was a cop-out. Maybe it wasn't a lie, but it definitely wasn't the whole truth. "I'll bet you Gigi B will miss you today."

A shrug. "I suppose."

So that was the way of things. He could only imagine what had prompted her avoidance of the elderly woman, but there was no arguing that avoiding was exactly what Kate was doing. He knew it as sure as he knew he needed to leave it alone. If Kate wanted to talk about it, she would. If not, there was no way he was going to drag it out of her.

KATIE'S THOUGHTS meandered through the subjects of her father, Gigi B's worries, and the sermon she'd just heard when Nathan brought her back to the present.

"It's a beautiful day. How'd you two like to have a picnic with me at the park?"

Sammy chimed in with his opinion from the back seat. "A picnic! Can we have a picnic?"

Katie wasn't ready to head home. "I don't see why not. Sure we can have a picnic. Should we go back to the house and throw some sandwiches together?"

Nathan shook his head. "I don't think this is a sandwich and chips kind of day. I think it's more of a chicken nugget kind of day. Don't you Sammy?"

"Yay! Chicken nuggets! And French fries?"

Nathan laughed. "Of course. You can't have nuggets without French fries."

Katie smiled. After the initial permission was granted, she'd been effectively cut out of the decision making process. Nathan's attention bounced back and forth from the road in front of him to the little boy behind her. Not once did he look to her for input. She smiled. It warmed her heart to see the pleasure Nathan was taking in befriending her son. He was a man who loved and served God, and Sammy would do well with a godly man like Nathan taking an interest in him.

With a death grip on the kid's meal bag, Sammy dashed across the grass to an unoccupied picnic table. Katie took off after him with Nathan sauntering along behind with their meals. In the few seconds it took them to catch up, Sammy plopped down on the metal seat and plunged his pudgy hand into the bottom of the bag he carried.

Katie watched as he rooted through the bag. She scooted across the bench as Nathan dropped into place next to her.

"Look! I got a ball!"

Katie pulled the forgotten apple juice from his bag. His excitement would wane soon enough, and his currently neglected meal would be eaten in record time. "That's a nice surprise."

"A nice surprise? That's more than a nice surprise. Do you know what you've got there, Sammy?"

Sammy's frown was adorable. His voice was tinged with confusion. "A ball?"

Nathan reached across the table, waiting for Sammy to drop it into his hand. The toddler complied. Nathan turned the tiny ball over in his hands. "What you've got here is more than a regular ole' ball. This here is a football. You ever play with a football before?"

His pale green eyes were the size of saucers as he shook his head. Katie bit her lip. It wouldn't do to laugh and ruin her son's enthusiasm. You'd have thought Nathan had told him he'd won a million dollars. Not that Sammy would have appreciated the idea of a million dollars. But the look of awe on his face was adorable.

"Well, sir, we've got to fix that. How 'bout I say a blessing so we can eat? Then, I'll show you what you do with a football."

Sammy's head immediately bowed as his hands clasped together in front of his chest. Nathan's eyes twinkled as he looked at her before bowing his own head. His prayer was over and Sammy was munching a chicken nugget before Katie realized she hadn't bowed her own head. Watching the simple interaction left her heart flooded with thanksgiving. They'd have to take time for more picnics in the future.

THE TODDLER'S weight in his arms was next to nothing. How in the world could such a huge amount of energy be contained in someone so small? After eating, they'd tossed the miniature ball back and forth and chased each other around the park long past the time he'd have guessed would've tuckered the little guy out.

He stepped through the door Kate held open and headed up the steps to Sammy's room. His stores of energy had finally depleted on the way home, leaving him sound asleep in his car seat. Nathan placed Sammy in his toddler bed and pulled a light blanket over legs that had immediately curled his body into a ball.

Kate watched him from the doorway with a small monitor in one hand. She paused long enough to fasten the tall gate attached to the doorframe before following him down the stairs. Nathan turned toward the living room at the bottom of the stairs, but quickly rerouted to the screen porch when he saw Cal stretched out on the couch and heard soft snores.

He should go. Kate had to be worn out too. She chased that

little boy and worried about her father all by herself every day. It had to be exhausting. He should let her rest while she could, but he hated to see the afternoon end.

"I'm guessing its Sunday afternoon nap time in the McGowan and Blake house?"

Her shoulders lifted. "Dad and Sammy need the time, but if I let myself take a nap, I won't be able to get to sleep tonight. My mind won't slow down enough to allow my body time to rest."

He tapped the monitor in her hand. "Will that thing reach outside?"

"Sure. I'd never get anything done if I got a cheap one that had to be kept inside."

He tilted his head toward the door. "Want to walk?"

"There's plenty of shade in the garden. We could sit out on the swing for a while."

He held the door for her to pass through before falling in step beside her. The silence was comfortable as they made their way around the house to the swing. Her head tipped back to rest against the high wooden back as the gentle back and forth motion relaxed her. Her eyes drifted shut. The cool of the shade and movement of the swing tempted him to do the same, but she'd said she didn't want to nap. Maybe he should wake her.

Her voice stilled the movement of his hand toward her arm. "This is nice. I can almost convince myself everything is right in the world. It's almost as peaceful as my waterfall."

"The one you told me about?"

"You should see it. Though I guess it's only special to me and maybe Dad. It's always been my place to think or just be. With Sammy and Dad, I've not been able to go there for quite some time."

"Sounds just about perfect. What would you be thinking about if you were sittin' there today?"

He couldn't tell if the breath she sighed was frustrated or

simply thoughtful. Her eyes remained closed but her full lips curved down into a small frown. He waited in silence.

"I'd probably be thinking about the one thought I can't escape no matter how hard I try."

"And what's that?"

"Gigi B."

If he hadn't already surmised something was amiss between them, her answer might have been confusing. Should he probe further for information or let her bring it to him on her own? She'd refused to talk about it earlier. Pushing might not give him the outcome he wanted. He waited and was not disappointed.

"The other day with Dad was a rough one. I needed someone to talk to, and Erin's dealing with her own stuff. I called Gigi B." Her head shot up without warning and she speared him with those clear, green eyes of hers. "Did you know she thinks Dad has Alzheimer's?"

Careful. There was a lot of angst wrapped up in that simple question. "I don't know that she ever used the word Alzheimer's, but yes, she's shared her concerns with me. She wanted to know if I'd seen the same things she had before bringing them up to you. She was trying to be cautious about a difficult situation."

"And do you?"

The strain in her voice tempted him to lie. The last thing he wanted was to put space between them. Lying didn't sit right though. It never led to good. "I don't know that your dad has Alzheimer's."

"See I knew it. Gigi B is over-reacting."

His voice was quiet but firm. "I wasn't done. I'm not a doctor so I can't diagnose something like that. But there are major concerns. You've seen them. We've talked about some of them. Whether its dementia or Alzheimer's really makes no difference. The problems are real, and they need a real answer. Seeing a doctor could give you some of those answers."

Pain flickered in her eyes even as her jawline became rigid.

She wound a curl between her fingers. Her feet crossed, uncrossed, and crossed again. Nathan knew at any moment she could flee the swing and keep running from the truth. *Lord, let her hear me. Let her hear the truth.*

He watched her, hoping she could see in his face how much it pained him that she had to go through this. Her hand dropped to her lap and her shoulders fell.

"It's not going away is it?"

The helplessness in her voice ignited a desire to protect her. He draped her shoulders with his arm and guided her toward him until her head rested right above his heart. He gently stroked the top of her arm.

"No. It's not."

He felt the faintest shudder against his chest. He knew his shirt would sport a damp spot when this was over. He pulled her closer.

Her voice was muffled against his chest. "How much does God think I can handle?"

"I'm not sure I follow."

She pulled away to look at him. Damp cheeks and puffy eyes confirmed what he'd suspected. The way her brows knit together added confusion to the hurt emanating from her eyes. "You know. It's that old saying that God doesn't give you more than you can handle."

Nathan ran a hand through his sandy blonde hair as he considered his answer. "I've never quite understood why people would say that. It's supposed to be hopeful, but what happens when someone is given something they can't handle? Where's the hope then?"

Her tears resurfaced. He brushed one from her cheek with his thumb. He hadn't meant to make her feel it was hopeless. *Lord, let me get it out there right this time.*

"It isn't about what we can handle or not. Job was given more than any man can handle. The earliest believers faced persecutions that no man can handle. Even today in some countries, believers are being tortured and tested in ways men aren't equipped to deal with. But it's okay. It isn't about how much strength we have. It's about how much of God's strength we accept into our situation. In my opinion, the saying should be God won't give you anything that you and He can't handle together. He's the strong one. We just need to learn to lean on Him in the tough times."

Kate looked over the field beyond the garden. Her jaw worked as she sat in silence. She fidgeted with the monitor in her hands.

"I know you're right. He's been my strength and my sanity through every storm. I know He doesn't leave me alone. But sometimes, it'd be nice to have flesh and blood arms to hold onto. Someone you can look in their eyes and know they're right there with you, praying for you and supporting you in whatever way they can. Is it wrong to want that? Does it make me less faithful?"

His heart beat faster as her gaze met his. The yearning he saw created a physical ache in his chest. Was she opening the door he thought she'd sealed shut for good when Austin died? He'd be lying if he said he hadn't felt a shift in their friendship over the last few weeks, at least on his part. Had it changed for her too?

He swallowed hard. "It isn't wrong. And it doesn't mean your faith is weak. It means you're human. God created us to need Him first and foremost, but He also created us with a need for each other. He made us to experience laughter together, to support each other in our hurts, to know...to know a picture of His love for us through loving another."

So far so good. Kate's features seemed to relax a bit. She didn't turn away. She hadn't flinched when he mentioned love. It was now or never.

Another hard swallow followed by clearing his throat of

nothing more than the knot that had settled in his vocal cords. "You've always been my kid sister's friend. Especially in the last few months, that's changed. I'm thankful God brought you back into my life and allowed us to become closer friends. But I'm open to more. Back then we flirted and played around, but now, it's more than adolescent attraction. Don't get me wrong, you're more beautiful than ever. But it's who you are that makes me want to be with you. And I do want to be with you, Kate. I want to be the one praying with you and supporting you through this hard time with your dad and every other hard thing that comes. I want to be the flesh and blood arms for you to hold onto. I'm not proposing marriage. Neither of us is ready for that. I'm asking for a chance to see where we can go together, to see if I could be the one you want beside you through everything. Will you let me be that man for you?"

The green of her eyes was swallowed by white as her eyes grew. Shock. There was definitely shock in them. Hesitancy too. But at least there wasn't regret or worse, pity. It meant there was still a chance she'd accept his awkward declaration.

When the silence continued, he couldn't fight the urge to fidget. He needed to give her a way to bow out gracefully. He forced a smile in direct opposition to the weight settling in his stomach. "It's okay. I know this is outta the blue. But I needed you to know, and now you do." He shrugged. "It's fine. It's not all or nothin'. No matter what, I'm going to be your friend and help you through this. Got it?"

Her eyes dropped to the wood slats they sat on. That was it then.

∼

THE SWING SHIFTED with Nathan's nervous movements. Katie refused to look up. The anticipation in his eyes was palpable.

Where had this come from? What had possessed him to make

such an outrageous declaration? Then again, was it so unthinkable? She'd just poured out her heart to him once more. She'd leaned on him time and again, physically and emotionally. His friendship meant more to her than she'd ever thought possible.

He was right. They'd been attracted to each other as teenagers, and truth be told, he was as good looking as ever, maybe more so. Katie had caught herself admiring him more than once in their encounters over the past few months, though she'd only recently admitted it even to herself. But it was more than a schoolgirl crush on a cute guy. Nathan had become a treasured friend. His way with her, her father, and Sammy were full of care and understanding.

She'd just told him she didn't want to be alone anymore but did that mean she wanted a new relationship? To want it and not at the same time made no sense, but relationships were a big deal. Katie knew that better than most. Could she put herself out there again? What if she ended up losing their friendship, or worse, what if she lost the man himself?

Nathan said it wasn't all or nothing. She could choose to simply go on the way they had been. But she didn't want that either. If only she could wring a guarantee out of God that this one would last, that devastation wouldn't come. She couldn't, and He wouldn't anyway. Was the chance to love again worth the risk?

The swing shifted again as Nathan stood. Could she let him walk away? If she did it would mean her choice was made. There would be no going back. A deep inhale. She grasped his wrist while pulling herself to stand.

She hoped the tremor in her voice would go unnoticed. "Don't go."

He stopped but didn't turn. Of course, she hadn't told him anything that meant anything yet. "You're an amazing friend and a wonderful man." The drop in his shoulders was almost imperceptible. She needed to come out and say it, let him out of limbo.

Without loosening her old on his wrist, she stepped around to face him as she spoke. "But I'd like you to be more than that. I'd like to give us a chance."

While his lips barely registered it, his eyes shone with happiness. He freed his wrist from her grasp before drawing her into his arms. She looked down, away from his eyes. Meeting his gaze would only bring a kiss, and she wasn't ready for that.

Nathan's lips pressed a kiss to the top of her head before his cheek rested in the same spot. "I get it, you know? You've loved before, and you've lost a lot. This can't be easy, but I'm patient. We'll take everything as slow as you please."

"Thank you."

Katie relaxed against him. Though she knew she'd battled fear and won, she knew the war was far from over. Even now, a shadow of doubt lingered behind the hope trying to grow in her spirit.

Chapter Fifteen

"Aren't we in a good mood today."

Katie smiled at Mildred and stopped humming the praise song that had been on her heart through her morning routine. "It is a beautiful April morning. Why shouldn't I be happy? I may even sit with the children outside in the reading garden for story hour today. They would love that. Don't you think?"

Katie fought a smile as Mildred's pursed lips raised with a tilt of her chin.

"I suppose that would be allowable if you get permission from the parents."

Katie dropped her purse onto the breakroom table. "I'm sure it won't be any problem at all. Now, if you'll excuse me, I need to go find a story about a mouse, a bear, and a ripe strawberry for our outdoor adventure."

Katie left without waiting for an answer. She knew where the book was just as sure as she knew Mildred wouldn't have a clue which book she was referencing. Maybe it would entice her to come outdoors and find out for herself. Story-time with the little ones was always a fun time. With the book in hand, Katie scribbled a note about the change in location and taped it to the library door.

Outdoor story time was a success. She'd found the perfect, grassy spot under a big oak tree, and the children had listened as raptly as they did every other week. Mildred hadn't joined them, though Katie thought she'd seen her watching through one of the windows. Maybe one day she'd find out why the woman was so straight-laced and get her to enjoy her job a little more. But that would have to wait. Katie had more important things to do.

Gabe and Anna were near the back of the crowd, and Katie wanted to speak with them before they left. She spoke briefly to each child she met as she made her way to the pair. She ruffled Gabe's straight, dark hair when he smiled up at her.

"Did you enjoy the story today, Gabe?"

The little head bobbed up and down.

"What did you think of our visitor?"

His brown eyes grew wide. "I like strawberries too."

Katie smiled. A local pet store owner brought a tiny white mouse to story time and let each child take a picture with it safely enclosed in its clear, plastic travel cage. Both mouse and child were given strawberries to snack on. Next week she'd have the pictures printed and the children would make a scrapbook page for the reading scrapbook they'd begun after her first week on the job.

She leaned down next to Gabe and her voice became a stage whisper. "I'll tell you a secret. I love strawberries too." She rose and directed her attention to Anna. "Would you and Gabe like to come to my house for a playdate this afternoon? I pick up Sammy at noon today, and we'd love for you to come have lunch with us."

Anna shifted her weight from one foot to the other. "Thank you for the offer, but I don't think we can."

"That's okay. Maybe some other time?"

"I don't know. You said you live outside of town. The buses don't usually go out that far."

Katie could see the girl's discomfort at the situation, and she spoke quickly to ease it. "You don't need the bus. I'd be happy to take you and bring you back home. I know Sammy would love to play with Gabe. I can run inside, get my stuff, and we can head out to pick him up if you like. If you can't or don't want to, I understand. But if it's just the ride, I'd be happy to have the company today."

Katie was rewarded with a full smile. "I think Gabe and I would like that a lot."

After grabbing her purse Katie led Anna and Gabe to her jeep. Katie lifted Gabe into the booster seat she kept secured in the back seat for Sammy. "If you'll tell me where to go, we can stop at your house and pick up Gabe's car seat."

Anna's mouth twisted to the side as she bit her cheek. "There isn't one there."

Katie shrugged. "That's okay. We can go wherever we need to. I don't mind. My gas tank is full."

Anna brushed long, black bangs away from her face and looked out the passenger side window. "No. That's okay. Gabe will be fine just buckled into the seat."

"That's illegal, Anna. We can go get his seat."

She sighed. "No, we can't. I don't have one."

Katie pulled from the parking lot, stealing a glance at Anna as she checked oncoming traffic. She wasn't looking in Katie's direction, but the face reflected in the window showed resignation to her situation. "Do your parents have one for him? Or a friend?"

"No. All my old friends are still in high school. They don't really need a car seat. And I've not seen my parents since before Gabe was born. They didn't approve of me keeping him."

"I'm sure they thought they were doing the best for you. An adoption is a wonderful option for some people."

Anna looked at her from the corner of her eye. "Adoption was not the option they were pushing."

"Oh."

Anna picked at the skin around her thumb. "It's fine. I didn't need them then, and I don't need them now. There wasn't room for Gabe in their lives, and I wasn't about to give him up for adoption or anything else."

"Where do you live then?"

"It changes pretty often. You find out who your real friends are, but you don't want to overstay your welcome. Babies and toddlers are cute and fun at first, but midnight feedings and temper tantrums can really put a strain on relationships."

As Katie drove the rest of the way to Sammy's day care, Anna continued to share about her life. The only interruption was a quick stop at the store so Katie could purchase a second booster seat. Anna protested on the basis of not having a car and therefore not needing one, but Katie insisted. Soon, both boys were safely buckled in and on their way to a picnic playdate at Sammy's house.

"She doesn't have anything."

Nathan had arrived at her house thirty minutes earlier, and Kate hadn't stopped talking about the girl from her story group, recounting every detail of her difficult situation. It was obvious that the young mother had made an impression on her.

Kate rose from where she sat beside him on the swing. She paced in front of him, her hands a flurry of motion as she spoke. "I just wish I knew some way to help her. She never finished high school. So there aren't prospects for jobs better than the one she has at Burger Hut. The only reason she can keep that one is that she gets government help with childcare. Did I tell you she didn't even have a booster seat for Gabe?"

Nathan smiled. "Yes, but that's okay. You can tell me again if you want."

"What in the world are you smiling about? Here I'm telling you about this sad situation, and what do you do? You smile."

He pulled her into his lap and brushed her curls behind her ear. "I'm not smiling at her situation. I'm smiling at seein' you so fired up about it. You've got one of the biggest, most caring hearts. I love that about you. I know if you keep searching for it, God's going to show you exactly what He wants you to do for Anna and Gabe."

He punctuated his announcement with a quick peck on her mouth. The way her lips parted into a surprised "o" begged him to kiss her again, long and lingering. He wouldn't though. Pink crept into her cheeks. She was still as skittish as a colt about their new relationship. As much as he'd like to kiss her again, it would be better to move into safer subjects.

"And her family?"

The change was immediate. Her lips formed a hard, straight line as her jaw tensed. Her usually bright green eyes turned dark. Maybe it wasn't a safer subject, just a different kind of danger.

"They pretty much disowned her. She's a kid. Their kid! And when she wouldn't agree to an abortion, they kicked her out. Gabe is an adorable, loving little boy. But they wouldn't know that. They won't ever know that, because they refuse to even meet their grandchild. How can people do that?"

Nathan shook his head. "I don't know."

Before he could say any more, Sammy came around the side of the house holding Cal's hand. Kate slipped from his lap to the swing beside him. Nathan smiled and took her hand in his between them.

"Mama!"

Sammy broke free of his grandpa's grasp and launched himself across the remaining yard into Kate's arms. Letting go of Nathan's hand, she wrapped Sammy in her arms and squeezed until he squealed. Nathan had never been one to chafe at what he didn't have. Life brought what it brought, both good and bad, and he thought he was okay with that. As Kate tickled Sammy's sides and that contagious, childish giggle filled the air, Nathan knew contentment deeper than anything he'd ever known. Their little family had worked its way deep into his heart in an incredibly short period of time, but Kate was only now open to testing the waters of something more. Taking it slow was necessary, but Nathan wondered if it was going to be possible.

"And who might you be young man?"

Nathan looked up into the concerned face of the only man that had been in Kate's life for the last three years. From the corner of his eye, he saw Kate glance at him but chose to keep his focus on Cal. "My name's Nathan, sir. Nathan Phillips."

His face screwed up momentarily before the fog lifted. "Well, of course, you are. Why would you think I wouldn't know you, son?"

Nathan lifted his shoulders. "I don't know. Guess I wasn't thinking about it."

The elderly man's attention shifted to Kate. "Now that you've got our little man with you, I'll go make dinner."

Nathan looked to Kate who continued to snuggle her son. She looked up at her father with surprising calm. Nathan's adrenaline, however, was pumping with the memory of smoke and burning grease. He forced himself to stay quiet until Cal made his way around the corner of the house.

He fought to control the concern that wanted to creep into his tone. "Your dad is making dinner?"

Kate looked sheepish. "Sort of. I make it first thing in the morning and put it in microwaveable containers with instruction cards taped to the top. It helps him feel useful, and I don't have to worry about fire hazards. The worst we might do is eat a rubbery entrée if he puts it in too long. But we have back up meals in the freezer for those occasions."

"Hmm. That's a pretty creative way of problem-solving."

Kate released Sammy to play on his slide. "I do what I have to do. I've tried to keep things as normal as possible, but it's getting harder each day. He's constantly worried about people coming into the house when things are exactly where he put them. He just doesn't remember doing it. I can't leave him with Sammy for more than a few minutes while I'm out hanging clothes or running to the mailbox. He keeps talking about my mom like she's in the other room or out running errands."

She leaned forward, her elbows on her knees. He placed his hand on her back and rubbed it in gentle circles. "I can't imagine how difficult it must be for you."

"And now, I either have to switch churches again, or he can't go to the one he loves attending."

"Why is that?"

"The pastor has picked him up the last several months, but he told me this week would need to be his last. Dad wandered away from him while he was shaking hands with everyone after service. It's not the first time it happened. I can't hold it against the pastor. He's got a job to do, and he can't focus on the congregation as a whole if his focus has to be on one."

"I can understand that."

She sat back up and turned her head to look at him. "I don't know what I'm going to do. Dad knows Gigi B and a few others at my church, but I know he's going to balk at it. And he doesn't understand how much care I've had to give him lately. I have neighbors and friends check in on him regularly during the few hours a week that I'm working. When I'm not working, I'm pretty close to home."

"I'm sure he appreciates your help."

A frustrated huff. "Not likely. On the rare occasions he realizes I am doing something for him, I get an earful about how he knows how to care for himself and I need to stop treating him like a child. It's not personal, but it does wear on you after a while."

The idea popped into his mind at the very moment it popped out of his mouth. "Let me take Cal on Sundays."

"I can't ask you to do that. You have your own church family."

It may have been less than pre-meditated, but Nathan knew in his spirit that God was prompting his offer. "You're not askin'. I'm offering. I want to do this for you. Help you carry your load. I mean it. We're in this together. I enjoy Cal, and he seems pretty comfortable with me. Let me do this for you both."

She eyed him with suspicion. He fought a smile as her bottom lip tucked under her teeth. He could almost see the war that was waging inside her to let him step in and help or continue doing it all herself. It was a big step for her in realizing she didn't have to be on her own anymore.

"Fine. If you're sure. We'll try it this Sunday, but you have to be completely honest with me. If it's not working out, you have to tell me."

He was sure they would have no problems, but he wouldn't belittle her concerns. "Deal."

Chapter Sixteen

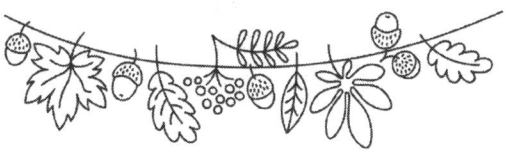

Gigi B dismissed the apology with a wave of her well-manicured hand. "Tsk. Don't you know me better than that by now? There is absolutely nothing to forgive. Discussing your father is a heart matter discussion, and those always tend to get messy. Lots of emotions and memories and fears tied up in those talks. Agree or disagree, I knew you'd not hold my opinion against me forever."

The weight of guilt lifted from Katie's shoulders. "Still. I shouldn't have shut you out, and I'm sorry about that."

"It's forgotten, child. Let's move on now. Have you talked to my Erin lately?"

A new helping of guilt replaced the previous one. Katie walked beside Gigi B down the sidewalk without looking at her. "I was going to the day I talked to you, but she's had so much on her own plate lately. I told myself I didn't want to add to her stress, and I know that's true. But I could have called and talked about her life. I should have. Just as soon as we're done here, I need to give her a call."

Gigi B placed a hand on her arm, stopping her entry into the nursing home. "You were right not to call then. Erin would have known something was eating you up inside, and she wouldn't have let it rest until she knew. She'll be a mite testy with you when you finally tell her, but she'll be quick to forgive and move on."

Katie smiled as she opened the door and waved Gigi B in ahead of her. "Must run in the family."

The elderly woman's head raised and Katie laughed as she heard her say in complete seriousness. "Of course it does. She gets all her best qualities from me."

"I CAN'T BELIEVE how much has been happening in your life, and you're just now thinking to tell me about all of it!"

Katie cringed at the dramatic whine and adjusted the blue tooth in her ear. At least it was over the phone, and she didn't have to see the disappointment in Erin's wide eyes. No, that wasn't true at all. She would have loved some face to face time with her friend. But after her talk with Gigi B, conviction hit hard. The conversation couldn't wait, and a phone call while she walked the path at Campus Lake was as good as it was going to get.

"It's not that much. And you've had your own issues to deal with. You didn't need mine."

If possible, her pitch rose even higher. "Not that much? Not that much? You can't be serious right now. Your father's mental capacity is deteriorating, and you're struggling with whether or not it's regular old-age stuff. You've got a job leading story hour at the library and heading up the children's activities. You're starting a reading time for the residents of the nursing home. You're befriending a teen mom and her son. How is any of that 'not much'?"

Katie adjusted her stride to make sure she could keep up her side of the conversation without gasping for breath at every other word. "Okay. I admit. It seems like a lot."

"Yes, it's a lot. And you've been going through it all alone."

"Not totally alone."

"Of course, you're not totally alone. You have a great church for prayer support, and I know Gigi B has your back. Maybe not always with blind support and adoration, but you wouldn't want that anyway. The truth is sometimes hard to hear, but it's always better in the end."

Katie adjusted the ponytail she'd hastily pulled her hair into before beginning her walk. Erin was completely missing the point. "Gigi B is great, but she isn't who I was referring to."

Silence hung heavy in the air. Maybe she wasn't ready to broach the subject with Erin. Not that she could avoid it now that she'd brought it up. Why didn't she consider that Erin had been a close friend of Austin before wading into this topic? What if Erin didn't approve or worse, what if she thought it was disrespectful to Austin?

"Are you going to tell me about this mystery friend? Is it anyone I know? Someone you met at work?"

"You know him."

"Him? Your new bestie is a guy?"

A sigh escaped before she could stop it. "He's not my new bestie. Never fear. You've got that title now and forever. But Nathan's been there for me a lot through all of this."

"Nathan? Nathan Phillips is the new shoulder you've been leaning on?"

She couldn't tell if it was shock or disappointment. "Nathan and I practically grew up together with his sister being my best friend back then. The Phillips family was a second family to me."

"So he's like a brother to you?"

"Umm...not exactly a brother."

Katie gave up all pretense of trying to walk and dropped onto one of the benches dotted along the path. If Erin disapproved, it would hurt more than she'd like to think about. But Katie trusted Erin, and she would have to consider whatever she told her.

The high-pitched squeal caused Katie to rip the blue tooth from her ear. She switched it off and put the phone to her ear. "What was that?"

"You cannot be serious. Oh my goodness! You and Nathan? You're seriously going out with Nathan?"

"Simmer down. It's not that serious. He's been there for me, and I don't know what I would've done without him the last little bit. And he's wonderful with Sammy and Dad."

"Not to mention he's as cute as they come. And he's got that whole cowboy thing going for him. Who doesn't love a cowboy?"

The image of Nathan riding beside her on the trail played in her memory. He definitely sat a horse well. And his baseball cap was fine, but there was something about the way his cowboy hat looked on him. She fought a grin. "Who said anything about love? We're taking things slow. Dating with a toddler and elderly father presents some unique challenges, but Nathan seems fine with spending most of our time hanging out at the house or going on picnics with Sammy."

"Okay, you've given me the boring facts, but you've left out the most important piece of information."

"What's that?"

Erin giggled like a schoolgirl. "Is Nathan Phillips a good kisser?"

Katie knew Erin couldn't see it, but she rolled her eyes anyway. She debated whether or not to tell her friend the whole truth. "I'm not sure I know the answer to that. A quick peck on the lips is the most kissing we've done."

"Why?"

Leave it to Erin to be blunt. How could she explain it when she didn't really get it? Nathan wanted to kiss her. She could sense it every time he looked at her with his heart in his eyes. But he refrained. She hadn't asked him to, but he did anyway. "We're taking it slow."

"You don't want him to kiss you?"

Katie moved a stray strand of hair from her face but weaved it through her fingers instead of releasing it. "I do. At least I think I do. It's not like I asked him not to kiss me. He just doesn't."

"Maybe he isn't sure if it would be welcomed or not. It doesn't sound like you're sure about it, and if he senses that, Nathan would never take that step." She adopted an over-the-top southern accent. "His mama taught him better than that."

The discomfort of the conversation fled as Katie laughed at what would most assuredly be Nathan's catchphrase if real-life people had catchphrases. "It's true, you know."

"Yeah, I know. There are precious few men out there that can honestly say their mama's raised them to be gentlemen, but Nathan is one of those men. I'm happy for you."

"Did I tell you he's going to start taking Dad to church for me?"

"What happened to the pastor?"

Katie explained the situation and her fears that his confusion was progressing. Erin listened in silence. "Nathan and I were discussing how we could help keep Dad as comfortable as possible, and he offered to take him for me. He knows I'm still not comfortable with the idea of returning to Orchard Hills Church, but it's where Dad is happiest. I think I'll start inviting him to lunch each week as a sort of thank you for taking Dad."

"I know Gigi B loves having you and Sammy at church. Sometimes, I think she's more excited about that than when I used to go with her."

Katie sensed a "but" coming in. She didn't want any naysayers at the moment. She and Nathan had a good plan worked out.

Erin continued when Katie refused to take the bait. "However."

Close enough. It was the fancy version of "but."

"Gigi B would completely understand if you wanted to take your dad to his church since he can't get there on his own."

"I told you I can't. It's too different."

"I know it would be different without Austin preaching, but that's the thing. It wouldn't be Austin's church anymore. I just thought since you're moving on in other areas, you might be ready to look at the whole church thing from a different perspective too."

Other areas. It was Erin's roundabout way of referring to her decision to pursue a relationship with Nathan. It was not Austin's church anymore, just like she wasn't Austin's wife anymore. She hadn't considered it in those terms before, and she felt the familiar pain of loss. It had been close for quite a while after Austin's death, but recently, the feeling hadn't come as often or stayed as long. Time had dulled the intensity, and Nathan's presence in her life had lessened the frequency. The realization caused Katie's stomach to ache.

"I'm not ready." She didn't want to talk about it since she was less than sure of her own feelings at the moment. "But enough about me. What's going on with you and Paul?"

Mercifully, Erin allowed the switch in topics and her words flowed without a breath to separate them. "You would not believe everything that's happening. Paul didn't want me to say anything until it was finalized. It nearly killed me. Literally, I was about to burst I wanted to tell you so badly. I never even thought about it until Paul brought it up. I mean, I thought about it for sure, but I never really told him about it. And then, he just comes up with it on his own. It had to be a God thing."

Was she finally pregnant? Her excitement certainly ranked up there, but her wording would be a little strange for her news to be about pregnancy.

"We're moving back to southern Illinois."

She hadn't heard right. She was sure. "You're doing what?"

"Paul's decided to expand. He's going to put Pages under a manager here in Bloomington kind of like you did when you moved in with your parents, and he's going to open another store down in Cape Girardeau, Missouri. But he doesn't want to live in Cape. So, we're going to look for a place in Anna. We'll be about thirty minutes from you and thirty minutes from Cape."

Her best friend was moving home! "I'm so happy for you and Paul. When are you moving? How can I help?"

Erin laughed. "I knew I could count on you to be as stoked about this as I am. The lease on the store begins in June, and Paul wants to open for business in July. That gives us roughly a month to find a place to live."

"A month? I can't believe I'll get to have you back in a month. You let me know what you need, and I'm there for you. Maybe we can get Gigi B and Nathan to help. Together we make a pretty great moving team. We could even help get the store set up. Whatever you need."

"Sounds great. For now, though, I have to run. Paul and I are supposed to be finding a house to rent. I'll talk to you later."

Katie stared out at the lake. Erin was moving home. She and Paul were still unsuccessfully trying to conceive, but at least they'd be close by where she could console and encourage her until their family dreams came true too. A sigh escaped her lips. Not even the niggling feelings of unease Erin had inadvertently set loose in Katie when they talked about moving on from Austin with Nathan could shake her contentment. Things were finally falling into place for everyone.

Chapter Seventeen

How did things go from good to having storm clouds on the horizon in such a short period of time? Just two weeks prior Erin had called with her good news. Both the reading program at the library and the nursing home were going well. Sammy's time in daycare was filling up with fun summer field trips and projects. She and Nathan were not moving forward quickly, but their relationship was solid.

The man in question watched her from across her kitchen table. He sat back in his chair with his arms crossed across his chest. "I know you don't like the idea, but it's time."

Katie occupied herself with a smudge on the otherwise clean floor. The toe of her sandal slid back and forth over it.

"Kate?"

She glanced up before returning her attention to the spot. He wasn't going to let this go. "I know he needs to see a doctor, but it's not as simple as all that. He doesn't even realize there's a problem. I can't imagine how he's going to react or how I'll even get him there. He never goes to the doctor."

"But you've got to find out if something more serious is going on and what can be done to alleviate the symptoms."

She rubbed her hands over her eyes and cheeks until her chin was cupped in her palms. "I know." She groaned. "Slide my phone over here."

He pushed it across the table. She found the number in her contacts and hit send. In a few moments, the deed was done. "Happy?"

"I understand it's hard, but you and I both know it had to be done. When's his appointment?"

"Three weeks."

She didn't need to tell him how hard this was on her. He always seemed to sense her emotions. As he came to her and pulled her up into his arms, she knew this time was no different. For the moment, her concerns faded as she soaked in the comfort of his embrace.

NATHAN PULLED into the drive early the next Sunday. The whole time he was at the barn feeding and watering the horses, he couldn't shake an uneasy feeling in his spirit. He'd prayed about it, turning the undecipherable concern over to the One who knew exactly what was happening.

When the feeling didn't subside, he decided to head over to Kate's house. He wouldn't need to leave for church with Cal right away, but he could help her out with him or even Sammy if she needed it. Being with Kate felt like being home. Maybe that was what he needed to calm his spirit.

His unease turned into full-blown concern as he rounded the bend in the driveway to find Kate toe to toe with Cal on the front lawn. Cal's face was set in a stubborn scowl while Kate gestured wildly, her eyes wide. As he crossed the drive to join them the conversation became clear and his heart pounded in his chest.

"Where is he, Dad?"

"I'm not telling you. You're just going to let them take him."

She threw her head back as she attempted to keep some semblance of control before looking him in the eyes once more. "There is no one here. No one has been here. No one has been in the house. No one has been in the yard. There has been no one here but me, you, and Sammy. Now tell me where he is!"

Nathan had no trouble understanding that Sammy was missing and that Cal had something to do with it. But what had happened and how could he help diffuse the situation? He laid a hand on Kate's arm. The fire in the green eyes she turned on him left no doubt that words would be had if his intervention didn't help solve the problem.

He turned his attention to Kate's dad. "Cal." He waited until the man looked at him. "Cal, I know you're trying to keep Sammy safe. You love Sammy, don't you?"

Cal glared at his daughter before nodding. If it hadn't been a serious situation, his offense at not having his daughter understand such a simple concept might have been humorous. But it was serious, and Nathan had found the door into what he hoped would be earning Cal's trust.

"I love Sammy too. He's a very special little boy. I don't want anything to happen to him either. We've got to work together to keep him safe. Don't we?"

Cal's bushy eyebrows nearly met as he frowned. Nathan stood still letting him assess his motives. A slight tilt of his head and relaxing of his features seemed to indicate his approval.

"I want to keep Sammy safe too. I can't do that right now, because I don't know where he is. But you do. Can you tell me where he is? Can you show me so I can help keep Sammy safe?"

The stubborn set of his jaw almost caused Nathan to lose hope of gaining Cal's help. "Please?"

The old man broke eye contact, focusing on a point over Nathan's shoulder. What was he looking at? Nathan followed his gaze to a run-down little shed sitting outside the barnyard fence. Could it be?

He patted Cal's arm in an effort to reassure him that everything was fine, that they were on the same side. With more restraint than he felt, Nathan started a leisurely walk down the drive toward the shed. He grasped Kate by the wrist as she took off past him in a rush.

Before she could tear her arm away or kick him in the shin for standing between her and her son, Nathan shook his head and nodded toward her dad. Cal paced two steps to the right and then two to the left as he wrung his hands in front of him.

"No. No. They'll take him. They'll take Sammy."

Nathan didn't wait for Kate's attention to come away from her father before speaking. "I know you want to find Sammy, and we will. I have a hunch, but I'm not sure it's going to be right. Cal could've taken him anywhere. If I'm wrong, Cal isn't going to be able to help us in this agitated state. You can calm him down. Let him know you aren't mad. That everything is okay. I'll get Sammy. You get your dad inside and get him calm."

He raised his brows in question. She looked from her dad to him and back to her dad. The decision wasn't an easy one. After seconds that felt like minutes of wasted time, Kate removed her arm from his grasp and moved to her dad's side.

"Dad, why don't we go inside and get a nice glass of iced tea. Nathan will take care of Sammy for us."

Nathan wasn't sure if she was saying it for Cal's benefit or her own. Maybe it was a little of both. He waited only long enough to see them walking arm in arm up the walk before turning to his own task. It took everything in him not to sprint to the building, but he couldn't risk upsetting Cal any more than he already was. He twisted the latch to unlock the metal plate holding the door closed. *Please, Father, let Sammy be safe inside.*

It took a moment for his eyes to adjust to the dim interior. Outdated farming equipment and containers of tools and hardware littered the floor. Scuff marks in the layer of dust on the floor indicated someone had recently been in the building, but he didn't see Sammy. He stood still as he scanned the single room one more time. In the silence, he could hear a whimper from behind barrels grouped together in the back corner.

Nathan kept his voice calm and quiet. "Sammy? It's Nathan. Are you in here?"

"I'm here."

Thank You, God. He was not a man given to tears but hearing fear in that little voice was almost too much. He moved quickly to find Sammy huddled on the floor in his pajamas with his knees pulled up to his chest and his arms wrapped around them. Dusty streaks on his cheeks and a quivering lip broke Nathan's heart. He reached his arms out to the toddler, and in a swift movement, Sammy launched himself into them.

Nathan used the sleeve of his shirt to wipe as many of the tear stains from Sammy's cheeks as possible before exiting the building. Kate must have gone into the house while he was retrieving Sammy because she came through the door as he stepped away from the building. Seeing her son in his arms, she ran to meet them slowing only as she drew near.

Sammy reached for her, and Nathan was only too happy to pass him to Kate. She held him tight. Though tears streamed down her cheeks, she kept her demeanor calm for her son.

With Sammy's head nuzzled into the curve of her neck and shoulder, Nathan barely heard his tiny voice repeating a single word. "Mommy."

AN HOUR LATER, Sammy had been bathed and fallen asleep. The strain of waking up in a dark, strange place had taken its toll on her son. Of course, her nerves weren't much better. While bathing him and checking for injuries, Katie's shaking had finally stopped. Now, she wanted nothing more than to climb into bed herself and pretend this horrible morning was a nightmare she would be able to forget in time. But her father was off pouting in his room last she checked, and Nathan sat at her kitchen table waiting for her return.

She sat across from him and shook her head when he tried to pass her a steaming mug. "The last thing I need right now is caffeine."

His grin was tinged with sadness. "That's why I made you mint tea instead of coffee. You need something to help you relax."

Something that sounded like a strange mixture of laugh and sob escaped before she could stop it. "Relax? I don't know that I'm ever going to be able to relax again."

"What happened? I mean, I know Cal's been a little paranoid lately. He's complained about people being in his house and moving things around and stuff like that. But what prompted him to hide Sammy?"

She inhaled the fragrant steam rising from the mug before blowing on the hot liquid and taking a careful sip. She played with the handle as she relived the experience. "I'm not sure. I've not left Sammy in Dad's care for months now, for obvious reasons. I would go outside to hang clothes or get the mail or whatever while Sammy was sleeping. You know that. We've sat outside talking while Sammy slept. Sometimes I'd take the monitor, but today I was just hanging a load of towels on the line. It wasn't going to take ten minutes. When I came back around the house Dad was on the walk with his hand on the door like he couldn't remember if he was coming or going. Even then, I didn't think anything of it."

She paused and cleared her throat. When that didn't clear the knot forming, she took a long drink of her now warm tea. She blinked a few times before continuing. "I came inside because I needed to get Sammy ready for church. Seeing his empty bed."

Katie couldn't force herself to finish the thought. All her

fears came rushing back in, mixing with the relief and causing a war of emotion. It was over now. She didn't need to worry. It was over. She laid her head on her arms and allowed the sobs she'd been fighting. She barely registered the hand rubbing her back or the way that same hand took her arm and pulled her out of her seat.

The smell of the dusty shed clung to the shirt she was pressed against as Nathan wrapped her in his strong arms. She'd avoided that creepy old shed as a child. It was dark, and it was dirty. And her son had woken up to find himself in that place alone. The sobs were so strong her chest hurt but still, they didn't stop. Nathan didn't try to quiet her or tell her everything was okay now. He simply held her up in his arms as her body purged itself of the residue of the morning's events.

Tears ended and energy spent, she remained in his embrace. Silence enveloped them. His heart beat under her ear, and Katie found comfort in the steady rhythm. If only she could stay there forever. She breathed out a final ragged breath.

The shrill call of her cell phone broke the tenuous peace. She sniffed and moved from his arms to answer it. Gigi B. She and Sammy had missed church. Of course, Gigi B would worry especially after they'd smoothed things over between them.

"Hi."

"Don't you 'hi' me. Where are you at, girl? Did you forget this was the Lord's Day?"

Katie was too spent to find humor in Gigi B's delivery. "It's been a long day. I'm fine. Sammy's fine. But we had a scare with Dad today, and it's kept us at home."

"Is Cal okay? Do you need someone with you? I can be there in ten."

"Dad's fine, relatively speaking. But I'm going to have to make some decisions, and I don't have the luxury of waiting to speak with his doctor first. Nathan's here with us. We'll be fine.

No. On second thought, I'd appreciate your input. Can you come now?"

"As I said, I'll be there in ten."

~

GIGI B STARED at Katie then to Nathan then back again. "Mercy. You have had quite the eventful morning."

Nathan moved to stand behind Katie. His hands kneading the taut muscles in her neck and shoulders felt wonderful. "Kate's handled everything like a pro. She kept it together until Sammy was asleep. I've checked on her dad a couple of times since we came in. He's holding a grudge, but he has no idea why. Just says he wants to stay in his room. It works in our favor though since it gives us time to figure things out. Sammy could wake any time, but I doubt it. The poor kid was spent."

Gigi B nodded toward her while addressing Nathan. "I don't think Sammy's the only one wore out by all this. I think maybe we should let Katie get some rest before she tries to make any decisions."

"I can't sleep." A realization hit hard. "I really can't sleep, ever. I was awake when Dad did this. I can't let Sammy out of my sight. What if Dad wakes in the middle of the night and decides someone is out to get him again? What if we aren't fortunate enough to be able to figure out the hiding spot next time and something awful happens to my son? Sammy was terrified. I can't imagine what this is going to do to him. And I'm powerless to keep it from happening again."

As her mind ran through the possibilities, Katie began to shake. Nathan ran his hands up and down her arms. It eased the shaking on the outside, but her insides still quivered in fear.

"Go up to bed. Gigi B is right. You need some rest before we figure all this out. I'm here. Gigi B is here. If Sammy wakes or your dad needs something we will take care of it."

She opened her mouth to argue. Nathan cut her off. "I'm not asking, Kate. You need this. Let us take care of you so you can take care of Sammy and your dad."

She nodded without a word and climbed the stairs. Each step felt like her shoes had weights in them. Her mind spun with all the details of the day and the questions they brought. She doubted she would even be able to sleep, but she would take a few minutes of quiet to thank God for keeping Sammy safe. She'd barely made it past 'Thank You' before falling asleep.

Chapter Eighteen

"I don't want to go. This is my home, and you can't make me leave it."

She prayed for patience. Thank the Lord she'd been made medical power of attorney after her mother's injury. Neither parent had wanted to leave her with her hands tied in case of an emergency. None of them had foreseen this situation though.

"Dad, we've talked about this. Your mind isn't working the way it should right now. You need a place where they can help you in the best ways. Sammy and I will visit every day after school."

Nathan's presence at her back brought comfort to an otherwise comfortless situation. How could she make her father see there was no choice in the matter? He was cognizant enough to know the facts about what was going on but was incapable of thinking logically through the reasons for the move. The situation with Sammy had given the doctor reason enough to see him earlier than scheduled, and his advice coincided with what Katie had determined. If it was just her and her father, he was capable enough that she could theoretically give him twenty-four hour a day care at home. Realistically speaking, Katie knew she couldn't do that with Sammy also living in the home. Her dad wouldn't want to hurt him, but his behavior was unpredictable at best. Sammy had experienced nightmares every night since the incident with the shed. She couldn't do that to her son, but the tears welling up in her father's eyes were almost more than she could take.

Gigi B stepped in. "Cal, I know you're going to love this place. I'm there every day for at least a couple of hours and will come to visit you. There's a beautiful garden we can walk in and enjoy the sunshine. And do you remember Mr. and Mrs. Taylor from your church? You'll be living right down the hall from them. Won't it be nice to see them again?"

His brow furrowed. "Mr. and Mrs. Taylor? Do I know a Mr. and Mrs. Taylor?"

She patted his arm. "Why sure you do. In fact, I think there's a church picture on your wall with them in it. Why don't we go see if we can figure out who they are? It might even be nice to wrap up the picture and take it with you. Nothing better than keeping your memories close by."

She led him from the room. Katie's shoulders sagged under the weight of what she was doing. She hated the tears that came without warning. She'd cried far too often lately. It seemed like all she was capable of doing.

Nathan's arms circled her waist, and she leaned into him. She felt his warm breath on her ear as he spoke. "It's going to be okay. It doesn't feel like it, but this will become his new normal."

"Maybe I'm doing the wrong thing. Maybe I should try to get around the clock in-home care."

"Possibly. Why did you decide against it though?"

She tilted her head back against his shoulder. He knew why. He wanted her to remember. "Dad becomes obstinate and angry when anyone tells him what he should or shouldn't do or tries to help him. He does it with me, and it gets worse when it's someone he doesn't consider family. Besides, he's already paranoid about strangers in the house. He would not take kindly to having someone new here."

She felt his lips press a gentle kiss above her ear. "This is your decision. Gigi B and I can't tell you what you should do. If you've looked at your reasons and decided this is your best option, then as tough as it is, we'll stand behind you. If you change your mind and decide on getting around the clock care, we'll still stand behind you. You've prayed about it?"

"Nonstop since the doctor's visit. And I had a peace about the nursing home until Dad realized what was happening."

"And what would happen if you got in-home care? Would he be at peace?"

She lifted her head from his shoulder. "No. He wouldn't. He would be mad that people were coming into his home and telling him what to do."

It didn't matter what she did. The disease stealing her father from her would prevent him from accepting either situation with grace. As understanding and patient as he'd been throughout her life, Alzheimer's was twisting his personality into something new. He couldn't be patient and understanding because he couldn't logically work through the details. His mind was constantly lying to him about what was happening and why. With faulty information, he couldn't make a rational choice.

The realization removed the shroud of doubt and regret from Katie's heart. For the first time in the months of dealing with her father's declining mental capacity, she felt free to make the hard decisions she knew would be best for all involved. She turned in Nathan's arms and threw her arms around his neck. The scant inches between them was too much distance in light of the freedom she felt. She used the hands clasped behind his head to pull him towards her raised face. She paused when he was near enough she could almost feel his lips on hers.

"Thank you."

His lips were soft against hers. He tightened his arms around her, holding her close, but didn't deepen the kiss. She pulled back enough to place a light kiss where his smile caused dimples to hide under his stubble before moving back to his lips. Still, he let her set the tone of the kiss. How did she end up with such a caring man in her corner?

"We best be getting back into the living room."

Gigi B's too loud voice stole the moment. Katie laughed. The woman was sharp, and she was discreet enough to give them the opportunity to retain their privacy. Looking at Nathan as she moved away stole her breath. His blue eyes regarded her with an intensity that left no question as to his feelings for her. Left on their own, she didn't have a doubt that he would have pulled her right back into his arms and continued kissing her.

Katie felt her cheeks heat and turned from him. Her dad entered followed by Gigi B. Katie nodded toward the picture frames her dad carried. "Did you find some pictures you want to take with you?"

He held them out to her. "I need to take these. I want them with me."

She accepted the frames from his outstretched hands and flipped through them. The church photo was on top. A picture of her and Sammy taken at his birthday party was underneath that one. Katie had to clear her throat as she looked at the portrait of her mom and dad on their wedding day in the final frame. He was taking everyone he loved with him.

"I think these are great, Dad. I'll wrap them up in bubble wrap and put them where they'll be safe until we get to your new place."

He allowed her to do exactly as she said, watching her intently as she did. She would have to thank Gigi B later for her insight. She didn't know what else had been discussed but her dad seemed more at ease with the move, at least for the moment.

She was learning moods changed with the wind. But for this moment, he was resigned if not content. She would take it.

"I think that's everything. Let's go get you moved in. As soon as we do, if you want me to, I'll pick up Sammy from school so he can come to see your new place."

His eyes roamed the room. Katie tried to ignore the tightness in her chest at the wistful look. How would it be to say good-bye to the only home you'd known throughout your adult life? She hated that it had come to this but was thankful for the time they'd had together. He wouldn't have been able to be on his own this long if she and Sammy hadn't moved in after Austin's death. She needed to remember to look at the blessings in the middle of the mess.

She placed her arm around his stooped shoulders. "Come on, Dad. It's time to go."

THE GROUP GATHERED around the kitchen island laughed as Gigi B regaled them with dramatic retellings of the adventures of her past. The scent of the pizzas they'd polished off for lunch hung in the air. Katie watched them as she filled her cup at the sink. It was amazing how different the tone could be from one moving day to the next.

Her dad's moving day was fresh in her mind along with the mix of emotions it evoked. He was settling better than she expected. He regularly asked about going home but seemed resigned to his new place in the nursing home when she reminded him it was his home now. These last few weeks had been hard, and Katie reminded herself to count her blessings, four of which were currently trying to top each other's stories.

Nathan moved his bar stool next to hers as Erin told her story. Katie grinned at him and he took her hand in his. It lasted until she leaned forward on her stool and rested her arms on her thighs, giving her attention fully to Erin's tale

"So there we were with a flat tire and no spare in a town we'd never been in before. While Paul put on the baby spare, I ran across the busy highway to a gas station to get a number for a place we could get the tire changed. Would you believe there was only one place open? I mean, seriously, what kind of town doesn't have a place to get a tire changed at five o'clock on Friday night? Anyway, they changed the tire, and we maxed out our spending limit for the day on our debit card. Then, we'd barely been back on the road when Paul realized we needed gas and tried to pull over at a station only to misjudge the intersection and end up straddling the median! All I could do was pray, 'God please don't let him pop another tire!'"

Paul rolled his eyes. "C'mon. It wasn't nearly that dramatic."

"That's easy for you to say. You weren't the one seeing your life flash before your eyes as the car careened toward oncoming traffic!" She slapped her hand over her heart. "I thought I was going to die."

Katie laughed. Erin could make going to the market down the road to get butter sound like a chapter out of the *Odyssey* or some other epic tale of adventure. Nathan and Paul merely shook their heads. Gigi B wiped happy tears from her eyes.

As the stories ended, the others went back to work unloading the moving trucks and sorting the boxes into the appropriate rooms. Erin and Katie finished worked together to wash the cups they'd used and wipe down the counters.

"It's going to do my heart a world of good to have you home again."

Without a word, Erin wrapped her in a bear hug. Katie had learned early in their relationship to accept these unscripted invasions of her space. It would do no good to fight it. God had given her a friend with absolutely no concept of personal space, and Katie decided He must have had His reasons. Besides, with the way things had been going lately, Katie wasn't totally against receiving a little extra love from a friend.

Katie started to pull away only to have Erin's hold on her tighten. "Okay. Hug received. Moving on."

Erin released her but the smile on her face kept Katie from walking away. What was that old phrase her dad used? The cat that ate the canary? Yep, that was the only way to describe the look on Erin's face.

"What's up with you? This is more than moving home."

Erin giggled. "I've got the best news."

Katie's eyes involuntarily went to Erin's middle before finding her eyes once more. Erin shook her head, but her smile remained content.

"No. I'm not pregnant. The IUI's didn't take. But Paul and I came to a decision. We prayed about it, and we're going to adopt. We've started the process. I know it can take a long time, but we've started. We're on our way to finally having a family."

Katie shut her mouth as she realized she was gaping at Erin like a wide-mouth bass. "That is so awesome! You two are going to make wonderful parents. I know it. You're already the best godparents a boy could ask for. Just let me know what I can do to help."

"You might want to be careful with a blanket offer like that. Adoption is really expensive. Paul's parents have helped us, but we're going to have to do fundraising in the future. I will call on you to help."

"Call anytime. It would be my honor."

Katie drew Erin into another hug as they squealed with each other like junior high girls at a slumber party until Nathan and Paul came into the room.

Paul looked at Erin with mock irritation. "You told her, didn't you? I thought we were going to wait, but I should have known better."

Erin bit her lip and shrugged. "It's too good to keep to ourselves."

Nathan's gaze flicked to each person in the room before settling on Paul. "Would someone like to fill me in?"

"And if we're telling secrets, I'd like to know too." Gigi B's voice entered the room seconds before she did.

Paul shook his head. "Go ahead. You know you want to."

The flurry of questions following Erin's announcement covered everything from when to what agency they were using to how they decided to adopt. When every possible avenue of discussion was covered, Katie stood and gathered her purse from the corner.

"Though I know this won't be the last time I'll say this, I am happy for you guys. But, right now, I have to go pick up Sammy and stop by the nursing home to see Dad."

Nathan stood as well. "Want me to come with you?"

"You don't need to. I've got to finish prepping for tomorrow's story time at the library after we get home. I probably won't be great company. By the way, are you still going to watch Sammy tomorrow while Erin and I have a girls' afternoon?"

"You bet I am. Sammy and I have plans to go riding tomorrow. But since I'm not going to be seeing you, I'll go ahead and walk you out."

They bid the others good-bye. Katie slipped her hand into Nathan's as they walked out together. "You do know you're welcome to come out to the house tonight. I just don't want you to be bored when I can't pay you a lot of attention. I have about a million green and red circles to cut out for our caterpillars tomorrow."

His head raised in false arrogance. "I'll have you know I'm an expert circle cutter. I got an A-plus in the subject in kindergarten, and my skills like the rest of me have only gotten better with age."

"Well then, by all means, come ahead. I can use the extra hand."

He fished his keys out of his pocket. "I'll meet you over there in about an hour and a half. Will that give you enough time to pick up Sammy and go visit Cal?"

Katie nodded. "That should be just about right. See you there."

Chapter Nineteen

B y the time Nathan knocked on the door, Katie had her crafting supplies spread out on the coffee table in the living room. Sammy was engrossed in his favorite movie about a talking train that got into trouble without even trying. She'd given him some apple slices and string cheese to snack on while she and Nathan worked on cutting circles from construction paper.

Katie fought a smile as Nathan worked the small pair of scissors in a nearly perfect circle on the page of red paper. The tip of his tongue barely showed between his lips as he concentrated on cutting along the pre-drawn line.

"You know these are for small children, right?"

He nodded, keeping his focus on the paper. "Yep."

"They aren't going to care if the circle isn't absolutely perfect."

"Yep. But if you're going to do it, might as well do it right. That's how my mama taught me to do things."

"Well, your mama is a pretty wise woman. And she did raise a pretty great son."

She didn't have time to react as he looked up from his circle and leaned in for a quick kiss on her mouth. She looked quickly to Sammy, but he was oblivious, lost in his movie.

"Getting these circles cut is going a lot quicker than I thought it would. It must be due to my extra help."

"Yep."

The dismissive tone in his voice caught her attention. She watched him working on the next piece of paper. Something had changed in the last few seconds. All signs of playfulness were gone as sure as if someone had flipped a switch. He was too relaxed for his expression to be angry, but there was something there she couldn't quite identify.

Maybe a change of subject was in order. "Dad was doing really well today. He recognized both me and Sammy. He was in a pretty good mood too. We sat in the garden and ate the frozen yogurt Sammy and I picked up from Cool Spoons on our way over there."

"That's good. I'm glad Cal is adjusting to his new place. Seen it go both ways in my years of volunteering out there. But it helps that you visit him regularly. There's a big difference in those that get visitors and those without."

He set aside the scissors and piled up his finished circles. "I'm gonna go get a drink if that's okay."

"You know where everything is."

Katie finished cutting her stack of circles. Nathan hadn't returned from the kitchen. Making sure Sammy was still focused on his movie, Katie joined Nathan. He stood at the sink staring out the window. What was he looking at? She moved behind him. His gaze wasn't distant like he was searching the fields. It was close and low. She scanned the yard but didn't see anything of interest, not even a deer or rabbit.

She rubbed her hand across his shoulder. "What's so interesting out there? I thought I'd lost you."

He ran a finger along the edge of the wooden ornament hanging in the window. "You're not ready are you?"

"Ready? Ready for what?"

A knot formed in the pit of her stomach. She knew what Nathan was referring to, but she couldn't bring herself to say it. Better to play it off instead.

His hand dropped to his side as his head swiveled to look at her standing next to him. "You're not ready to see where this relationship is going to go. To give us a chance."

She fought the urge to huff at him, but she couldn't quite control the defensive tone to her voice. "I'm not ready? Why? Because I have an ornament with sentimental value hanging in my kitchen window? That means I'm not ready?"

His brows drew together. "No. It's not about the ornament. I get it. That's a reminder of the man you loved and all your good times with him. But when I kissed you in the living room, why did you look at Sammy?"

She raised her chin. "I'm not sure it's the best thing for him to see our displays of affection. He's little, and I don't want him confused by our relationship."

"And the other day at Erin's? It seems an awful lot like you're having issues with us as a couple. I'm not upset or anything. I'm only makin' sure you're not having second thoughts about us."

His concerns echoed those Erin had expressed not so long ago. Could there be something to it? Could doubt about moving on be what created the little catch in her mind that snuck up on her at the most inopportune times? Of course not. Austin had been gone for years, and Katie enjoyed being part of a duo again. She rolled her eyes and grinned. "Don't be silly. I'm not having second thoughts. You can understand why I wouldn't want Sammy to see a lot of PDA at this point. I have to think of him. And the thing at Erin's wasn't even a thing. I was getting comfortable is all."

When he continued looking at her with such intensity that she felt he was trying to read her thoughts, she did the only thing she could think of to reassure him. She moved to stand toe to toe with him before looking up to find his head tilted down toward her. She gave him a flirtatious wink before wrapping her arms around his neck and pulling his lips to hers. The muscles in his shoulders remained stiff. She deepened the kiss as she played with his hair. His arms tightened around her waist drawing her closer. When she felt the tension in his shoulders release, Katie knew he got her point. He was being silly. Would she be able to kiss him like that if she wasn't sure about their relationship? Absolutely not.

Katie barely registered the tiny footsteps pitter-patting across the living room's hardwood floor before Nathan broke their kiss and stepped away from her. She smiled. He was so sweet to simply accept her desire to keep their signs of affection away from Sammy's young eyes. Leaning against the counter, she took his hand. A gentle squeeze told her Nathan understood it for the compromise it was.

Sammy's socked feet slid as he went from hardwood to linoleum and tried to stop. Katie started toward him as his feet did an unsteady dance but Nathan's grip on her hand held her back. Sammy righted himself as she was about to pull away.

"The trains are over."

"You know what that means."

His lips pushed out in a pout. "Bed?"

"Yes, sir. It means bed, but if you go without any arguments I'll tell you a bedtime story first."

Pale green puppy dog eyes assured her Sammy wanted to argue. Instead, he gave an exaggerated sigh and turned to the stairs.

"Sammy, don't forget to tell Nathan bye first."

Nathan crossed the room to scoop him up before he could turn around. Holding him with one hand, he used the other to tickle the little boy's side.

"Stop! Stop!"

"What's the magic word?"

"Pleeeeeaaase!"

Nathan laughed and kissed his cheek before returning him to his feet on the bottom stair. "Close enough, buddy. You get a good night's sleep, and I'll come to get you for our trail ride tomorrow. Deal?"

His head nodded sharply. "Deal."

Katie shook her head. This could go on indefinitely. "You've said goodnight. Now to bed, little mister."

"Yes, mommy."

Though her dad would've said his pace was slower than molasses, Sammy started up the stairs. Katie moved to follow, stopping next to Nathan.

"This could take a little while."

He pulled her in for a side hug and kissed the top of her head. "That's alright. I'll head home for the night and see you both tomorrow."

She kissed his cheek. "Good night. See you at one."

Only when sitting in the silence with her sleeping son cradled in her arms did Katie allow the sliver of doubt to slip back into her mind. She missed Austin more than she could say, but she couldn't deny the rush it gave her every time Nathan looked her way. The two couldn't be more different. How could they both turn her head and win, or in Nathan's case be working to win, her heart? Surely Austin would understand even if she was having a hard time doing that very thing. But was it disrespectful to his memory to choose someone who was nothing like him? And if their relationship followed the typical progression, would Austin think a man like Nathan was capable of raising Sammy as he would have?

Oh well. They were questions she wasn't likely to find answers to in one night. Katie rose from the rocking chair and laid Sammy in his bed, carefully placing his satin edged blanket beside him. She smiled as his pudgy hand instinctively reached for the security giving blanket. If only peace and security were as easy to come by for adults. She would surround herself with piles of the softest blankets. But her questions and fears were not erased with items of comfort, nor were they as free of consequence as her son's usual dilemma of whether to have chicken nuggets or a cheeseburger with his kids' meal.

Katie turned on his monitor, grabbed her receiver, and made her way downstairs. She needed a steaming cup of herbal tea and some time in her Bible if she was going to quiet the storm brewing in her heart and mind so she could rest throughout the night.

Chapter Twenty

"Everyone grab a wipe for their hands. Get all the glue off, and we can go have a special snack."

Katie used one of the cloths to scrub the glue from her fingers before moving to help the children who did not have parents present. She glanced at the table covered in sticky red and green caterpillars with wiggly eyes, making a mental note to return and clean the glue off the table before Mildred saw it. If she didn't, the poor woman's blood pressure might never return to normal.

Once hands were clean and wipes discarded, Katie led the children outside for their special snack. In keeping with the book, each child had the correct number of pieces of apples, pears, strawberries and the other fruits mentioned in the story on their napkins. As a special treat, Katie even had a sucker for each child to take home, since she'd requested they leave their caterpillars to display on the library bulletin board for the next two weeks.

While the children ate their snacks, Katie made her way to each of the parents. She wanted their in-put on story time but also to let them know their participation with their children was an important part of growing life-long readers. She purposefully left Anna for last.

"Is Gabe enjoying story time?"

Anna looked to where her son sat next to Sammy on the quilt. The two were becoming fast friends. "He always enjoys the stories and crafts. You have such imagination."

"Thank you. I love what I get to do with the kids. I know for some it's just a little free babysitting, but I enjoy having parents like you who will stay and participate with their kids."

"It's been wonderful for him. With us moving around so much, story time is the one constant he has. I hate that we may have to miss it for a couple of weeks."

Katie swallowed a bite of apple before she spoke. "Why is that?"

The younger woman shrugged. "We've been staying with Callie's family. I grew up with her. She's a senior in high school, and her parents are very nice. We've been there for about a month now, but next week they're going out of town for a couple of weeks. As wonderful as they are, I can't blame them for not wanting someone living in their home with them not there."

"Where will you go?"

"I've got a couple of possibilities. I'm waiting to hear back from them with a definite answer. Callie's family will let me come back when they get home, but I don't want to wear out my welcome there either. I may need them again down the road. Know what I mean?"

The concept was easy enough to grasp. The reality was foreign. "Sure, I do. If there's anything I can do, let me know. And if you end up living too far out and need rides to story time, I'd be happy to pick you up. I'd hate for Gabe to lose the constant in his life, especially when he enjoys it as much as he seems to."

Sammy ran to them, pulling the subject of their discussion along with him. "Mommy, can Gabe ride with me?"

Katie knelt in front of the boys and looked up at Anna. "Our friend Nathan is taking Sammy on his first horseback ride today. As you can tell, he's very excited." She shifted her gaze to her son. "I know you like to have fun with Gabe and riding a horse sounds very fun. But Nathan invited you to ride. We can't invite our friends to someone else's house. Nathan is only one person, and he can't teach both of you to ride at the same time."

His bottom lip started to puff out. "I'm sorry, but not this time. Maybe we can speak with Nathan and ask for a time when we can all go. Then we would have enough adults to watch everyone. How does that sound?"

Gabe jumped up and down. "Can we, Mama? Can we ask?"

Anna looked at her. Katie nodded. "Of course, we can ask, Sweet One."

Katie interrupted. "How about I ask today? We'll try to get something set for after things settle down in your life."

"That sounds perfect."

Katie looked at the clock on her cell phone before addressing the whole group. "Thank you for coming to story time today. I hope you enjoyed our story. It's time to clean up. Parents, don't let your children forget to pick a sucker from the sucker tree before you leave today and come back through the week to see our caterpillar bulletin board with all your beautiful caterpillars on it."

With children and parents set into motion, Katie moved to pick up the leftovers and picnic blanket. Anna stayed to help while Gabe and Sammy chased after a squirrel until it ran up a tree leaving them in fits of giggles.

Anna held up a plastic zipper bag of assorted fruit. "Where should I put this?"

"Why don't you and Gabe take it with you? We have more at home than we can eat before it goes bad."

"If you're sure."

"Positive. Thank you for your help cleaning up. We've got

everything put away. Nathan will be here any minute to pick up Sammy. You two should go ahead. I'll walk up front with you to see if Nathan's gotten here yet. After he gets Sammy, I'll put up the bulletin board and head out myself."

As they rounded the corner of the library, Katie was pulled from her conversation with Anna when Sammy tugged on her hand.

"Nathan! Nathan!"

She quickened her steps so Sammy wasn't yanking her arm quite so hard. He frantically waved at Nathan across the parking lot.

Nathan made a show of looking all around the parking lot. "Sammy? I hear Sammy, but I don't see him." He looked at Anna and Katie. "Have you seen Sammy? He should be here somewhere."

As Nathan neared, Sammy broke her hold on his hand. Launching himself at Nathan, he bear-hugged him at the knees and laughed. "I'm here!"

"Oh, there you are. Are you ready to go ride some horses today?"

His answer was muffled by the blue jeans he was plastered to.

"Sammy, please look up at Nathan before you answer."

His head tilted back at an impossible angle. "I'm ready. Can Gabe come with me next time?"

Katie shook her head and addressed her son. "Maybe you should at least wait until after your ride today to ask for more."

Nathan squatted in front of the boys and addressed Sammy's friend. "You must be Gabe. I'm Nathan. Pleased to meet you."

Dark, straight hair shifted with Gabe's nod. His brown eyes were wide. Nathan put out his hand. Anna nudged her son's shoulder. His small hand inched away from his side. Nathan shook it vigorously.

"My, my what a strong grip you've got there, Gabe. That's

perfect for riding horses. Maybe next time you can come with Sammy and take a ride yourself."

"Do me. I'm strong too."

Katie placed a hand on Sammy's shoulder. Her son had rarely had to share the admiration of the adults in his life. They would have to remedy that to help him get rid of the flicker of jealousy she recognized in his interruption.

Nathan went with it and shook Sammy's hand. "Wow. You are strong. You two will both make excellent cowboys."

"Speaking of which, shouldn't you guys be heading out? I've got to decorate a bulletin board before it's time to meet Erin."

Anna chimed in. "And Gabe, we have to get home. I need to get ready for work."

Katie waved to each pair before heading into the library. Time to scrub glue off tables and staple caterpillars to the bulletin board. She'd have to hurry to meet Erin on time.

~

"You pour some drinks and grab some spoons. I'll run these upstairs and meet you in the living room."

Erin saluted. "Aye, aye Captain. But you better hurry. I'm not going to pause the movie if you don't make it back before the opening credits are over."

Katie took the stairs two at a time. She tossed her shopping bags on the bed and turned to join her friend. How did Erin still have the power to make her do things she'd never enjoyed? They'd spent two hours in the mall, and neither of them had had one thing they needed. Still, Katie had come out with three bags and an emptier bank account. The new pair of boot cut jeans, two button-up blouses to wear with them, and pair of cowboy boots would wait to be put up until after the movie if she didn't talk herself into returning every item.

Katie took her pint of dark chocolate gelato from Erin's

outstretched hand as she made her way to the other end of the sofa. Just in time. The bouncy theme music faded as the main character walked confidently across the screen. Katie criss-crossed her legs on the cushion, dipped her spoon into the silky, cold confection, and settled in for the show. The rom-com had been in and out of the theaters before Erin moved back to the area. Katie had been disappointed at the time, but rounding out their girls' day out with it was as near perfect as they could get.

"They have got to be the most adorable couple in the history of rom-coms." Erin touched a hand to her heart for dramatic effect while the ending credits rolled.

Katie pressed the power button on the remote. "And the looks they gave each other were priceless. You knew what they were thinking."

"It had all the feels."

"The feels?"

Erin rolled her eyes. "You know. It had all those moments when your stomach gets butterflies for them when something amazing happens between them. Or your stomach drops like you're on the downward slope of a roller coaster when one of them screws up and leaves the other heartbroken. The feels."

Katie laughed as she scooped up the long since empty gelato containers and spoons. "I guess I've never heard that phrase before, but I know what you're talking about."

Erin picked up the glasses and followed her to the kitchen. "And don't you agree this movie is full of those moments? I'm for sure going to add this one to my collection. I think I could watch it a million times and never get tired of it."

"I'll admit it. I'm a little bit sorry I only rented it. I thought I would swoon at the end when Jill looked up, and then Peter wasn't there…"

"But he really was. He was just behind Jill. And that kiss! You could feel the electricity between them."

They had wandered back into the living room and flopped

onto the couch. Giving in to the theatrics of the conversation, Katie laid her head back on the cushions with her eyes closed. "It was perfect."

Erin's next words snapped her head up and her mind back firmly into reality.

"What did you say?"

Her well-shaped blonde brow rose high over one eye. "I said, 'You know all about perfect kisses, don't you?' Or maybe I'm wrong. Is a kiss from Nathan still only a fantasy you allow in your weakest moments?"

Katie smacked her in the shoulder with a throw pillow. "Not funny."

Erin snatched and held the offending pillow against her chest, where it couldn't be brandished as a weapon any longer. "No, it isn't. I don't understand why you insist on straddling the fence on this. Nathan is smitten from the top of his cowboy hat to the tip of his boots. He dotes on Sammy. He's fiercely loyal to you and your family. He's a godly man and leading man cute to boot. Why are you holding him at arm's length?"

"For your information, we have kissed. So there."

Erin gave her the same look Katie gave Sammy the day he ate a chocolate chip cookie without permission. He denied it vehemently, but traces of chocolate around his mouth told a different story. "You've kissed, and what? That proves you've decided to move on, and now it's all sunny skies and butterflies in your love life? You've held nothing back and have no reservations?"

Katie's previous conversation with Nathan played on a loop in her mind. She hoped the heat she felt in her cheeks didn't mean tell-tale red tinged them. "No. I wouldn't, uh, I wouldn't exactly say that. I still miss Austin every day."

Erin placed a hand on her shoulder. "Who said that's ever going to end? You loved Austin. He's your son's father. Some days it will feel like a shadow in the background of your lives, but on other days, the important days, I'm sure the sting of losing him will be sharp enough to steal your breath. But that doesn't mean it has to steal your future joy or keep you from moving forward with someone else."

"I remember one day before Sammy was born, we were discussing whether our child would be a boy or girl. Talking about the possibility of a boy, we realized neither of us could teach our son football."

Erin bit her lip momentarily before speaking. "I'm not sure I understand what you're getting at."

Katie sighed and mindlessly played with a stray curl. "The other day at the park, do you know what Nathan did?"

Erin shook her head.

"He taught Sammy how to throw a football. A football. Sammy has someone who can teach him football."

"Isn't that good?"

"Yes, but Nathan isn't Austin. And Austin couldn't have done that. He didn't know the first thing about sports. Does the fact that I sat there and happily watched another man teach our son how to throw a football mean I've betrayed Austin's memory in some way?"

Erin's eyes glistened with tears. "No, Katie. You can't believe that lie. It's okay for Austin and Nathan to be different. It's fine to be happy that your son has a man in his life who can teach him some of the things his dad didn't enjoy and might not have taught him. And if you want Sammy to know the things Austin could teach him that Nathan can't, tell him about his dad. Find classes where he can experience those things and decide for himself what he's going to love and go after. You wouldn't want Nathan to be Austin's twin. You'd constantly be putting them in competition with each other, and one would always be lacking. This way you can appreciate their differences and celebrate the fact of how they're alike."

"They're nothing alike."

Erin shrugged. "Maybe they're not in the way they look or their interests, but those are just the wrappings. Both men have a heart to serve God. Both place a high priority on ministry, though their mission fields look nothing alike. Both love you and Sammy and would give anything to be able to walk through life with you, celebrating the good times and comforting you in the bad. Where it counts, Austin and Nathan are very much alike."

Katie fidgeted with the hem of her shirt. Maybe Erin had a point. Surely it was okay to move on, even if moving on with someone else would look very different than the life she'd imagined with Austin. Then again, if it was right, would she have these doubts?

Chapter Twenty-One

"I'm ready. Hand Sammy up here."

Chris tipped back the brim of his hat and looked up at his business partner. "You sure about this? Katie seems pretty careful with the boy."

Careful. Nathan was sure it was Chris's polite way to imply Kate was over-protective of Sammy. "Kate'll be fine with it. She knew we were going riding. I'm sure she'd be fine with a short trail ride. Besides, we're being careful. We're riding double, and Sammy's got a helmet on. Don't you, Sammy?"

Pudgy toddler fingers patted the hard black helmet. "Sammy's got a hat."

Chris shook his head and lifted Sammy to him. "If you say so. You two have fun on your trail ride."

Nathan gave a little wave that Sammy promptly imitated. As soon as Buck moved, those little hands dropped to the saddle horn and gripped it tight. Nathan felt the child press against his chest. He was as tense as his mother had been on her first ride, but what he'd seen then he now felt as rigid shoulders pressed against him.

Nathan had no doubts that Sammy could handle a trail ride as comfortably as he'd ridden double in the corral. Not even sitting alone on Buck while the horse stood tethered to the fence unnerved the little guy. However, it was understandable that riding outside the boundaries of the fence felt less secure for Sammy. Nathan's free hand encircled the child's middle. After a few moments, some of the starch left his body. A short time later, Nathan decided it was safe to speak.

Without loosening his hold on Sammy, Nathan tilted his head down and to the side to speak to him. "Are you liking the ride, Sammy? Buck's a good horse, isn't he?"

The little black helmet nodded while Sammy's eyes remained trained on some spot ahead of them. "Buck's big."

"Yes, Buck is big. But Buck is also a very nice horse. Would you like to pat his neck and tell Buck he's a good horse? I've got you, and you aren't going to fall. You can even keep holding the saddle horn with one hand if you want."

Little fingers stretched open on the saddle horn before promptly closing again. It was going to take a bit more coaxing.

"It's okay, Sammy. I've got you, but Buck needs to know he's a good horse. Can you tell him for me? And pat his neck?"

The boy's hand loosened its grip on the saddle. Slowly, Nathan watched as it inched forward. Fingers quickly patted the horse's neck.

"Good, Buck."

The hand quickly found its way back to the saddle horn. Nathan smiled. It was a start. Sammy had overcome his fear, and that was enough for now. They continued riding with Nathan pointing out every tree, bush, and bird as calmly as he could. After a while, Nathan noticed Sammy joining in the conversation. When Sammy reached his hand to pat Buck's neck unprompted with a hearty "Good, Buck", Nathan knew Sammy was totally at ease.

They rode down the same trail Nathan had taken with Kate. With Sammy feeling comfortable, it was Nathan's turn to listen as the boy pointed out and commented on everything they passed. When a bright red cardinal flew by, Sammy's excited gestures pulled Nathan's attention from the trail. Nathan's muscles tensed as Buck's front leg buckled beneath him. Nathan fought for control, but when Buck was unable to recover, both riders went tumbling to the ground.

Nathan twisted in the air to keep Sammy from a tree on the side of the trail, leaving his shoulder to ram into it and turning his body further. He contorted his lanky frame to take the brunt of the fall, continuing to clutch Sammy to his chest. Pain shot through his head behind his ear. He heard Sammy scream before everything went black.

Nathan grimaced. His head throbbed, and his eyes didn't want to open. What happened? He heard Buck whinny. It sounded strained, weak. Buck? What was Buck doing with him? That's right. They were on a trail ride. Buck stumbled. Was his horse okay?

He started to sit up, pausing as he heard a whimper that didn't belong to his horse. He became aware of the weight on his chest. His eyes flew open. Sammy. Sammy had ridden with him.

He bit back a yelp as he tried to move his left arm to hold the crying child. His memory of what happened was fuzzy, whether it was from pain or hitting his head, but he was pretty sure a tree had connected with that shoulder. As he gingerly tested the right one, he realized he already held Sammy, safe in his arm. "Shhh."

He rubbed the child's shuddering back as softly as he could. The whimpering increased as he rubbed the boy's left shoulder. It wasn't a fear-filled sound. It was pain, and Nathan realized the tiny arm was caught under his own body at an unnatural angle.

Fighting dizziness, Nathan forced himself to sit up. It did nothing for his pain level, but it would free Sammy. It would also allow him the opportunity to survey both of their injuries. His head throbbed where the sharp pain had been behind his left ear. He let go of his hold on Sammy to reach back and massage the spot. The hair was sticky and matted against his scalp. He wasn't surprised to find fingers smeared with blood when he drew his hand back. He rubbed them down the leg of his jeans. A three-year-old did not need to see blood when he'd already been through a frightening experience.

With gritted teeth, he forced a smile for Sammy who'd moved to sit between his legs, looking up at him with tear-filled green eyes. He hoped the child wasn't astute enough to see through the gesture. Of course, the tiny face twisted with pain. Tears ran down his cheeks as he cradled his left arm with his right.

"It's going to be okay, Sammy. Can I take a look at your arm, buddy?"

He shied away from Nathan's hand. He wanted to leave him alone, but Nathan knew he had to get a look at that arm. He grasped it lightly between the shoulder and the elbow. The joint seemed to rotate without pain. That was something anyway. But his wrist didn't look quite right. His whimpers grew sharp, indicating an increased pain level the closer Nathan got to the spot of potential injury.

Nathan struggled to unbutton his shirt and remove it. He fought the urge to vomit as he worked it from his left shoulder. Gulping in a few deep breaths reminded him to slow down. He shut his eyes. In through the nose. Out through the mouth. In through the nose. Out through the mouth. Okay. Now he needed to fashion his shirt into a makeshift sling for Sammy.

"I'm gonna need you to be brave, buddy. I'm gonna slide my shirt under your arm." He eased Sammy's arm away from the injured one. Careful not to jostle his forearm, Nathan worked the body of his shirt under Sammy's arm and draped the sleeves over his shoulders.

"Can you turn around for me?"

Wide eyes stared at Nathan as Sammy's head dipped up and down. His bottom lip jutted out in a pained pout. "Go ahead. I'm just going to tie this around your neck. so your arm doesn't hurt as much."

Slowly Sammy turned until his back faced Nathan. With Sammy's gaze averted, Nathan didn't try to hide the jolt of pain that ran down his arm when he attempted to move it. Nathan took a deep breath. He tried again to lift his left hand to grasp the sleeve. It barely moved before Nathan's injury left him wanting to cry out in pain. He stifled the urge knowing it would frighten Sammy. He couldn't do that.

This would require creativity. Nathan crossed the sleeves with his good hand and grasped one sleeve. Leaning in, he took the end of one sleeve between his teeth and pulled in the opposite direction. Then he repeated the procedure to secure the knot. It wasn't perfect, but it would do for the time being.

"How's that, Sammy? Does that feel better?"

"Mmhmm."

It was little more than the previous whimpers, but he would take it. "Good. Now let's see about getting us home."

With Sammy's arm immobilized and his own out of commission, getting them home would be an interesting adventure. He just wasn't sure it was anything close to the good kind of adventure.

Though he knew deep inside Buck would not be able to help in their endeavor, Nathan hoped he was wrong. He shifted his attention to where Buck lay on the ground. A knot formed in his stomach.

There wasn't a contest when the decision was between seeing to Sammy and seeing to his horse. Sammy would win every time. But the sounds of pain coming from his horse, who'd been a faithful companion on the trail since Nathan was a teen, had been hard to ignore while he tended to Sammy's injuries. Now that Sammy was taken care of, Nathan wished he could do something to help his horse. Anger surged through his body at his inability to even move to examine the extent of Buck's injuries.

From where he sat, Nathan could see the mole hill that caused the issue. All that weight on the underground tunnel collapsed it causing Buck's fall. Though he couldn't move to assess the damage, Nathan's best guess was a break in his foreleg. Recovery would take time. But first, he had to get all three of them home to get the medical help they needed.

He looked at Sammy. His wide eyes were fixated on Buck writhing in pain on the ground. Great. More emotional trauma for the kid, as if a fall from a horse and injured arm weren't enough for the day. But he couldn't worry about that now. "Sammy? Can you look at me, please?"

Sammy faced him, and Nathan used his free hand to unbuckle the helmet and lift it from his head. His curls were plastered to his head with sweat. It wasn't unusually warm, but fear and pain could do a number on a little one. Who was he kidding? They could cripple a lot of adults.

He set the hat on the ground. "There. Is that a little better?"

"That's better."

"Good. What d'ya say we get some help and get home?"

"I want to go home."

He fished his cell phone from his pocket. Chris was at the barn. He dialed the number hoping his friend's phone was on. After four rings, his mind began running through his other options.

"Hello. Whatcha need, Nathan?"

"Thank God, you answered. Sammy and I are in a little bit of a pickle and need some help."

Nathan explained the situation. Chris flew into action on the other end of the line. "I'll be right down with the truck to get you and Sammy. I'll have one of the other guys ride down and see to Buck until the vet can get down there. But you don't have to worry about him any. They'll take good care of your horse. All we've got to focus on is getting you and Sammy patched up. You can call Katie while you wait, or I can do it once we get to the hospital if you give me her number. It's up to you."

"I'll call. You just get here with the truck."

He pressed end and settled Sammy on his lap to wait. He explained who was coming to help and followed it up with a silent pep talk to brace himself for what would most definitely be a difficult conversation. With each number he keyed in, Nathan prayed for God to give him the right words to say.

Chapter Twenty-Two

"I feel horrible for her, you know?"

Katie had finally gotten Erin away from her relationship with Nathan as a topic of conversation. The subject of Anna and Gabe wasn't what she'd term light and easy, but at least it wasn't her personal life. They'd walked around the yard while Katie told her about story hour and the teen mom and now sat on the raised brick border of one of the flower gardens.

"I mean, it's hard enough to raise a child on your own, but to do it as a teen. That's a tall order. And they don't have a steady place to live. They bounce around, and she doesn't have a lot of help. Her job won't pay for much beyond their immediate needs, and she doesn't have the education to get anything better."

Erin played with a blade of grass she'd plucked. "And you want to do more than befriend her? You want to help her in some way?"

Katie stared at the house she'd lived in for most of her years. "I'd like to give her a home. A place she and Gabe feel safe and wanted. A steady place where they don't have to worry about having to leave because people are getting tired of them. We had that, and we took it for granted. Think about what kind of comfort that would be for someone like her."

"What can you do about it?"

Katie frowned. "Got an extra thirty thousand dollars to get her a starter home?"

Erin snorted. "If I had that kind of money do you think I'd have jars out in the local businesses raising money for me and Paul to adopt? You're going to have to come up with that on your own!"

Katie bit her lip. "I'm sorry. It was a joke, but I shouldn't have said it. I know you two are doing all you can to come up with what you need to adopt. That was insensitive of me."

Erin shook her head. "I didn't take offense. I know you were joking. No apology is necessary. Besides, with both of our families helping, we're well on our way to meeting our goals. A lot of people are not so lucky."

"I'm sure. And you've got to keep me updated. I'm looking forward to being Auntie Katie. I can't wait to meet your baby."

Katie's phone rang before Erin could answer. Why was Nathan calling? It wasn't pick up time yet. "Hey, Nathan. Are you ready for me to pick up Sammy? I wasn't expecting it yet, but Erin and I can come to get him now if you want us to."

A deep breath. "There's been a change in plans. I don't want you to worry. Sammy's just fine. But I'm going to need you to meet us at the hospital."

"I'm sorry. Did you say you need me to meet you at the hospital?"

"'Fraid so. Buck took a tumble, and we're all a little banged up. It's nothing serious, but Sammy's wrist needs to be checked."

"His wrist?"

"Yep. Chris, one of the guys who works with me, is on his way to pick us up in the truck. We're going straight to the emergency room. I need you to meet us there."

She heard some rustling, and what she thought was Sammy's

voice. Nathan grunted, or maybe it was more a groan. His voice sounded farther away from the phone.

"Yes, it's your mommy. Yes, you can talk to her."

"Mommy?"

She could hear the strain in his quiet voice. "Yes, baby?"

"Mommy, my arm hurts."

"I know, but Nathan's going to take you to a doctor that will make you all right in no time. You be brave for Mommy, and I will meet you there. Okay?"

"I'm brave."

"Good boy. I love you, Sammy."

"Love you, Mommy."

"Now hand the phone back to Nathan, please."

She heard more rustling and far away voices and something else she couldn't quite make out.

"Chris is here with the truck. We'll meet you at the hospital in Carbondale. Got it, Kate?"

"Get Sammy to the hospital. I'll meet you there."

Katie's hand shook as she hung up the phone. Her mind was already at the hospital questioning the doctors who hadn't even seen Sammy yet. Was he going to be okay? Would he need surgery? Would there be permanent damage? She shook herself. Dwelling on the what ifs wouldn't get her answers, and it certainly would not get her to her son.

"I know I only heard half the conversation, but I'm sharp enough to understand you're going to the hospital and that Sammy's involved. You're shaking like a leaf. Let's grab our purses and your car keys. I'll drive."

Katie didn't argue. In seconds they were pulling out of the drive in the direction of the hospital.

Chapter Twenty-Three

Katie followed the orderly down the U-shaped hall. The
glass-walled rooms draped with flimsy curtains for
privacy looked the same to her. The only difference was their
position around the desk and computer filled command center in
the middle of the space.

The man dressed in pale green scrubs waved her into a room
at the back of the U. She fought the urge to rush to Sammy's side
as she saw him lying in the first bed. He was tiny under the
sheets but seemed in good spirits. She didn't want to cause him
undue worry by seeming panicked. It took him a second to
realize who entered his room.

"Mommy!"

Katie and Erin flanked his bed from both sides. Katie, unsure
of his injuries, hugged him as gently as she could. When she
tried to pull away, his little arm refused to release her neck. She
noticed the other lay unmoving on the bed beside him.

Erin came to stand beside her and took the bed railing in her
hands. "Here, let me help you." She dropped the bed railing so
Katie could climb in bed next to her son.

With Sammy cuddled against her side and her arm around

him, she looked to Erin. "Can you find a doctor or nurse? I'd like to know what they've found out about Sammy. And I'd also like to find out where Nathan is. It doesn't seem like him to run off and leave Sammy, especially when he's in such an unfamiliar place and situation."

Erin nodded and left the room. Katie gently stroked Sammy's hair. "Does your head hurt, Sammy?"

She could feel his head shake against her chest. "Can you tell me where you hurt?"

He carefully lifted his arm from the bed. Someone had immobilized it from his elbow to his fingers with a splint. "My arm hurts."

Erin returned with a nurse.

"Is his arm the only thing injured?"

The man nodded. "Seems when they fell from the horse, your son's arm got trapped under Nathan. We've x-rayed it, and we think he may have broken his wrist. We're waiting on the doctor to read them and give us the final diagnosis. But we've checked over Sammy well and decided he must be a superhero in disguise. Isn't that right, Sammy?"

Sammy's chest puffed out. "I'm strong like Superman."

Katie chuckled. The emergency room staff had taken extra time with her son to make sure he was comfortable and at ease. "I have to agree. I think you must be Superman or maybe Superman's little brother." She looked at the nurse. "Thank you for taking such good care of my son."

"You're welcome. He's been a real trooper. The doctor will be in as soon as he reads the x-rays."

Before the nurse walked out the door, Katie asked the other question that had been on her mind. "Could you tell me where the man went that came in with Sammy?"

The nurse paused only long enough to answer. "Nathan will be back momentarily."

Erin sat in a chair next to Sammy's bed and entertained him

with the tiny television on a moveable arm that hung over his bed. Katie listened to them giggle over the animated antics of a moose and squirrel. How was that show still on? It had been popular long before she was a child, though its reruns were seen more often then than now.

With the assurance that Sammy was going to be okay, Katie's mind wandered to Nathan's absence. He knew how much her son meant to her, and she'd trusted him to take care of him. How could he have left him alone, even for a minute before she arrived? Sammy was a toddler for Pete's sake. You didn't leave a toddler to fend for themselves in a big scary hospital with monitors and wires and tests. A responsible adult stayed by their side, played with them like Erin was doing to distract them from all the other stuff.

When five more minutes had passed without his arrival, Katie fought the urge to march herself through the entire hospital until she found him and give him a piece of her mind in regards to his care for her son. The only thing that prevented it was her need to stay with Sammy. Whether Erin was there or not, Katie needed to be present when the doctor came in. Besides, what if Sammy wanted her for something? She wouldn't abandon her child the way Nathan had.

Several more minutes passed before Katie heard Nathan's voice in the hall. She seethed as it drew closer.

"Our outfit's not as big as some, but it ain't too shabby either. We have a girl, Jessica, who works a lot with the riders themselves. Chris and I tend to work more training the horses."

An unfamiliar female voice responded. "I may have to give you guys a call later. It sounds like you might be just what I'm looking for."

Katie didn't hear his answer. She seethed at the idea that Nathan had left her son alone while he meandered through the hospital flirting and drumming up business for his ranch. She'd just shot out of Sammy's bed to chase Nathan down in the hall

and give him a piece of her mind when a nurse pushed a wheelchair around the corner into the doorway.

"You made it." Nathan gave Katie a weary smile from his
position in the wheelchair before turning to Sammy with a wink
and a nod. "Have the doctors been in about my little partner
here?"

Katie stood slack-jawed as she mentally ran through her
phone conversation with Nathan. Not once had he indicated he
had an injury from the fall. She was sure of it. Yet here he sat in
a wheelchair wearing a flimsy hospital gown with a sheet draped
over his bare legs. Why didn't he tell her he was hurt? She
wouldn't have gotten so upset at him.

She fought through the residual anger now that she understood the situation better. When Nathan's brows drew together,
he switched his gaze from Katie to Erin and back again. She
realized she hadn't answered his question. "No." It was the best
she could do under the circumstances.

The nurse pushed him to the other side of the room and drew
back the curtain halfway. "Time to get you settled back in your
bed, Mr. Phillips. Can you do it, or do you need help?"

Katie watched him struggle to pull himself forward in the
chair. After a second, he sat back and panted quietly. "Much as I
hate to admit it, I think I'm gonna require some assistance."

The nurse went to his right side. He draped his arm over her
shoulder. Katie approached his left side and started to lift his
arm. His growl of pain made her drop it immediately, causing a
deep grunt to rumble from his now tightly closed lips.

She felt the blood drain from her face. "I'm so sorry, Nathan.
I didn't realize your arm was hurt." She nodded to the nurse. "I'll
get out of the way and let you do your job."

The nurse smiled with practiced tolerance as she repositioned
herself and Nathan. With practiced ease, she helped lift him from
the wheelchair and, in moments, had him settled in his bed. She
adjusted the covers over him and hooked him up to various wires

causing movement on the monitors to his right. Before she left, she pressed a button to raise the head of his bed to a slightly reclined sitting position.

"You've got a buzzer here." The nurse pointed to a spot on the inside of the bed rail. "If you need anything at all, press that button, and one of us nurses will come running. Got it?"

Nathan rested his head against the pillow and yawned. "I've got it. Thank you."

The nurse left the room, nodding at Katie as she went past. Katie made her way to the newly vacated side of Nathan's bed. "I'm so sorry."

Nathan's smile was weak. He rested his good hand over hers on the bed railing. "You didn't know. It's fine."

"What's wrong?"

"That's what I'm waitin' to find out. Doc thinks it's possible I broke some ribs or something when my shoulder hit the tree. And he said something about a possible concussion and stitches where my head maybe hit a rock. At least, I think it was a rock. And I'm not sure if he ended up stitching me up or not. They've given me enough pain pills I can't think straight."

"Would you like me to check?"

His eyes slid shut. "No. Right now, I want to rest."

Katie wanted answers. She wanted the doctors to give them answers in regards to their tests. She also wanted Nathan to wake up and tell her what happened. How did he and her son go from riding horses to lying side by side in hospital beds?

Katie didn't realize she was staring at Nathan's sleeping form until a voice on Sammy's side of the room startled her.

"Hello. I assume you're Sammy's mother?"

"No."

Katie came around the curtain. "No. I'm Sammy's mom. Are you his doctor?"

A man who looked too young to be practicing medicine smiled at her. "Hello. Yes. I'm Dr. Adams. I've just finished looking over your son's x-rays. Everything looks great, except for his left wrist. It looks like Sammy broke his radius in the fall. But the break is clean and should be easily reset. At this time, I think we're looking at setting and casting it. With his young age, where the break is, and the type of break I doubt very seriously, we will need to look at further measures."

"Further measures?"

He blinked. "Yes. Further measures like surgery. That doesn't look likely."

"And how long will he be in the cast? And when will all of this take place?"

Dr. Adams flipped through Sammy's chart. "It looks like you're in luck. The orthopedic doctor is making rounds right now. The nurse has contacted him, and he's on his way. He's going to set and cast Sammy's wrist today, and we're hopeful that the cast will come off in eight weeks."

Eight weeks with a three-year-old in a cast didn't sound great, but at least it wouldn't involve surgery. "Thank you, Dr. Adams."

"You're welcome. I'll check in again after the orthopedic doctor has been here to make sure we have everything we need to get you and Sammy home tonight. How does that sound?"

"That sounds perfect."

He ruffled Sammy's hair and shook her hand before moving on to Nathan's side of the room. Katie didn't move from Sammy's side, but she did listen to the conversation without a trace of guilt for eavesdropping. The curtain would have been open anyway if Nathan hadn't fallen asleep. She'd closed it to give him some semblance of privacy.

The doctor's voice, though hushed, carried across the flimsy barrier. "Good news, Mr. Phillips. Your x-rays show no fractures or breaks in your shoulder or ribs. That was our major concern about the trauma you suffered when you hit the tree. You do have some bone bruising, but we can take care of that with ice and rest. Give it a couple of weeks, and you should be as right as rain. You do have a mild concussion from your head injury, and the area with your stitches will need to be taken care of properly to ensure they don't get infected. However, if you have someone staying with you through the night, I don't see any reason for you to stay with us any longer. Do you have someone?"

"Chris can stay at my place. He brought us in, and he's coming back just as soon as he's checked my horse. I'm ready to go whenever you are, doc."

"Great. I'll get the nurse started on your discharge paperwork, and we will get you home and into your bed."

Katie busied herself with straightening Sammy's covers as the doctor came around the curtain and made his way out of the room. As soon as he was gone, Katie drew back the curtain between the beds.

"Were you asleep when the doctor first came in?"

"I musta been. I'm pretty sure he woke me up to talk to me. Did you find out anything about Sammy?"

"His wrist is broken. He'll need a cast for several weeks, but it doesn't look like he'll need surgery."

"Thank God. It could've been much worse. And I suppose you heard what the doc told me?"

Katie nodded. "I'm glad it's nothing more serious. I know you'll be feeling it for a while, and I don't envy you that. As you said, it could've been much worse. But what happened out there?"

Nathan leaned his head back against the pillow as he spoke. "I took Sammy out for a trail ride after we rode in the corral. I took him down the same trail we went down. Only we rode double with him in front of me. There was a molehill, and I didn't see it. Buck stumbled and fell. It sent us to the ground, and Sammy's arm got caught under me when we landed. Buck couldn't get up, and neither could I. I managed to call Chris, and he brought the truck down the trail to get us. I'm so sorry, Kate."

Katie heard every word Nathan said, but her mind could only focus on the fact that the danger was right in front of him, and he hadn't seen it. Because of his failure, Sammy's wrist was broken. Riding was too dangerous for a child, and Nathan should have realized that. She knew her thoughts might be a little hard toward him, but she needed time to sort out what she felt and why. Yet he'd apologized. She needed to say something encouraging, at least until she figured everything out. "It's fine. Accidents happen. Sammy's going to be okay, and I'm glad you are too."

She tried for a reassuring smile as she pulled Sammy a little closer. At least part of what she said was in complete honesty. She was glad Nathan and Sammy were both going to be okay. Accidents did happen every day. She simply tried to make sure they didn't happen to Sammy on her watch. She might need to try harder. But whether it was okay or not was still up in the air.

Other than Erin keeping Sammy distracted, silence reigned in the room for the next thirty minutes. The silence was broken by the nurse coming to release Nathan. Once freed from medical care, he stood next to Katie. When he didn't immediately speak, she looked up at him.

He cleared his throat. "Would you like me to stay until Sammy gets his cast on and gets released too? I can always lie back down for a few minutes."

"No. You need your rest. Let Chris take you home, and we'll check on you tomorrow."

"You sure?"

"Positive. It's what's best for you. You do have to look after yourself."

She ignored the disappointment reflecting in his eyes. "Okay. I'll go meet Chris out in the parking lot then. He texted to say he's pulled around by the door. I'll talk to you tomorrow. And Sammy, you take care of yourself. Okay, partner?"

Sammy perked up. "Okay, partner."

Nathan waved to Erin on his way out. Erin returned the

gesture before turning questioning eyes on Katie. Katie turned away and fooled with the monitor cords as if they were in the way. When she turned back, Erin still watched her. Katie smiled before turning her attention to the television she'd all but ignored the rest of the afternoon.

"It's not going to be that easy. You know that, right?"

Katie flicked her gaze to Erin and back to the screen. "I don't know what you're talking about."

From the corner of her eye, Katie saw Erin sit poker straight, looking at her. "Don't play dumb with me."

Sammy's mouth dropped open. "We don't say dumb, Auntie Erin. It's not nice."

Erin smiled at him. "You're right. Dumb isn't a nice word to say, and I'm sorry." She returned to Katie. "What I should have said was that you know what I'm talking about, and we will discuss it. Like it or not."

Katie lifted one shoulder. "Maybe. But we're not going to discuss it now. As my dad used to say, there are ears in the cornfield."

"You're right. I'm dropping it. For now."

NATHAN HAD NEVER BEEN HAPPIER that Chris wasn't the chatty sort. He'd given Nathan a detailed report on Buck's injury along with the prognosis that he would be fine in time, but after putting Nathan's mind at ease about his horse, he kept to himself. The silence suited Nathan. The pain in his head and shoulder was enough to staunch the flow of words, but it was more than that. He needed the long drive home and the silence. They gave him the space he needed to think, or at least try to.

Kate's behavior at the hospital had seemed off somehow. He couldn't quite place his finger on it. She'd asked about him and checked on him. Even sending him home rather than asking him to stay was within reason. He was injured too. She wanted to make sure he was taken care of. So why did he have a sneaking suspicion that there was more to it?

He replayed their conversations in his head. They weren't full of gushy sentiment, but she was distracted, as well she should have been. Her son was in the hospital. Was he jealous of the attention and care she gave to Sammy? No. She was his mother. He'd have been concerned if her attention was not focused on Sammy.

Every muscle tensed as the truck unexpectedly swerved to the left. The pull and strain on his already injured body caused a sharp growl before he was able to grit his teeth against the shooting pain. The truck's path evened out, but his head swam with the sudden movement.

He shot a look at Chris, whose eyes darted to him momentarily before refocusing on the road. "Sorry. I had to swerve or hit a deer and send us back to the emergency room. You okay?"

He took a couple of deep breaths. "I can't say it felt like heaven, but I'll be fine."

"Good. Hopefully, we can get you home without any more incidents. I'd hate to give you more pain considering you probably already feel like you've run headfirst into a brick wall."

A wall. That was it. That was the issue at the hospital. Kate went through all the motions, and he knew she cared. But for some reason, she'd put up a wall. It didn't seem possible at this point, but she was putting space between them. He felt that disconnect. But why?

He could just ask her, but he didn't think she'd give him a straight answer. Kate didn't like being pushed. He'd like to think she was unaware of it, but that'd be a lie. He had a calm assurance she knew precisely what she was doing and why. Now, if only he could figure it out.

Chapter Twenty-Four

K atie said a silent prayer of thanks for the slowness that pervaded care in most emergency rooms. God was merciful with her. The late hour Sammy was released was the only reason Erin agreed to go home rather than come inside and finish the chat she wanted to start at the hospital. She would have the night to think things through on her own. She didn't need someone else in her head until she figured out her mind.

With Sammy nearly asleep on her shoulder, Katie locked the door behind her and proceeded to turn off all the downstairs lights before taking the stairs to his room. Careful not to jostle his wrist, she changed him from his dirty clothes into a fresh set of pajamas that snapped down the front. Without having to pull them off over his head, Sammy might be able to get in and out of them on his own. She'd have to go through his closet and find out how many shirts of the same style he had.

She pulled his blankets up around him and handed him his special blanket to hold in his free hand. She lifted his injured hand out of the covers and laid it on top so it would be less likely to get tangled in the sheets.

His eyes closed. Katie placed a kiss on his forehead. "Love you, little man."

She barely heard him whisper. "Love you, Mommy."

Katie flipped off the light and turned on the monitor before going across the hall to her room. Her stress and fear throughout the day left her fatigued. She plopped down on the edge of her mattress and let her arms dangle between her knees. They felt heavy, and she almost dropped the monitor receiver. Thinking better of keeping it in her hands, she tossed it on the bed beside her.

"Dear Lord," she whispered. "Thank you for protecting my son from further injury and for the professionals who treated him. Help him heal quickly." Her prayer dropped off as her mind began to shut down for the night. Without taking the time to change, Katie scooted up the mattress and lay down on the pillow, covering herself with an afghan.

Long before her body had gotten the rest it needed and before the sun had a chance to rise, Katie was pulled from sleep by the sound of Sammy crying. Groggy, she stumbled down the hall and bumped into the small table kept halfway between their rooms. Quicker than she would expect her tired body to react, she grabbed the decorative pitcher right before it toppled from the table to the floor.

Memories of another restless night flooded her mind. She'd fallen into the table then and ended up in a sling for weeks. Maybe it was time for the table to find a new home. If she wanted to decorate the hall, she could pick up something soft like a bean bag chair! But redecoration would wait for daylight. Right now, she had her crying son to attend.

She kept her voice soft as she entered his room. "It's okay, Sammy. Mommy is here."

The cries continued though they had eased some and sounded more like whimpers. The nightlight created a shadow of his eyelashes on his cheeks. He was still asleep. His arms jerked as his head moved from side to side in an irregular beat.

Katie debated waking him from the nightmare. Had she read or heard something before about it being harmful to wake someone from a scary dream? It seemed cruel to let him remain in a frightening situation even if it wasn't real. But she didn't want to compound the problems either. Maybe waking dreamers before their minds had worked through the nightmare to comple-tion would make them repeat the dream until it was finally able to reach its end. She wouldn't want to subject Sammy to his fears again because she was trying to help.

She lowered herself to the floor beside his bed. Maybe some-thing between ignoring and waking would help. At the very least, it would make her feel like she was doing something to help her son. She retrieved his satin edged blanket from where it had fallen to the floor in his discontent and placed it beside his hand. Immediately his pinky finger found the material, and he clenched it in his fist before bringing up to rub his face.

Katie couldn't help the tiny smile. She'd seen him perform the same calm-inducing act while wide awake. It was sweet to see the action on a more instinctual level. It was Linus and his blanket come to life. Wouldn't it be nice if adults had the same option for chasing away their bad days?

As the thought entered her mind, Sammy's face scrunched up. His limbs twitched again. He cried out, and his eyes shot open, wide with fear. His breath came out in frantic pants.

"Shhhhh. It's okay, Sammy. Mommy's with you."

Katie rubbed his hair. His frightened eyes sought hers. She swallowed the knot forming in her throat as she saw his eyes fill with tears.

His voice was mewling and pitiful. "Fall."

"I know, baby. But you're home now. You're safe. Shhhh."

The hand still clutching his blanket raised to reach out for her. "Hold you."

"It's okay. I've got you."

Katie picked him up from his bed and carried him into her room. She managed to pull down the comforter with one hand and placed Sammy underneath it before crawling in beside him. With his casted arm on the outside, she pulled him close beside her to snuggle him. She stroked his hair and calmed him by softly singing her assurance that he would always be in her heart. Realizing it was a lullaby from one of the animated movies he loved, Katie made a mental note to download the soundtrack for him. She could play it on loop for him as he went to sleep each night.

When he finally found peaceful sleep nestled next to her, Katie found herself fully awake. She shouldn't be after the day she'd had, but sleep eluded her. Instead, her mind swirled with all the thoughts she'd tried so hard to keep at bay. The worst of which threw a healthy dose of mommy guilt in her face.

If she'd been with Sammy, this wouldn't have happened. Because she wanted a girls' day out with Erin, her son now had to suffer through a nightmare causing experience. If she'd only told Nathan no about horseback riding, Sammy would be sleeping comfortably in his bed right now. But she'd said yes, and that was on her. She'd come to rely on Nathan, first in friendship, and now in this new relationship they were exploring. Maybe she shouldn't have.

She'd had her misgivings about letting Nathan assume such a prominent place in their lives. She'd considered moving on might involve risks, but she'd foolishly hoped if those consequences came, they would fall only on her. Nathan was not Austin. He was not Sammy's father. Despite Erin's insistence that their spiritual similarities were more important than their physical differences, Katie was now learning otherwise.

If Sammy had been in Austin's care, he wouldn't have been on a horse. He wouldn't be experiencing this trauma. Austin had a quieter, gentler nature than Nathan. His pursuits were not as physical and uncontrollable. For the first three years of his life, Katie had done all in her power to keep dangers at bay in Sammy's life. He played and enjoyed life, but not once had it crossed her mind to teach him football or put him on the back of a horse or any other activity that came with a higher risk of injury. He was only three!

No. It wasn't until Nathan came along and started pushing her boundaries that she'd even considered pushing Sammy's. And look where it landed them. She took the chance, and her son paid the price. She'd followed the cries of a lonely heart rather than the mind of a mother who wanted to keep her son safe. She couldn't be with a man like Nathan without accepting risk into their lives, and Katie wasn't sure she could do that anymore.

Chapter Twenty-Five

"Don't ya think you should give 'em some peace and quiet this morning? I'm sure they had a long night and might appreciate sleepin' in."

Nathan ignored Chris's advice and continued cleaning his breakfast dishes. Chris didn't understand the sick feeling he'd had in his stomach since he left the hospital. He was knotted up inside, and it had nothing to do with his injuries. Kate wasn't okay, no matter what she'd said. There was something wrong, and he had a sneaking suspicion it had to do with him. If he'd done something unintentionally, he needed to take care of it.

"Don't pretend you don't hear me. The bump on yer head didn't affect your hearing one bit."

Nathan swiped a kitchen towel over the wet bowl in his hand. "I heard you all right. But you're wrong about this one. You don't know Kate as I do. There was something stuck in her craw last night. And the more time that woman has alone, the more time she has to work herself into a tizzy over whatever it is."

Chris swirled the coffee in his cup into a black whirlpool. "Still. Will it help if she's plumb wore out?"

The bowl clanked onto the plates in the cabinet with enough

force Nathan thought he might have cracked one or the other. He took a deep breath. "I appreciate the concern, but I've gotta get this done. If I don't do it now, whatever's eating at her is going to devour her whole before I get there. Trust me on this. Besides, what good am I here right now? I can't do anything for Buck, except wait for him to mend. I can't help with the other horses either. Until this shoulder heals, I'm benched. While I'm on my way to Kate's house, I need to call a couple of the boys from the youth group and see if they'd like a temporary job filling in with some of my chores. They can't train the horses, but they can muck out the stalls."

Chris took a swig of his coffee before rinsing the cup in the sink. "Calling in some of the boys is a sound plan. I've said my piece, and that's all I'm going to say. Good luck, buddy."

"I'd rather have your prayers."

Chris lifted his cowboy hat from a peg on the wall and dropped it into place on his head. Starting out the door, he paused. "Always."

Nathan tried to distract himself on the way to Kate's house. It did no good trying to guess what was on her mind. He used the hands-free options on his phone to start calling the youth group boys, but when the first one agreed to take on all the hours he needed, Nathan was left to his thoughts. Unable to stop them completely, he decided to herd them in a more helpful direction.

"Lord, I'm not sure what's going on with Kate, but I'd like to know what I did and how I can fix it. Give me the words to say and the wisdom to know when to say them and when to keep my mouth shut. Lord, if Kate's less than open with what's going on, I pray for the discernment to read between the lines. Guide our conversation today. Amen."

He tapped the button on the stereo, and praise and worship music filled the cab of his truck. There was no better way to end a time of prayer than with music meant to remind you of how great a God you served.

As he pulled into the driveway, he found himself in the middle of a particularly good song and waited until it finished before he stepped from the truck and headed up the walk. He was pretty sure Kate had seen him coming from movement in one of the windows. When she opened the door while his fist was in mid-air, poised to knock, he was sure of it.

"What are you doing here?"

Not the reception he'd hoped. Not by a long shot. "I came to see how Sammy's doing and find out if you need help with anything."

"Shouldn't you be in bed yourself? You were hurt, too, weren't you?"

He tilted back his cowboy hat as he thought about the best answer. "I'm useless at the ranch right now, but I'm not an invalid. I've got to go slow and careful to keep my shoulder pain and headache under control, but they've got me on enough pain meds to take the edge off. My concern is you and Sammy. Now, are you gonna invite me in or leave me standing here?"

He hid a satisfied grin as she waved him inside. At least he was in the door. It was a start. "How is Sammy this morning?"

She ignored his question as she went to the coffee maker. "Coffee?"

He shook his head.

"Sammy's sleeping peacefully. Finally."

He watched her sit at the kitchen table before joining her. He lifted the cowboy hat from his head and plopped it onto the table as he sat. "Was he in a lot of pain last night?"

Angry eyes underlined with dark circles, glared at him over the top of her mug. She moved the rim away from her lips to answer with enough heat to scald more than the coffee in her cup. "No. He did not have pain. The medicine helps with that, as you pointed out only minutes ago. He had nightmares. Sammy kept dreaming about falling off a horse. He's scared out of his mind."

Easy. Don't respond to the emotion. She's tired, and she's a protective mother whose baby is in pain. He fiddled with the brim of his hat. "I'm sorry about that. The first fall is bad enough without the added injury and emergency room visit. It'll help as soon as we get him back on a horse."

"Back on a horse?" She clamped her mouth shut after yelling loud enough that Sammy should have been disturbed. Her eyes shut as she sucked in a deep breath. "I've no intention of Sammy getting on a horse again, ever."

"You can't do that to the boy, Kate."

"Watch me."

"He needs to get back on."

"Don't you sit there and tell me what my son needs. He is MY son, not yours. He has a daddy, and you're not it. We've been playing at it, and now Sammy's suffering because of it."

Nathan cleared his throat, refusing to give in to the surge of defensive anger coursing through him. "This isn't about who Sammy belongs to. I know he's not my son. I've never said he was. Sammy needs to get back on a horse as soon as possible so he can get over the fear."

The pitch of her voice rose along with the volume. "He has every right to be afraid! He's a small child that got injured falling off a horse that's more than twice his size. Who wouldn't be afraid after that?"

"I'm not trying to upset you. But I know horses, and I know how people react to them. If Sammy doesn't get on a horse pretty soon, his fear could very well solidify into a phobia. He won't get on one again."

"So?"

"So, until he fell, Sammy was having a great time. Do you want him to go through life scared of something he could get a lot of enjoyment from?"

"He doesn't need horses to be happy. He doesn't need horses to be well-adjusted. He'll be fine."

He ran his hands through his hair. "Please listen to me on this."

"Like I listened to you on whether or not Sammy was old enough to ride? Am I just supposed to take your advice on this and hope it works out better this time? You've had a lot of advice for me lately. Let Sammy ride. Put my father in a nursing home. Pursue a relationship with you. What else is going to blow up in my face? I think I'm through taking your advice."

"Kate…"

Her next words snarled through clenched teeth. "It's Katie, and I think you need to go."

"Don't do this, please. I know you're angry, but we can figure this out together."

She crossed her arms in front of her chest and refused to look at him. Instead, she stared out the window over her shoulder. "Together is what started this mess. It's time we admit this isn't going to work. You're not a good fit for our family."

"Why? Because I'm not Austin? I know that. But Austin's not here, and I am."

Nathan was thankful shooting daggers was only an expression because Kate's green eyes blazed with anger strong enough he had no doubt daggers would fly if they could. Her voice was as icy as her eyes were fire-filled, and the quiet tone sunk her message deep. "Get out, now."

She was making a mistake. She was hurting, and she was afraid. He met her eyes, hoping she could read the disappointment and understand his silent plea to reconsider her decision. Words weren't going to make a dent. Maybe if she took another minute to think about it, but her features didn't soften. A single eyebrow raised in challenge. He nodded and picked his hat up from the table to place it on his head.

"Relationship or not, I'm here for you. If you need a friend, just give me a call."

"I've got Erin, thanks. Please, leave."

He refused to look back as he made his way out of the house for what he knew might be the last time. *Lord, this is wrong. Please, let her know this is wrong. Even if she doesn't want a relationship with me, let her see what she's doing to herself and Sammy. And Lord, help me. I love her, and I'm not sure how to let her go.*

∼

ERIN SCOOPED Sammy up in her arms and placed him on the platform attached to the short slide of his playground. "There you go, buddy. Be careful not to bump your cast."

"'Kay, Auntie Erin. I'll be careful."

Sammy launched himself down the slide, tottering to regain his balance as his feet hit the grass at the bottom. "Again?"

Erin laughed. "Come on over here, hotshot. One more time, and then Auntie Erin needs a break. Maybe you could crawl into the cave underneath and build with your blocks."

Sammy flew down the slide one more time before running around the structure to the opening. Three sides took up a slide, a miniature rock wall, and the ladder leading up to the slide's platform. The fourth side was left partially open to create a clubhouse for Sammy to play in the shade. It even had a pebble floor to keep it from being so dirty for him. Sammy loved to build with his wooden blocks inside his tiny man cave.

Erin joined Katie on the garden bench. "I've got to give Nathan props for creating that special play place for Sammy. I wouldn't have thought of it, and it's perfect when he needs to get out of the sun."

"Or when he has a broken wrist and can't climb up the structure and go down the slide on his own."

Katie refused to acknowledge Erin's look. She kept her gaze locked on Sammy's play place.

"What's eating you?"

Katie lifted one shoulder. "I don't know what you're talking about. I just think that a person doesn't need to be praised for the foresight to make something that comes in handy when another of their choices renders the rest of something useless."

"Wow. Could you be any more bitter? And nothing is eating at you? That's an obvious lie. So why don't you go ahead and spill it now? Save us both the trouble of me having to pull teeth."

She blew out a frustrated breath. "I guess I'm just tired of everyone treating Nathan like he's a knight in shining armor, and I'm some kind of damsel in distress that can't raise my child or live my life without him."

Erin smacked her hand to her forehead and ran it over her head through her blonde hair. "Oh, no. Tell me you didn't."

"I'm sure I don't know what you're talking about."

Erin jumped up from the bench and stood directly in her line of sight. "Don't you play dumb with me, Katie Blake. You know what I'm talking about, and these evasive maneuvers aren't going to work with me. Did you or did you not break up with Nathan?"

"Is my love life suddenly your business?"

Erin threw her head back. "You did! You broke up with Nathan. Why on earth would you do something like that?"

Katie mercilessly twisted a curl in her fingers. "I don't need this from you, Erin. It wasn't easy. It had to be done. Nathan isn't the right fit for our family. Look what happened when I left Sammy with him for an afternoon. He obviously is not the man Sammy and I need in our lives. There's too much risk."

Erin sighed and sat back down. Her voice was as calm as it had been exasperated seconds before. "Too much risk for Sammy or too much risk for you?"

Katie lost her fight against a sudden onslaught of tears. She forced her words past the tightness in her throat. "It's too much. Period. For Sammy. For me. I can't do it."

Erin drew her into her arms like a small child. "Oh, honey.

I'm so sorry. You've loved and lost so much. I know it's hard. I just hate seeing you shut yourself to the possibility of finding love again. You've got so much love to give and life to live, but you can't do either if you aren't willing to take the chance."

Katie sniffed and sat up. "I took the chance once. It brought me pain and loss as I've never known before. Nathan nearly convinced me to try again, and Sammy got hurt. I'm just glad I got the wake-up call before it went any further."

"But you can't avoid pain. No matter how hard you try."

"Do you know Sammy's been having nightmares since the fall?"

Erin shook her head.

"Every night. I tuck him in and within an hour he's restless and crying out in his sleep. He's ended up sleeping next to me every night since then. I hate seeing him like that, and I can't allow anything into our lives that can create that kind of pain. He's going to have it hard enough growing up without his daddy."

The pity she saw in Erin's eyes would have irritated her in anyone else. With Erin, Katie knew it was born out of empathy for her situation. Either way, it wasn't easy to see.

Erin covered her hand with her own. "I'm sorry. I know this is hard. I can only imagine how hard. What can I do to help?"

"I'm not sure. Do you have a remedy for nightmares?"

The faint signs of a smile formed on Erin's lips. "Not usually, no. But considering these seem rooted in his fear of falling, do you think facing those fears would help end the dreams?"

Katie shifted. She wasn't sure what Erin was saying, but she felt it was dangerously close to something she'd heard before. She almost didn't want to pursue it. "What do you mean?"

"I mean, if it's a fall from a horse that started the dreams, maybe he should get back on a horse. That way, he can see that horses aren't bad, and they don't have to be frightening. He can have a positive experience to take the place of the negative one he had."

Yep. That's what she thought Erin was getting at, and she didn't want to hear it now any more than she did when Nathan suggested, no demanded, it. "Whoa there, Freud. My son is traumatized by a huge animal, and I'm supposed to put him back in the path of that same animal? I don't think so."

Erin shrugged. "It was just a suggestion. I don't know. I'm not a therapist. I'm just working off that old adage that if you fall off the horse, you're supposed to get back on it. I figure it has to be a phrase for a reason."

Katie rolled her eyes. "I think I'll find a less common way of dealing with my son's fear. Thank you, though."

"Like I said, I'm no therapist. I'll be praying for you and Sammy both."

"That's the best help I've heard all day."

Chapter Twenty-Six

Nathan wasn't sure what he was doing sitting in the nursing home across from Kate's father. Sure, he volunteered at the home. And he'd even visited Cal on numerous occasions without Kate, but that was before she'd decided he wasn't good enough for her. And he'd backed off, given her the space she wanted. He hadn't even considered contacting her in the two weeks following their breakup. The distance hurt more than his head and shoulder combined, but it was what she wanted. Did he have a right to visit her father now that she'd kicked him out of her life?

"How's my Katydid?"

Nathan hid his shock. The clear times were few and far between with Cal anymore. Of course, just because he'd used her nickname didn't mean his mind was completely clear. Sometimes it meant he'd slipped into the times when Kate was a child. Cal watched him expectantly.

"Tell you the truth, sir. I'm not sure. Kate and I aren't really on speaking terms right now."

Cal chuckled. "That's Katie for you. She's full of fire."

Nathan grinned. "Yes, sir, she is at that."

"I mean it, son. It's a fire that will singe the hair right off your head when she's mad. I've seen it many times, usually directed at her mother."

"Well, I wish it was directed at someone else, but right now, it's aimed straight at me and means there's not a place for me in her life. And I don't know how to put it out."

Cal shook a finger at him. "You don't want to put it out. Don't ever put out the fire. When you put out the fire, you lose the passion. Without the passion, there's no love. Without love is she even living?"

Nathan felt immediately humbled. Here he was being schooled by a man most of society would label as having outlived his usefulness. "Thank you, Cal. I think I needed to hear that today."

The older man looked him in the eyes and smiled. "Why hello, young man. How's my Katydid today?"

Nathan tried to smile. It was a never-ending cycle of confusion. He felt blessed to be present for the day's ray of clarity, mainly since it spoke directly to him. Cal might never know it, but God had used him to answer Nathan's prayer for understanding and give him direction for how to pray for Kate in the future. The least he could do is give Cal some peace about his loved one.

"I think Kate's doing just fine. If she sticks with her usual habits, you'll probably see her a little later today."

"Good. Good." Cal's attention turned from Nathan to the window.

In the silence, his eyes grew heavy, and his head dropped to his chest. Nathan rose from the chair as quietly as he could and made his way down the hall. Miss Paula's light was out again. Somehow a light was always out whenever he was at the home to volunteer. Nathan couldn't help wondering if it had to do with the fact that when he'd fix her light, he would give her a few extra minutes of his time. From what he'd seen, Miss

Paula wasn't as blessed as Cal to have visitors every day. He couldn't remember the last time he'd heard of her family coming to see her. He determined to take their place, if only for today.

~

KATIE SCANNED THE ROOM, but Anna and Gabe were not present. She knew their absence was a possibility, but she was hoping things wouldn't come to that. She enjoyed her time with them, and it seemed to her that Anna found encouragement through their friendship.

It was time to start story hour with or without them. She picked up the featured book and did her best to make the story of a little fur family who lived in a tree come alive for the children. After the story, Katie helped the children draw pictures of their own families, taking time to appreciate the differences in each one.

"Wow. Do you have two older brothers, Emily?"

The little girl nodded her head and held up two fingers. Her mother sat beside her, helping her color.

"Darren and Derrick are twins. Rambunctious ones at that. Some days I'm surprised we ended up having more, but I'm thankful we have our sweet little Emily. She balances them out a bit!"

Katie laughed. "Boys can be a handful." She noticed Anna enter the room. "If you'll excuse me."

Anna was already making her way across the room when Katie moved her direction. "I'm so glad I didn't miss you."

"Where's Gabe today?"

"Since I knew we would miss story time, I left him with my friend. She didn't have school today, and I told her I would be right back."

Katie placed a hand on the teen's arm. "I'm glad you could

make it for a few minutes anyway. I've been thinking about you. How are things going?"

Her shoulders drooped. "It looks like we won't make story time any time soon. My friend Tami, the one who has Gabe right now, got permission for us to stay with her family."

"That's great."

"But we could only stay for a week. That ends tomorrow. After that, we're going to another friend's house, but only for a night or two. Who knows after that? All this jumping around has made me late at work a couple of times, and I'm afraid I could lose my job."

Katie could only imagine the burden this teenage mother must be carrying. It was too much for an adult, much less someone on the edge of adulthood. "I'm so sorry. Is there anything I can do for you?"

"No. I just wanted you to know what's going on since we won't be here for a while."

"Do you have a phone or any way I can get in touch with you? I'd like to check in every once in a while, until you can join us again."

"Sure."

Katie took out her cell phone and keyed in the new contact information before Anna had to leave. At least she had a way to contact her now. If only she could come up with a way to help.

Anna's plight still weighed on Katie a few hours later as she waited for Sammy to wake up from his nap. He'd been grouchy when she'd picked him up from daycare, and she'd thought better of taking him to see his grandpa in that condition. Instead, they'd come home and eaten lunch together before she put him down for a nap. They would visit the nursing home after he woke if he was in better humor.

Katie reminded herself to be patient with him. He was three years old with a broken wrist and an uncomfortable cast in the heat of summer. Add to that the continuing nightmares, and her son had to be exhausted. She was, too, but there was too much she needed to get done around the house to waste her time with a nap.

Instead, she worked at dusting and straightening the living room while her mind wandered to Anna's predicament. Being a single parent was tough, but the thought of doing it as a teenager without any family support was enough to make Katie wonder how the girl managed to do so well with Gabe. He was always clean and well-behaved. But she could see how resigned they were to their situation every time she looked in their eyes. Life was what it was for them, and they didn't believe it had any hope of getting better. How could it? Anna hadn't finished her education and worked at a dead-end job. They didn't even have a home. They needed a home.

Or a room.

It was rare for Katie to hear God speak to her spirit as clearly as if He were standing beside her, but she had a sneaking suspicion that was what He was doing. She looked up from the picture frame she was dusting and directly toward the doorway to her parents' room.

She decided if God were going to address her so clearly, she would return the favor. "Yes, God, they need a room. I understand."

You have a room.

"I'm aware I have a room, and I want to help. But I can't."

They need a home.

"I can't be the one to give it to them. I have to think about Sammy. What if I brought them here, and Sammy and Gabe didn't get along? Or what if Anna isn't as motivated to get them out of the situation they're in as I've thought? What if it didn't work out? How could I be one more person to tell them to leave?"

They need a home. You have a home.

"But it's not my home, is it? It's my parents' home. What

would dad think about having a stranger in his home?"

They need what you have.

"But those are things. God, there's a lot of people out there who have a room and a home. There are people better equipped to deal with situations like this. I'm not that person. I want to help, and I'll spend every day trying to find them a place. But that place is not here. That's not a risk I can take. Please, understand, I'll do anything I can to help them, but I can't do that."

Katie waited in the quiet. The moment had passed, and her relief mingled with the weight of the unresolved issue. Of course, she could have heard wrong. Maybe God was simply telling her to reach out to others to find a place for Anna and Gabe.

God knew what she was up against in her own life. He wouldn't ask her to give more than she had to offer. He knew she couldn't risk herself or Sammy to an endeavor that was as uncertain as this one.

She had to have misunderstood the words He spoke to her heart. She breathed out, releasing the last vestiges of concern she'd had when she thought God was asking her to take them in. She was positive that wasn't what He meant at all.

With that settled in her mind, Katie decided to forgo cleaning the rest of the house. She had one problem she could do something about, and after two weeks of restless nights, it was high time she did. Booting up her laptop, she typed "dealing with fears" into the search bar. For the next hour, Katie scoured every article she could find on how to deal with fears from the real to the imagined and took extensive notes on what each recommended.

Looking back over the three pages of information she compiled, similarities in what each site suggested became apparent. She groaned. With few exceptions, each ended up in the same place. To get over a fear, one needed to face it. She hated to admit Nathan and Erin might be right. Of course, several sites spoke of working up to the actual facing of the fear--small steps to increase comfort levels before taking the giant leap.

Katie brainstormed several small steps she could take with Sammy. Pictures of horses and stories about horses were the first on her list. She would also go to the store and buy Sammy some play horses, and she could drive by the local college's equine center. She and Sammy could stop by the side of the road and watch them in the fields. Maybe all of these ideas would blend and help Sammy get over his fear. Perhaps she wouldn't even need to push him to the final facing of the fear. It was worth a try, and Katie decided she would start implementing her plan right after they visited her dad.

FROM THE MOMENT Sammy launched himself into Cal's arms, Katie had known the day was not a good one for her father. Instead of hugging Sammy and smothering him with love, Cal had barely touched him.

"Papa, it's me. It's your Sammy."

"Sammy?"

Her son's confusion over his grandpa's lack of response broke her heart. She took his hand and led him to the place on the bed where he could sit. "Grandpa's not feeling well today. Why don't you sit over here while I talk to him for a minute."

"Kiss it better?"

Her smile tinged with the pain she felt. "I wish I could, but kisses don't make Papa's owie go away. Papa loves you, but he can't tell you that right now. And he knows you love him even if he can't hug you back."

She moved to sit in front of her dad. He acknowledged her presence only with a glance. She covered his hands with her own.

"Hey, Dad. How are you doing today? Sammy and I thought

it was a great day for a visit."

Her greeting met with silence. She smiled at him and looked over at Sammy. He sat on the end of his grandpa's bed staring at Cal. His eyes were wide, and he'd placed his thumb in his mouth. Katie wished she'd brought his special blanket with him. It always calmed him when he was stressed. She had to admit her father's behavior was odd enough to warrant stress in her son.

"Everything is fine, Sammy. Grandpa is just tired today. Remember how tired you were after school today?"

"Papa needs a nap?"

Before she could answer, a familiar voice floated into the room. "Do I hear Sammy Blake in this room?"

Sammy's attention flew to the doorway, where Gigi B came around the corner. He was off the bed in seconds and in her arms. The enthusiasm he missed with his grandpa made up for in the bear hug she gave him as she scooped him up. While she held him close, she looked over him to Katie.

"Cal having a rough day?"

Katie nodded. "Seems like it. And someone isn't handling it well. I think it scares him a little bit."

She placed Sammy back on his feet and straightened her rainbow-colored tunic top. "Leave that to me, and you go ahead and have a good visit with Cal." She reached down and took Sammy's hand. "How about you and I go to the cafeteria? I hear they have cups of chocolate ice cream, and I bet if you show them your cast, they'll give you one even if you don't live here."

He looked at Katie.

"Go ahead. You can go get ice cream with Gigi B."

Never one to need to be told twice to eat ice cream, Sammy went out the door pulling Gigi B behind him. She called to Katie over her retreating shoulder. "Off we go. If we're not in the cafeteria, look for us in the garden."

With Sammy entertained, Katie could focus on her father. He

still hadn't done much to acknowledge her presence one way or the other. Noticing his Bible sitting on the bed table, she retrieved it and turned to the marked page. One verse was high-lighted, his life verse. Through the years, he'd spoken it into her many times. She smiled with the sweet memory.

Maybe it would be a good memory for him too. She sat back down in front of him. "Dad, do you remember all the times you used to share your life verse with me?"

His eyes flicked from the scene outside his room's window to her and back again. She held up the open Bible. "Here. Let me read it to you. Micah 6:8 'He has shown you, O man, what is good; And what does the LORD require of you But to do justly, To love mercy, And to walk humbly with your God?'"

As she read, she noticed her dad mouthing the words along with her. Tears stung her eyes. Even in a state of confusion, God's word still reached him. Katie knew how much she and Sammy meant to him, but they were physical. The physical was confused in his mind. But his relationship with God was spiri-tual, and God promised never to take His Spirit from His chil-dren. A feeling of peace surrounded her as she considered the truth she'd seen with her own eyes. God could still speak to her dad's spirit even though his mind and body were failing.

"Thank You, Jesus. Dad has lived this verse all his years, and we thank You for honoring Your promises never to leave him. He loves You, and it's a blessing to know You won't leave him alone. Amen."

Her dad bowed his head as she prayed and raised it only after her amen. The tears that threatened began flowing as she prayed. Alzheimer's stole the father she knew bit by painful bit. Half the time he was living in a reality only he could see and understand, and Katie wasn't even sure he understood it himself. Time was taking her father from her, but it was a comfort knowing the man she loved and remembered was still held in the arms of God. He hadn't forgotten her father, and God alone had the privilege of seeing beyond his brokenness to the man who'd followed Him faithfully all his life.

She wiped the tears from her cheeks, only to find more take their place. Her father had been her constant, pointing her to God when the questions and hurts of life threatened. He gave her comfort by merely being beside her when she hurt. His was a voice of reason when she was at her most unreasonable, and when she stopped fighting long enough to listen, she always realized it. How she wished she had that now.

Her head dropped as she fought for control. Gravity took her tears from her cheeks to the Bible, still in her lap. She gave up trying to wipe them away and folded her hands on top of the thin pages.

"Oh, Daddy. I love you so much."

She started when his wrinkled hand covered hers. She looked up to find his eyes trained on her. They looked clear, lucid. Her heart soared with hope. Had God seen fit to bless her with a moment with the father she missed so much?

"Your first love."

She fought to keep the confusion from her face. "What was that, Daddy?"

"Your first love."

"My first love?" He was looking for Austin. Could this get any more painful? She choked on her next words. "Austin isn't here. He died before Sammy was born."

Her father shook his head. His hands patted hers as he spoke. "Find your first love. Your first love. Your first love."

One hand slipped from under his to cover her mouth and the sob trying to escape. The pain in her chest left her panting with each breath. Her hope crushed beneath the weight of reality, it wasn't a moment with her father. It was another moment marred by this horrible disease, and it was made worse by the subject matter. Katie desperately tried to come up with something to derail from his singular focus.

"Yes, Daddy. My first love. I'll find him and bring him to see you. How does that sound?"

He kept patting the staccato rhythm on her hand. His voice grew more insistent. "Your first love. Your first love."

Father God, make it stop. I can't do this. I don't know what to do. Please reach him because I can't.

As soon as she turned her thoughts to prayer, the Psalm she'd used to calm her wayward thoughts during her most anxious times came to mind. She placed her free hand over his, stilling his movement. She looked him in the face. Knowing there was nothing he could do to make himself understood, the urgency she saw in his eyes broke her heart.

In a slow, quiet voice, she recited the verses that put her anxious mind at ease. "'I will lift up my eyes to the hills – From whence comes my help? My help comes from the LORD, Who made heaven and earth. He will not allow your foot to be moved; He who keeps you will not slumber. Behold, He who keeps Israel shall neither slumber nor sleep.'"

As she spoke the words, her father's hand stopped its restlessness under hers. The distress in his eyes faded. His stooped shoulders were relaxed. By the time she repeated it a second time, he'd calmed completely. His gaze transferred to whatever lay outside his window. It was far from what she wanted, but Katie was relieved she wouldn't have to leave him in an agitated state.

She kissed his papery cheek. "Bye, Dad. I'll see you tomorrow, okay? I love you."

He didn't look from the window, but he raised his hand to softly pat her cheek. "I love you."

It was so quiet she almost missed it. There were no outward signs that he'd said it, other than his hand on her cheek. That and the comfort she felt in her heart. Katie hugged him and went in search of Gigi B and Sammy.

Chapter Twenty-Seven

K atie rubbed the grit out of her eyes and looked at the clock on her bedside table. Six o'clock came too early after a night plagued with her son's nightmares. Three weeks of keeping horses in front of him hadn't eased his fears. He was fine playing with horses. He loved to watch movies and shows about horses. He was even fine watching them in the pastures when they stopped at the equine center. But no matter how great he dealt with them in his waking hours, he was hounded in his sleep by the trauma he'd faced.

Katie knew what she needed to do but dreaded it just the same. She slipped from the bed, careful not to wake Sammy, and went in search of coffee. It was too early to think about the phone call, especially without the fortification of caffeine.

While the coffee brewed, Katie took a quick shower. As much as the steam cleared her head, she knew Sammy could wake at any time. He was usually good about not wandering, and she had the gate up at the top of the stairs. But she didn't want him spooked if he called for her and she was unable to come to him immediately.

When he hadn't awakened by the time she finished her

shower and dressed, Katie knew the restless nights were taking their toll on him as well. She sipped her coffee with her cell phone taunting from in front of her on the kitchen table. If she had any other options, she would take them. For Sammy's sake, she would do what needed to be done.

Before she could talk herself out of it, she punched in the familiar number. She fought the urge to hang up as the first ring broke the silence. She took a sip of coffee to force the tightness out of her throat. The selfish part of her hoped he wouldn't answer.

"Kate. Didn't expect to hear from you. Whatcha need?"

Not a warm welcome, but what else could she expect. She cleared her throat. "It's been weeks since the fall."

"I'm aware."

He wasn't making this easy. "Sammy has had nightmares every night since then."

"I'm sorry to hear that."

It wasn't flowery, but it was sincere and filled with compassion for Sammy. She continued. "I've tried everything from movies and television programs featuring horses to watching them in the fields at the equine center. Sammy even has a new herd of toy horses, and they're some of his favorite toys. Nothing has worked."

"You know what I think."

She took a deep breath. It was time to rip off the bandage no matter how it might sting. "That's why I'm calling. Would you be willing to help Sammy ride again?"

"He's not going to like it."

"I know."

"No, you don't. It's going to scare the daylights out of the kid. He'll cling to you like you're the only thing between him and certain death. He may even beg you not to make him do it. Can you handle that? If not, it's better not to even try."

The idea of her child clinging to her in fear tore through her heart. But wasn't that what he did each night when the dreams came? If it were for his good, she would find the strength to do it. She raised her chin though he couldn't see it. "I can do it."

"Good. Bring him out this afternoon. You've got story time today, right? We can do it after that, maybe one o'clock?"

"We'll be there. And Nathan?"

"Yes?"

"Thank you for this."

"I'll see you at one."

With everything in place, Katie knew peace that Sammy's nightmares might soon be at an end. Now, she just had to get him up and ready to go to story time. She would wait to tell him about their afternoon plans. No sense in making him anxious and afraid before the situation left no choice.

KATIE DROVE toward the ranch with Sammy talking happily in the back seat. When Anna and Gabe weren't at story time, he'd been upset. She couldn't blame him. She'd been disappointed too. However, his spirits lifted when she told him they were going to see Nathan.

She felt like a fraud keeping back the information on why they were going for a visit. The only thing that kept her from it was the knowledge he would be upset either way. At least not knowing gave him a few minutes of excitement. His non-stop chatter confirmed how much he'd missed his "big friend." She missed him, too, but at the moment, the idea of facing him again left her stomach churning. She'd gotten Sammy a kid's meal to eat on the way, but she passed on a meal of her own. There was no way her stomach could handle food with her nerves going haywire.

Her nausea increased as each mile brought them closer to the ranch. When she stepped out of the jeep, she had to get a piece of gum from her purse to keep the urge to vomit at bay. She'd just set Sammy on the ground when she heard his voice.

"Sammy! I've missed you, buddy. Come, give me a hug."

She turned to see Sammy run into Nathan's outstretched arms. One arm went around his neck, while the one in the cast stayed at his side. Nathan scooped him up with ease before joining her by the jeep.

She met his gaze. She was surprised to find sympathy in their blue depths. Her tension melted away. "Hi. I've not said anything about, well, you know. I've not said anything."

"Are you sure you're ready for this?"

The words wouldn't come. No. She was not ready for this. Who in their right mind would be? She couldn't say it because she didn't feel it. Instead, she nodded, and he led the way to the corral. There was a beautiful chestnut and white splotched horse roaming inside the fence. She watched Sammy closely for signs of distress. So far, so good.

Nathan pointed to the horse. "Do you have a toy horse like this one, Sammy?"

Sammy nodded.

"Do you know what it's called?"

He shook his head.

"This kind of horse is called a Paint. Her name is Belle. Do you like Belle?"

Sammy nodded again.

Nathan made a clicking sound at Belle and stretched out one hand. Belle made her way to him. Katie watched as Sammy tensed in his other arm. She was sure Nathan could feel it, but he didn't give any indication.

"Belle's a good horse. I'm going to give her a treat." He pulled a sugar cube from his pocket. "Look how I keep my hand flat. That way, Belle can use her lips and just scoop it right up."

He showed Sammy how to do it. Sammy even grinned a little

RELENTLESS LOVE

when the horse's big lips picked the small cube off Nathan's hand. Nathan patted the horse.

"Good, Belle." He looked at Sammy. "Can you tell Belle she's a good horse?"

Sammy looked unsure. He watched Belle before looking at Katie. Nathan saw it and motioned Katie over.

"I think your mommy would like to give Belle a sugar cube." He fished one out of his pocket and handed it to her.

Katie mimicked the way Nathan had held his hand and lifted it to the horse's mouth. She grinned as velvety lips plucked it from her palm. Without thinking about it, she raised her hand to stroke Belle's face. "Good, Belle."

"Now, you try. Tell Belle she's a good horse."

Sammy's hand stretched tentatively toward the horse while Nathan held out another sugar cube to keep her still. After a small pause, Sammy made contact. "Good, Belle."

Nathan handed Sammy to Katie and stepped inside the corral. "Okay, now I want you to hand him to me or come stand in here beside me."

Step by step over the next hour, Nathan got Sammy acclimated to being around the horse. They walked around inside the corral with Belle, they petted her, and they talked to and about her non-stop. Katie held Sammy while Nathan saddled Belle. He continued speaking to Sammy, reminding him of all the saddle and bridle parts. Finally, he pulled out a small riding helmet.

"Do you remember what this is for, Sammy?"

Sammy nodded. "I wear it on my head."

Nathan knocked on the helmet. "Yes, you wear hats on your head. And this is a special hat. See how hard it is? It is made to keep your head from getting hurt. Can I put it on you?"

His curious eyes stared at Nathan. Katie could almost see his thoughts racing to find out if there was a catch. Nathan must have sensed his hesitation. He went back to where he'd retrieved Sammy's helmet and dropped his cowboy hat over the fence

227

post. He came back with a second helmet and made a show of putting it on.

"I've got one, too, Sammy. Would you like to wear yours? You can be my little partner again."

The draw of being his big buddy's little partner again was too much. Sammy leaned forward for Nathan to place the hat on his head, buckling the strap under his chin. Nathan mounted Belle. Sammy stiffened in Katie's arms.

"Want to join me up here on Belle? She's a super nice horse."

The coaxing voice did nothing to convince Sammy. He buried his head in the curve where Katie's neck and shoulder met. Katie winced as the hard edge of the riding helmet dug into her soft muscle. Nathan looked at her expectantly. She couldn't do it. She couldn't push Sammy. Instead, she attempted to soothe him by rubbing a hand in small circles on his back.

Nathan frowned at her before trying again with Sammy. "Hey, partner. I know it's hard, but can you sit up here with me? I promise Belle is a nice horse. We won't even move. I'll tie her to the fence, and we can just sit here. Want to try, for me?"

Sammy's voice muffled against Katie could barely be heard. "No."

Nathan looked to her for help again, but she refused to acknowledge it. He blew out a quick breath and dismounted. "Let's all take a little walk. Shall we?"

There was only one thing Katie wanted less than taking a walk with Nathan Phillips when she knew "walk" was code for him getting on to her for failing to live up to their arrangement. Seeing how that one thing was making Sammy get on a horse, she picked the lesser of two evils and followed Nathan from the corral.

They walked toward the barn in silence. Not even Sammy, whose head remained buried in Katie's neck, made a sound. What was Nathan doing? Was he going back a few steps to having Sammy pet horses before trying again? Were they going to throw out the plan all together and leave Sammy in his frightened state? While she didn't look forward to continued nightmares, she knew leaving the ranch would provide immediate relief for her and Sammy.

"Chris?"

A voice answered from one of the open stalls in the back of the barn. "In Storm's stall. What do ya need?"

"Can you come here a minute?"

Nathan waited for Chris to join them. Katie smiled as the man's eyes traveled from one person in their trio to the next and back. He shifted his weight to his left foot, and his hip hung slack while waiting to find out why he was summoned from his work.

"Kate and I need to talk. Could you take Sammy up to the house and get him a cookie? He's been brave today, and I think that deserves a celebration."

Sammy's head popped up with the promise of a cookie, making it easy for Chris to get his attention. "I think we've got some chocolate chip cookies up at the house. My wife sent them with me this morning fresh from the oven. I might even be talked into seeing if I can rustle up some chocolate milk. Want to come?"

Sammy started to reach for him but stopped himself. He looked to Katie for approval. "Go ahead. Chocolate chip cookies sound great."

Chris took him from her grasp and put him on the ground, grabbing his hand. Katie watched them walk across the driveway and the lawn before hazarding a look in Nathan's direction. "I know what you're going to say, but I can't. He's scared, Nathan. And he's three. What am I supposed to do?"

Hands on his hips, Nathan regarded her without saying a word. His jaw was tight. His usually bright, sky blue eyes were dark. He took Katie's hand, led her from the barn, past the corral, and a good distance down the driveway.

Tired of the silent treatment, Katie jerked her hand from his and planted her feet. She refused to take another step until he'd answered at least one of her questions. She would even lob him an easy one. "What are we doing walking down the driveway? Your barn and your precious horse are that way." She sliced through the air with her arm to point in the direction they'd come.

His voice was low when he answered. "I'm getting us away from the animals and away from where Sammy might hear things that will only make the situation worse. Is that all right with you, or would you rather spook both my horses and your son?"

Okay. There was wisdom in his line of thinking. Some of her anger dissipated. "Fine." It wasn't quite an apology, but it would have to do for now. "What do you need to say that you think may cause more conflict than what already exists?"

He removed the riding helmet and ran a hand through his hair. Because his hair was damp from the helmet, the motion caused his sandy blonde hair to stand in little spikes across his head. Katie felt an irritating urge to straighten it with her fingers. Mercy, where did that thought come from? She was the one who'd moved past their relationship. She didn't need or want to be the one straightening the hair of or taking care of Nathan in any way.

"Kate?"

The tilt to his head and frown pulled her wayward thoughts back to the present issues. She lifted her chin. "Well, are you just going to stand there, or are you going to answer the question? What's so important we had to march halfway down your drive?"

"You can't do this to him. I know he's scared, but you don't want him to stay scared forever, do you?"

"He could get over it. Maybe the interaction he had with the horses today did the trick. That's all he needs, and the night-mares will go away from now on."

He cocked an eyebrow. "You don't believe that, do you?"

"Maybe."

"No. You don't. I know this is hard for you, but you've got to help me get Sammy on that horse. You could even sit on it with him. I don't care, as long as he gets on a horse for a few seconds."

She practically shouted in her frustration. "Why? Why do I have to make him do something scary that he doesn't want to do?"

Nathan's voice was soft. "Because you love him."

What? Had she missed a crucial part of the conversation? "How does that make a difference?"

"I know you didn't see it, but before the fall, Sammy had a blast riding. He was so excited to see Buck up close. When it came time for riding, especially the trail ride, he was more hesi-tant. But he overcame that. He loosened up, and he enjoyed himself. Can you honestly say you think it's in Sammy's best interest to live in fear?"

Katie crossed her arms in front of her chest. "But there are things out there he should be afraid of, that he should stay away from. Fear isn't always bad. Sometimes it's a warning to keep you safe."

He stared over her shoulder. She could almost see the thoughts tumbling around in his head. He made eye contact once again before talking and kept it there until he finished. "And Sammy has you to teach him the difference between the fears he should pay attention to and the ones he can work to overcome. I know you want to keep him safe, but what if your desire for safety keeps Sammy from things he could really, truly enjoy in life? And what about the lessons he'll miss about working through the hard things to accomplish even greater things? It starts here, Kate. Do you love Sammy enough to do the hard thing, the best thing for him? Sometimes, we all have to work through the fear to get to a reward that's better than we imagined it could be. Do you want to miss that? For Sammy, I mean."

With everything in her, Katie wanted him to be wrong. She wanted a reasonable excuse to pack Sammy into his car seat and leave. She wanted to block out the discomfort his words caused and the flicker of intuition that told her Nathan might be speaking about more than Sammy's issue. She couldn't face that at the moment, but she couldn't ignore the wisdom in his words.

"Fine. We'll do it your way. And maybe it would help for me to be on the horse too. I could be behind you or in front, whichever is easiest and would get Sammy on the horse."

Nathan's lips relaxed into a smile that returned the clarity to his eyes and put dimples in the scruff on his cheeks. "Why don't you sit behind me? That way, Sammy's in my arms just like he was on the trail."

Katie nodded, her mouth suddenly too dry for words at the realization that she'd suggested being enclosed in Nathan's arms on the horse. Sitting behind him was the much better choice. She needed to remember to thank God for small blessings in her prayers later that night.

Sammy stood with Katie and Chris at the corral as Nathan removed Belle's saddle, leaving only the blanket underneath. He swung himself over the horse's back and reached a hand out to Katie. She joined him in the corral, leaving Sammy with Chris. After he pulled her up, she began to reconsider her previous praise of riding behind him instead of in front. Sure, she wasn't in his arms, but was having to sit against him with her arms secured around his middle any better? Maybe her son would take pity on her and quickly make his recovery so she could put some distance between her and Nathan.

Chris walked Sammy over to Belle. He made a show of patting the horse's neck and shoulder. "You're such a good horse, Belle."

He continued patting and complimenting the mare until Sammy mimicked his actions. Nathan followed suit from his position on Belle's back. Katie kept her hands firmly locked around Nathan's waist. She leaned around his shoulder only far enough to watch Sammy's reaction to everything. So far, so good. He seemed at ease with talking to and touching the horse.

Nathan spoke quietly for her ears only. "Encourage Sammy to ride. Tell him how much fun you're having. Remind him what a good horse Belle is."

She did her best to sound cheerful. "Wow! Belle is a nice horse. I love riding her and wish I had a horse like Belle. Sammy, would you like to get on Belle too? We can be a train riding a horse. You can be the engine, and I'll be the caboose."

Sammy loved trains. Maybe it would entice him to join them. The look he shot her was less than encouraging.

Nathan chimed in. "What can I be in the train? Can I be an engine too?"

Sammy giggled. "You can't be an engine. Trains have one engine. I'm the engine."

"What am I then?"

"You be a car for people."

"I'm a people car. Your mommy's the caboose. But we don't have an engine. Will you please be our engine, Sammy?"

Sammy's head dipped slightly. Chris held him up, and Nathan used one arm to scoop him up and into place in front of him. Katie couldn't see him without leaning far enough to the side, she felt she would fall off. Instead, she watched Chris's face for signs of concern.

"You're doing great, little partner." Nathan's voice was soothing. "That's it, lean back against me. I've got you. Tell me something, what does a train engine sound like?"

The distraction seemed to do the trick. Katie heard Sammy's quiet voice. "Choo. Choo. Chugga Chugga. Choo. Choo."

"Do you know what it means when you hear that noise?"

"Trains are coming."

"Do you think our train should be coming? Do you want Chris to help Belle move a little while you be our engine?"

Katie didn't hear an answer, but Nathan nodded at Chris, who took the lead rope. She tightened her grip as Belle inched forward. She felt Nathan shift his arms to increase his grip on Sammy.

"You're doing great. But I don't hear any train sounds. Have we lost our engine?"

Sammy's voice was barely a squeak. "Choo. Choo. Chugga. Chugga. Choo. Choo."

They continued moving in a circle around the corral. By the time they'd reached the halfway point, Sammy's volume had increased. Nathan spoke fewer encouraging words as their ride went on. Katie found her body matching the horse's rhythm, and she loosened her hold on Nathan's waist. Just about the time she found herself entirely at ease, Chris brought Belle to a stop.

Nathan handed Sammy down to Chris. "Ride's over, little partner."

As soon as Chris and Sammy moved away, Nathan extended his arm to help Katie dismount before doing the same. He took Sammy from Chris as soon as his boots touched dirt.

"Would you mind seeing to Belle? I want to make sure we're all good here."

Chris took the lead rope and headed for the barn. Nathan unbuckled Sammy's chin strap and removed his helmet. He did the same to his. "Let's go put these up."

After putting them in the tack room, he took them to his home's wrap-around front porch and made himself comfortable on the hanging swing with Sammy on his leg. He patted the seat next to him, and though she didn't relish being that close to him for a second time that day, she took the spot he offered.

Nathan rubbed Sammy's back. "I'm proud of you, Sammy.

You took good care of Belle today, and you even rode her around the corral. You're as brave as they come. Did you have fun?"

He nodded. "Ride Belle again?"

"Right now, Belle needs her rest. But after you get your cast off, if your mama says it's okay, I'd be happy to take you riding. Horseback riding is always better with my little partner."

He ruffled Sammy's hair. Sammy leaned against him, and his thumb found his mouth. The ease of the back and forth motion of the swing, coupled with Nathan rubbing his back worked their magic. Sammy's eyes grew heavy. It was the perfect excuse.

Katie stood. "I think it's time I get your little partner home. It's been a long emotional day, and I think he's past exhausted."

She reached for him, but Nathan shook his head. "I'll carry him for you."

Katie decided not to argue. It wouldn't hurt for Nathan to carry him to the car. Besides, Sammy was comfortable where he was.

Once Sammy was buckled into his seat, Nathan turned to Katie. "I've missed seeing him. I've missed seeing you, too."

Katie chose to ignore his comments and the flutter they produced in her stomach. "Thank you for taking all this time with him today."

She looked away from the intensity reflecting in his eyes. His feelings were all too clear, unsettling her. She needed to get away.

His voice, as calm as it had been with Sammy, brought her attention back to him. "What are you afraid of?"

She bit her lip. Her auburn curls danced as she shook her head. "You did a great job with Sammy today. I'm amazed at how relaxed he got by the end."

"It's amazing what can happen when someone faces their fears."

She refused to see the double meaning in his words.

"Tonight, we'll find out if it works. I'm hoping for no nightmares."

They regarded each other in silence. Katie knew he was waiting for the faintest encouragement to continue, but she couldn't give it to him. There was too much at stake. If it hadn't been for Sammy, she never would've reached out to him. She was grateful for his help, but it ended there. He needed to understand that. Their silence continued.

She climbed into the driver's seat and shut the door. "Thank you again for your help."

He opened his mouth to speak but shut it again. His frown spoke volumes, but his words were few. "Let me know if it works?"

"Definitely." She couldn't tell him "see you later" or anything like that. Without the hope of continued interaction, there was no way to exit this conversation gracefully. Instead, she started the jeep and drove away. A glance in the review mirror told her Nathan watched them go until they were out of sight.

Chapter Twenty-Eight

"You got a good night's sleep, then?"

Katie smiled at Gigi B as they watched Sammy slide from the park bench. Katie gathered the remains of their Sunday afternoon picnic and placed them in the picnic basket Gigi B had brought. "For the first night in weeks."

"So, you're glad you saw Nathan then?"

Katie rolled her eyes. "Don't push your luck on that one. I'm glad he was able to help. I'm glad Sammy enjoyed himself. That's it."

Gigi B raised a perfectly penciled brow. "I'm tickled it seems to have worked. But since you're delusional when it comes to your former beau, we'll have to change the subject. Did you go see your dad yesterday?"

She chose to ignore the dig at her feelings for Nathan. "Briefly. We had a lot going on between story hour and going to the ranch. We stopped in for a few minutes after Sammy's nap, but I was there a bit longer on Friday when you took Sammy for ice cream."

Gigi B brushed a minuscule speck from her flower-covered tunic and adjusted the bangle bracelet on her wrist. "I meant to ask you about that. You seemed a little shaken when you collected Sammy from me that day. Did something happen with Cal?"

"You could say that. I was looking through his Bible and stumbled across his theme verse. I read it to him, and I thought we were going to have a nice visit. I thought he might even recognize me. But then he started talking gibberish. He was asking about Austin."

"What about Austin?"

Katie watched Sammy, but her mind replayed the conversation with her dad. It was as uncomfortable in hindsight as it was at the time it happened. "That's just it. I couldn't quite figure out what he was talking about. The whole thing was strange. I was holding his Bible in my lap. He put his hands over mine and kept patting them and repeating the same three words over and over. Your first love. Obviously, he was talking about Austin, because he didn't care one little bit for my previous boyfriend. And the only other thing he told me was to find my first love. He and Austin were close enough, but he'd never acted as if he missed him before. It was weird."

Gigi B cackled and clapped her hands together as she jumped up from the bench. She strutted back and forth in front of Katie and raised her hands in the air. "Praise You, Lord. Oh, You are one amazing God!"

Katie could feel the heat rising in her cheeks. A woman and her child watched the show from where they played near the swings, but a quick check confirmed there were no others present to see what was going on. The attention-drawing behavior was too much for Katie's more introverted tendencies, but she couldn't deny something she'd said spurred on the praise and worship. She wished she knew what it was. She would make sure to avoid it next time they were in a public place.

"While it's impossible to ignore your excitement, do you

think you could reel it in just enough to let me in on this great revelation?"

Hands clasped in front of her chest Gigi B dropped to the bench as if she'd just run a marathon. "Revelation? Ironic choice of words."

The older woman giggled like a schoolgirl.

Katie's lips pursed to one side. She refused to smile at her antics. She would much rather have answers. "I'm waiting. Would you like to fill in the rest of the class?"

Gigi B immediately sobered. "I'd be happy to, but you have to agree to one thing first."

A groan escaped before she could catch it. She'd made too many deals in the last forty-eight hours. But Gigi B had a stubborn streak that would keep her lips sealed unless Katie agreed. Did she want to know? Curiosity was a strong force when left unchecked. "Fine. What am I agreeing to?"

"You let me take Sammy back to my house for a visit."

Simple enough. But Katie knew Gigi B better than that. She wracked her brain, trying to figure out the catch. Gigi B knew she could have Sammy visit any time she wanted. Why make a big deal about it this time?

"Sure. Sammy can go to your house. I'll drop you both off just as soon as you fill me in on whatever nugget of wisdom is bouncing through your brain right now."

Gigi B placed a hand on Katie's knee. "Your father, God, bless his heart, he wasn't confused, at least not the way you think he was."

"He made no sense whatsoever."

She pushed Katie's knee away playfully in her excitement. "Oh, he made sense, all right. He just couldn't get everything out in a way you could understand."

Katie rolled her eyes. "That would be the definition of not making sense."

Her dangly earrings swung back and forth in time with the

shake of her head. "You sweet thing. His delivery may not have made sense to you, but I guarantee the message was crystal clear."

She ignored the "sweet thing" that could have easily meant "poor, dense creature." "Would you mind filling me in? Because I don't find this crystal clear at all. Not even remotely. Think of the most unclear thing you can imagine and make it ten times less clear. That's how clear this is to me."

"Praise Jesus! Your father may not be as communicative as he once was with us, but God's Spirit is still in that man witnessing to his spirit."

"Gigi B, please, get to the explanation."

"Patience, dear. Patience. What I was saying is that despite his current physical condition, God has given your father insight into what ails you. His message isn't anything about Austin. It's about you and your heart. He's telling you where you've made a left turn instead of a right and how you can set it straight again."

"And that is?"

"Your first love isn't Austin. He's talking scripture, honey, plain and simple. You've had a heap of hurts in the last few years. And we're not talking piddly little hurts either. You've dealt with all the big ones earlier in life than lots of folks, and you've come through it with your faith intact. But your daddy noticed something else was missing. You've lost your passion for it all. You've left your first love, and he thinks it's high time you found it again. Once you find it, hold it tight. It's the only way to live."

Katie dropped her head into her hands. "You might as well be speaking in riddles. I don't have any idea what you're talking about, or how you got all this from what my dad said."

Gigi B's hand cupped Katie's chin and lifted it until they were eye to eye. Her smile was soft and full of caring. "Your daddy wasn't patting your hand. He was touching the word of God, but your hands were on top of it. He's referencing a verse in Revelation to one of the churches. I think it may be around chapter two. It's close to the beginning anyway. And now that you know, I'm going to take Sammy for the afternoon at my house. It will give you a little bit of time to marinate in the message your daddy, and quite possibly, your heavenly Father wanted you to know."

WITH SAMMY safely settled in for an afternoon of fun with Gigi B, Katie sought the seclusion of home and her waterfall. How long had it been since she'd sought God out at the favorite spot from her childhood? She wouldn't waste this opportunity. She slung a backpack over her shoulder and headed down the trail.

Even before she reached the rocky ledge, the woods worked their magic on her soul. The quiet sounds of nature soothed, putting her in the perfect mood for reflection. At the edge of the waterfall, Katie sat and removed her shoes and socks. The hot summer sun was beaten back by the canopy of leaves above her head, but the heat remained. She dangled her feet over the edge and stirred the cool water in the pool below with her toes. She leaned back on her arms with her face raised to the sky and sighed. Why had she waited so long to return to her spot?

Reality crashed in on her immediately. How could she have returned more often than she had? She had a small son who needed her nearly every hour of every day. Her father, when he was home, couldn't be trusted to care for his grandson and, in the end, not even himself. Even with Sammy in day care, her time was not wholly her own. She had story time at the library, and that was a godsend. She loved being home with her son, but he needed socialization with others his age. She needed time away from the house doing adult things, like working. The few hours she worked a week provided that outlet for both of them.

Katie felt her peace slipping from her grasp and tried desperately to derail the progression of her thoughts. Gigi B was right. Life had given her more hurts and changes in the last few years than some received in a lifetime. They had left her to manage the day to day on her own for the most part, and that left little time for silent reflection at the waterfall or anywhere else. It was merely the way it was now. And that wasn't what this time was supposed to be. If Gigi B was correct, Katie's dad wanted her to know something. This was the time to find that out.

Katie took her tablet from the side pocket of her backpack and tapped the Bible app she installed back when she still lived in Bloomington. She wasn't sure what she was looking for, so she clicked the magnifying glass and typed in "first love". The top reference was one from Revelation. That's where Gigi B said to look. So, that was where she would start her search.

Since the verse was near the beginning of chapter two, Katie decided to back up to the beginning for context. It was a letter to a church that seemed to be everything you could want in a church. They worked for God and didn't accept evil into their midst. Tirelessly, this church sought after God's truth and did the things God wants believers to do. It sounded wonderful. It seemed like the kind of faith Katie wished to exhibit in her life. When she reached verses four and five, the ones her father referenced, she read out loud. She had a feeling with all the good the church was doing for God and the way they lived their beliefs, God was about to sing their praises.

"'Nevertheless I have this against you.'" Wait. What? God had something against this church. How could He have anything negative to say about them? They were doing everything right. "'Nevertheless I have this against you, that you have left your first love. Remember therefore from where you have fallen; repent and do the first works, or else I will come to you quickly and remove your lampstand from its place –unless you repent.'"

Katie was stunned. She read the words a second time to make sure she hadn't misread or missed a vital piece of information.

No, she hadn't missed anything. God wasn't pleased with them. Even though they were getting high marks in their spiritual activity, God still warned them to repent and find their first love. What did that even mean?

Knowing God often used the physical to give a picture of the spiritual, Katie considered her first love. She and Austin had little time together, but the time they had was full. They had their disagreements, but they never stopped wanting to be with each other. Her best memories from those times were ones where she was with him. She looked forward to being with him. She longed for his nearness for comfort and strength. They planned, worked, and played together because they enjoyed each other's company, not because they had to. They didn't stop loving each other. They were in love with each other. Could this be what God was trying to tell the church? They served Him, but had they forgotten to be in love with Him?

Katie considered the validity of the direction of her thoughts. It seemed reasonable but left her with questions. If the people were doing the right things and believed God, would love make such a difference to God? She thought of what she knew about love from the Bible. The words emblazoned on everything from bookmarks to wall hangings ran through her mind. Love is patient. Love is kind. The list continued through many attributes of love to reach the pinnacle of love. Love never fails. Was God upset at the church in Revelation because their actions weren't full of these attitudes? No. The verses said they were patient and enduring. Those were characteristics listed in the First Corinthians chapter thirteen passage.

She spent the next hour doing internet searches on Bible verses about love and going back to her Bible app to read the complete passages to ensure she was keeping things in context. She pulled a journal out of her backpack and began scribbling the references and her notes about verses that caught her interest. When she found herself circling back to the same references, she started going through her notes to see if anything jumped out at her.

In Matthew twenty-two, Katie saw that loving God was the greatest commandment, followed by loving others. Loving God should be first. Like first love? It was possible. Maybe the church loved others but had forgotten to love God first. The passage's description of how to love God certainly sounded like the life-encompassing love she'd shared with Austin only on a grander scale. Did she love God with all her heart? Soul? And what about loving Him with all her mind? Just one passage and she fell short.

Katie had decided at the end of her search to seek out the Corinthians passage. Everyone knew it, but she didn't want to be guilty of overlooking something because of her familiarity with it. She'd seen what she'd expected in those verses, but her eyes drew to the ones above love's description. They were less familiar, but their meaning left her wondering why they weren't preached more often. They were a warning that spoke directly to the passage in Revelation. She reviewed her notes on the subject. It didn't matter what she did in life. Even if she fed the homeless and sacrificed herself for faith, if she did it without love, "it profits me nothing." Nothing she did or said mattered without love. But why?

As Katie looked to her final notes, she thought she could see it. "'We love Him because He first loved us.'"

God's love for people didn't leave them without hope when sin destroyed them. God's love made way for them to be brought back into a relationship with Him, even though people wronged Him over and over. His love never gives up. It causes Him to pursue people, forgive them, and also send His Spirit to live inside them. That love, that perfect, passionate, relentless love, was what spurs on believers to love God back with their hearts, souls, and minds.

Katie picked up her phone and looked up the passage one

more time. Excitement over her find bubbled up inside, and she didn't want to lose that or miss any other details God might have for her. She started in verse seventeen, but when something in eighteen caught her attention, she began reading out loud. "'There is no fear in love; but perfect love casts out fear because fear involves torment. But he who fears has not been made perfect in love. We love Him because He first loved us.'"

Katie was stunned. Looking back at verse seventeen, Katie understood she didn't need to fear the day of judgment. She could stand boldly before God because of the provision of His love. But it was more than that. There was no room for fear in a heart full of God's love. She didn't need to fear the what-ifs that came with choosing to love the way that God loves.

She might experience a loss if she chose to love with God's passionate, relentless love. She already had more than once. But God did too. He lost His Son to death on the cross. In Katie's opinion, there was nothing worse than watching your child suffer and being unable to stop it. Unless, of course, it was being able to stop it, but knowing you had to let it happen. God's love was perfect. Katie couldn't imagine allowing something like that to happen to Sammy.

God also faced daily rejection and disappointment from those He gave His Son for. People were continually ignoring and denying His gift. Even those who believed failed Him, often twisting His words and using Him as a cosmic reset button. But even with all this, God chose love. Not the kind of love that performs out of a sense of duty, but a love that gives everything regardless of the pain it might bring. It was fearless love, and Katie knew in her heart, it was the love she was called to give. Gigi B was right. Her dad saw her heart and wanted more for her.

Katie wasn't sure when she started crying, but tears flowed down her cheeks. When had she let pain steal her love? When had she begun erecting walls that kept her from giving love despite the possibility of hurt? How did she correct her path?

Make it about Me. Make it about love.

Katie allowed the reality of God's love to wash over her, refreshing her soul deep. When she was so full of His love, she thought she wouldn't be able to contain it any longer. She turned to Him in prayer. She offered herself as a conduit of His love, no matter the cost. She asked for strength and reminders of His love to fight back against fear when it tried to find a place in her heart. She asked Him to show her what she needed to do to move from frightened and ineffective to loving and life-changing for Him. Before her whispered "Amen," Katie received her answer.

Not even taking the time to dry her feet, Katie slipped her socks and shoes on. Now that she knew her direction, she didn't want to waste time. On her hasty trek back up the path to her home, she made the first of three phone calls asking Gigi B if she could leave Sammy through supper. The next she made to Erin, who was as excited about her self-discovery and new plan as she was the opportunity to do some particular shopping on Katie's dime. If anyone could get the things she needed in the short amount of time she had, it would be Erin.

She offered one last prayer for wisdom and strength before dialing the last number. It could still blow up in her face, but that was a risk she was going to have to take. It was time for Katie Blake to stop worrying about the pain and start living the life God had for her.

"Hello."

"Hi, Anna. This is Katie. I think I have the perfect solution to your housing problem. Got a minute to hear me out?"

THE NEXT MORNING KATIE, Erin, and Anna watched as Sammy and Gabe played together on the slide. To help Sammy navigate with his cast, Katie had placed a step stool in front of the ladder on one side of the structure. It was the perfect solution for the situation. The boys followed a circuit up the steps, down the slide, and back up the steps. The women chatted while the boys played.

Anna pulled her long, straight hair into a ponytail and secured it with an elastic band she took from her wrist. "I can't thank you enough for this. Knowing we have a home, we aren't going to have to leave any time soon, well, it's a weight off my shoulders." She paused as she tried to gain control of her overwhelmed emotions. "And, Erin, you did a great job making the room look like a home for us. Gabe isn't going to know what to do with himself now that he has a bed all to himself. He's always slept with me on whatever we had for a bed."

Erin beamed under the compliment. Katie smiled, thinking of Gabe's face when he saw the toddler bed decked out with superhero bedding. And the way Erin had coordinated it with a cover for her parents' bed was nothing short of amazing. "Who would have thought you could make a room fit for an adult and a child at the same time? That solid purple bedding with coordinating yellow sheets was a stroke of genius."

Erin swatted the praise out of the air with her hand. "It was nothing. Once I had the colors from Gabe's covers, it was easy to pick out the covers and curtains for the rest of the room. I just wish I'd been able to get the rest of Cal and Sharon's things boxed up and out of the dressers and closet before move-in time."

Anna shook her head. "Don't feel bad about that. Gabe and I've never really had a place of our own, much less dressers and closets. We'll be fine until I can finish the job. Katie's shown me what needs to be done, and I can probably have it done by tonight."

Katie grinned and shook a finger at her. "Now, don't stay up too late. You've got a big day tomorrow. You may be living-rent free, but we did make a deal about how you earn your keep around here."

Anna laughed. "I know. Tomorrow I'll go by the high school and find out about their GED program."

"And we'll go shopping to see if we can find a cheap but reliable car for you."

Anna rubbed the back of her neck. "I'm not sure about that one. A car is a big deal. I'm not sure I can afford something like that right now."

"I'm going to ask you to trust me on this. We live far enough out of town that public transportation doesn't run through here. It won't be fancy, and technically, it won't be yours. The car will be paid for and maintained by me. But it will give you something so you can get around. You'll need it to get to classes and work. You'll put gas in it when you need to and be responsible for getting the oil changed. Everything else will be taken care of by me as long as you're in school, working, and don't get any tickets."

Anna fought tears. Katie and Erin sat in silence, sensing the younger girl's need to process everything that was happening. It was a lot to take in.

Sammy and Gabe had stopped their circles up the steps and down the slide. They faced each other as both gestured wildly and spoke at the same time. Katie caught snippets of the conversation. Someone wasn't doing something right, that was for sure.

She'd seen those stances before. Macho men on a football field were puffing themselves up in front of the competition while asserting their dominance. Mercy, did such behavior start this young?

Katie stood at the same time as Erin. She put a restraining hand on Katie's arm. "Here. Let me handle this one."

Katie gladly returned to her seat. She and Anna watched as Erin knelt between the boys. Erin spoke quietly enough that Katie couldn't hear much beyond the calming tone. Giant frowns and sullen nods over drooped shoulders replaced the starched shoulders and emphatic gestures of only seconds before. A few more words and Erin had them grinning from ear to ear. Sammy took Gabe's hand, and the two raced off to the clubhouse under the structure.

Erin returned and took a seat on the bricks of the raised flower bed nearest the bench where Katie and Anna sat. "Those two are going to be a handful, that's for sure. They'll be the best of friends until they aren't."

"You did a wonderful job calming the storm. Do you have kids of your own?"

Katie shut her eyes as she inwardly cringed. She should have warned Anna of Erin's situation. Of course, she hadn't had time to do it and had no idea the subject would even come up. She glanced at Erin, who smiled sweetly at Anna without a trace of discomfort showing on her face.

"No. Paul and I've been trying for a while, but we've not been blessed like that yet."

Anna's bronze cheeks darkened with her embarrassment. "Oh, I'm so sorry. I didn't mean to bring up a hard subject."

Erin's smile widened. "It's fine. Don't worry about it. I've got some great news." She looked at Katie. "Not even Gigi B has heard this one yet."

Excitement radiated off Erin. Her eyes shone, and her smile was the brightest Katie had seen. Considering Erin's generally happy personality, her news had to be amazing. Katie couldn't help smiling in response.

"Don't leave us hanging. Out with it. What's your news?"

"The agency we've been working with has found a match for us!" The news came out in a squeal.

Katie jumped up and ran to Erin, pulling her up and throwing her arms around her neck. "That's wonderful! When will it happen? How does it happen? Oh, my goodness, I'm so excited for you!"

"I'm not sure I understand."

Katie broke her hold on Erin's neck and turned to find Anna watching them with a blank look on her face. "Erin and Paul have been working with an adoption agency. It can be a long process with a lot of waiting and hoping and praying."

Erin interrupted. "Yes. And we've been doing all three of those non-stop."

"But now, they have their match. I'm going to be Auntie Katie! I can't wait to hold the little guy. Or girl. Do you know? Will it be a boy or a girl?"

"Slow down there, Auntie Katie. We've been matched with someone who hasn't delivered yet. There's not even going to be a baby to hold for a couple of months. We do know the baby is a girl. She's due on October fifth."

Anna smiled politely. "I'm happy for you and Paul. I know you're going to make a great mommy."

Her lack of excitement did nothing to dim it in Katie. Anna didn't know Erin beyond this first meeting. She hadn't dreamed with her in the beginning or cried with her after each of her failed IUI attempts. She hadn't seen the yearning looks when Auntie Erin spent an afternoon with Sammy. She hadn't offered up countless prayers on her friends' behalf, asking God to bless them with a family or for peace to reign in their hearts if it wasn't God's will for them. Katie, on the other hand, had done all these things on a continuous loop. To know their dream of being parents was finally coming to pass was almost as sweet as her time spent alone at the waterfall in the presence of God.

Katie flopped back onto the bench. "So, tell us everything."

When the conversation finally wound down, Katie and Anna had a working knowledge of open adoptions and what Erin and Paul were facing to reach the adoption's completion. Their giddiness was under control. As they calmed, Anna had seemed more comfortable, even asking thoughtful questions.

"Mama!" Gabe cried as he ran across the lawn and launched himself into his mother's arms.

She held him close for a hug before pulling him away enough to see his face. "What happened, sweetheart?"

"My head. Bumped. My. Head." The words came individually between his gasps.

"Can you show me where?"

His lip jutted out as he placed a hand on the back of his head. Anna felt the spot before kissing it softly. "There, now. I think you're fine. Maybe a bit tired, though." She looked over at Katie. "Would you mind if I take Gabe in for a while. It's past his nap time, and I think we could both do with a little rest. There's been a lot happening today."

"I think that sounds like a great idea. Remember, you don't have to ask. I want you and Gabe to feel comfortable here. This is your home now."

She scooped Gabe into her arms. "Thank you."

Erin waited until the pair had moved from earshot before speaking. "I'm proud of you, girl."

"About what?"

"I know this isn't an easy step to take. But you listened to what God was saying, and you're embracing it with everything you've got. It's like your time with Him flipped a switch inside you."

Sammy crawled out of the clubhouse and skipped over to her and Erin. "Where's Gabe?"

Katie pulled him onto her lap. "Gabe had to go take a nap. And I'm pretty sure I know another boy who needs one too."

"I'm not tired."

Katie hugged him close. "I know you're not, but you need a nap anyway. And then, sometime, I have to work out a way to get over to the nursing home and see your grandpa." She switched her focus to Erin. "I owe him. Though I didn't understand at the time, he was setting me straight. He needs to know I finally get it."

Erin reached over and took Sammy from her. "I've got a great idea. Sammy hasn't seen my new house yet, and I think Anna and Gabe could use a little time alone to adjust to their new surroundings. Let me take Sammy. We can make blanket tents in my living room and watch a movie until we fall asleep. I'll keep him until you're ready to come get him. I won't even mind trying an overnight if you want the whole evening to yourself."

Katie had never been away from Sammy overnight. He was only three, after all. She chewed the inside of her cheek. The wrestling match inside her mind had no clear winner. Erin laughed.

"Fine. No overnight. I'll keep him, and if I don't hear from you by seven, I'll bring him back here and put him down. Anna and I can visit until you get home. If it's too late, I'll just crawl under your covers for some sleep. Just don't wake me if I do."

"Deal."

She leaned over to look Sammy in the face. "Hear that, Munchkin? You're coming to my house."

Chapter Twenty-Nine

Katie's disappointment ricocheted through her when she
arrived at the nursing home to tell her father what had
transpired. True, he could have been awake and entirely out of it,
too. Sleeping wasn't so bad. It left open the possibility he could
wake up bright and ready for a conversation.

Katie considered her choices before lowering herself into the
room's extra chair by the window. There was no telling how long
he would sleep. Sometimes she found him snoring one minute
and awake talking to whoever would listen about something only
he could decipher in the next breath. In the past, his sentences
would have been coherent, the thread of some conversation he'd
been having in his mind. Lately, it seemed random words slipped
out without any rhyme or reason.

It was surprising how quickly his Alzheimer's fueled
dementia had progressed over the last several weeks. Katie
couldn't help wondering if going from home care by a relative he
knew and loved to group care had hastened on the symptoms.
She struggled to hold guilt at bay as she watched him sleep.
She'd had no choice in the matter. The level of care he
demanded, along with the safety concerns home care created

with Sammy, made keeping him with her impossible. Still, she wished with everything in her, it could be different. Who was she kidding? She wished for more than having him home. She wished her daddy, the one who'd been in her corner from day one, was back. She loved him just as much now as she ever did, but the majority of who he'd been to her had been torn away from him kicking and screaming by this insidious disease.

She stared out the window, conscious of the comparison it drew. How many hours did Dad sit staring out this same window looking at everything and taking nothing into the tangled pathways of thought in his mind? Her heart broke every time she came, but she couldn't be anywhere else. Her daddy had loved her, been beside her as much as she would allow. Even in times when she was less than loveable. He may not even realize it, but he needed her now. And Katie was determined she would be there for him as long as he had breath. She couldn't claim love and leave him to fade away on his own.

"There's my Katydid."

She pasted on a smile and turned from the window. Just because Dad recognized her didn't mean he recognized her as she currently was. It wasn't unusual for him to know her as his daughter, but not realize she was a fully capable adult. In his mind, the way she looked physically didn't always play a part in how he perceived things. She could still be a little girl when he looked at her. Katie wondered if she would ever get used to the way his brain now merged the past and the present into some strange variation that kept him in the current time while dancing with the memories from long ago.

"Hi, Dad. How are you doing today?"

He eased himself up from the bed, and each movement marked with difficulty. Even his mobility had decreased in the last few weeks. He shuffled to his chair. "I'm fair to middlin'. How about you?"

Katie smiled. "I'm doing fine. But I have to tell you something. Do you remember when I came to see you the other day, and I read your favorite Bible verse to you? And you kept telling me the same thing about my first love?"

"I'm not quite sure about the conversation itself, but I know what verses you're talking about. My life verse is Micah 6:8, but the verses about your first love are from Revelation."

"Yes, they are. Dad, when you kept asking me where my first love was, I didn't get it. It took Gigi B to help me understand you were talking about the Bible and not something about Austin. But she pointed me in the right direction, and I wanted to say thank you. You were right. I'd left my first love, and I'd let my fears turn love into nothing more than duty. God's love is relentless. Nothing stops it. Not fear, disappointment, or heart-break. But I'd let those things, especially the fear, keep me from loving with my whole being."

"And now?"

"Now I'm not letting those things keep me from loving with everything I've got. Heart, soul, and mind completely. Whatever God asks, I'll do, but not out of duty. I'll follow because I love Him, because of the way He loves me."

Cal slapped his knee with more animation than Katie would have thought him capable of doing. A bubble of pure joy escaped his lips. "You can't imagine how happy that makes me. I may not remember the talk you're telling me about, but knowing God is working in you is a blessing. You've had your share of struggles, but God is good. He's growing you, Katydid, and I'm tickled to get to see it."

Katie lost track of time as she and her dad had a conversation reminiscent of their talks in the past. Though she knew he wouldn't remember what they spoke of, Katie shared about Sammy's fall and subsequent nightmares and how he overcame them. Cal's grandfatherly pride was fed in the knowledge of his grandson's bravery to face his fears.

"Course his mama had to be brave that day too. It's never

easy to let your young'uns hurt, even when you know it's for their best. And humbling yourself to ask Nathan for help when you'd already turned down his advice couldn't have been easy either. But now you two have worked things out?"

Katie hated disappointing her father, and he'd always liked Nathan. "No. We aren't mad at each other or anything. There's just not a place for him in our lives."

"Even with your newfound understanding of how fear can steal your love if you let it?"

"Even with. I think all of this just showed me that I couldn't have a man in our lives like that. He's too different."

"From Austin?"

"Yes, from Austin."

His eyes turned serious. "I want you to understand something. Life is going to hand you a mixed bag of good and bad. Don't miss having someone to go through it with, because they aren't the person you thought you'd be going through it with. And maybe that someone is only a friend. That's fine too. But open yourself up to the possibilities. Nathan made you laugh, and he was there for you when you needed someone to lean on. A new man in your life or old friend, it doesn't matter. Think twice before you throw that away."

She would give her dad anything, well, almost. She couldn't promise a reunion, heartfelt or any other kind, with Nathan. Was it even possible for them to return to the friendship they'd shared since romance had entered the picture? Did she even want that after the little touches he'd reserved only for her, and the kisses that left her heart pounding and wishing for more?

Regardless of the answers to her questions, one thing was sure. If she didn't force the subject from her mind, she would be thinking twice about it and maybe even a third time. Her answer to her dad was as honest as it could be. "I promise. I'll take time to think about the possibilities before I do anything irreversible."

He patted her hand. "That's my good girl. Now, what's going on with the rest of life outside these four walls?"

Katie left her dad's room over an hour and a half later, feeling completely at ease. She had filled him in on Erin's news knowing there was no one he could tell that would make any difference if he even remembered it. She also told him about Anna and Gabe. She'd worried a little about what he would think of opening his home to them. She should have known better.

He'd sat a little straighter in his chair, looked her in the eye, and said, "I can't think of anything more worthy to do with those empty rooms. You love that girl and her son right into God's arms, you hear me?"

Peace washed over Katie. The visit was the best she'd had with him in a long time, and his support over the use of his home was the cherry on top. It didn't matter that tomorrow would likely bring back the confused version of her father. It wouldn't make a difference if that man returned the minute she left. Katie had this sweet moment with him, and nothing could take that away from her. She could still hear his laughter and sense his love. She would hold onto those memories like a lifeline in the darker days to come.

Lost in her thoughts, Katie started when she reached out to push the door open, and it swung open on its own. She looked up into Nathan's equally surprised eyes.

He stepped to the side and held the door open for her to pass. "I'm sorry. I didn't realize you were on the other side of the door."

She tried to look anywhere but his face. His eyes always expressed what he felt, and she wasn't sure she was ready to know what that might be. "It's fine. I didn't see you either."

As she walked away, she had the sensation he was watching her. Hurried footsteps in her direction confirmed it. She slowed though part of her ached to run. She wasn't ready for this.

"Kate, please wait a minute."

257

She stopped and turned. He caught up with her but stood saying nothing. He adjusted the bill of his baseball cap. She raised her eyebrows in question.

"Did everything turn out okay with Sammy?"

She'd forgotten to call. She'd told Nathan she would, but she hadn't. "He's slept fine the last couple of nights. I'm hopeful the nightmares are gone for good. Thank you."

"I'm just glad it helped."

The way he opened and closed his mouth left her with the impression he might have something else on his mind. She crossed her arms over her chest and waited. The silence was as far from peaceful as possible. He had something to say but couldn't find the words. She wasn't sure she would be ready to listen, even if he did. She wasn't going to wait around to find out.

She dismissed him with a nod. "I'll see you later."

It was just a saying. It meant no more than "bye." She didn't need to feel like she'd made a promise she didn't intend to keep. Besides, they lived in the same town. They were bound to run into each other. She turned away and began the walk to her car.

"Can we get together and talk?"

She refused to turn around. It may have been a coward's way out, but she called back to him as she kept walking down the sidewalk. "I'm not sure that's a good idea. I've got to go. Bye."

Chapter Thirty

Nathan's muscles ached to chase after her. Keeping himself rooted to the sidewalk while she made her hasty retreat took all of his willpower. He'd been unprepared to see her. He knew she visited her dad every day, but they'd failed to run into each other in the weeks since their breakup. It was easy to forget her presence at the home was a regular occurrence.

Two days. It had only been two days since Kate had been at the ranch. She had told him she would let him know about Sammy, and she hadn't. He would have called her himself if he hadn't run into her first. But Sammy's recovery from the nightmares wouldn't have been his sole reason for calling.

When Kate broke up with him, he understood why. She was scared and confused. He couldn't imagine the emotions that must be warring inside her. He'd never lost as she had. He wanted to give her space to work through her issues. He hoped in the time they were apart, she would miss him as much as he missed her. In the end, if she didn't, he would have to bow out gracefully.

But Nathan had never been in love before either. He'd underestimated the power of his feelings for her. He kept picking up the phone to tell her some little something that happened. He missed laughing with her and Sammy over a little bit of nonsense. He longed to feel her in his arms again, giving her his strength on those rare times when she admitted she needed help. He even missed the teasing. Kate gave as good as she got most times, and it kept him on his toes.

Nathan wanted to tell Kate all of these things, but watching her walk away, he couldn't do it. She wasn't ready to hear anything close to what was in his heart. If she was, wouldn't she have called to let him know Sammy was doing better? It seemed clear she wasn't ready for friendship much less love.

"My, my, this nursing home is moving up in the world. They've gone and got themselves one of those fancy statues of a Greek god chiseled out of fine marble and placed right in the middle of their sidewalk!"

Gigi B's exuberant voice pulled Nathan from the tug of war going on in his mind. He ignored the heat in his cheeks as he opened his arms to draw her into a hug. "Greek god, huh? Not sure I qualify for that title, or even want to, but thank you for the compliment."

Wearing a tunic with as colorful a pattern as ever, he was surprised that alone hadn't alerted him to her presence. Gigi B indeed carried sunshine with her wherever she went, and her clothes were simply the overflow of her spirit. It made what would be outrageous on anyone else completely fitting on her.

She patted her hand against his cheek. "Don't sell yourself short, kiddo. I may be a hair past my prime, but I still know a swoon-worthy leading man when I see one."

Nathan shook his head. "Gigi B, you are something else. You know that?"

"Sure, I do. And people have been trying to figure out what since the day I was born!"

Nathan's laugh joined hers momentarily, but when it stopped, he looked down at her. Her head tilted to one side as she watched him with knowing eyes.

"I see the way of things."

"I'm sure I don't know what you're talking about."

"Don't try to pull one over on me, Nathan Phillips. I've lived too many years and seen too many things for you to get by with that. I'm just embarrassed it took me this long to see it. Must have been your handsome face confusing my radar."

"Gigi B, you're speakin' in riddles, and I've never been very good at figuring those things out."

She patted his arm sympathetically. "You've got it bad, my boy. Only one thing causes a young man like yourself to stand like a statue for all to admire in the middle of a sidewalk. And only one that I know of causes this particular gentleman to do it. I take it Katie's been in to see her daddy today?"

Nathan sighed. Perceptive didn't begin to describe Gigi B's powers. Her abilities of observation and deduction would rival Peter Parker's spidey sense. Might as well come clean. She'd figure it all out anyway. "Yeah. She was leaving right as I got here."

"Well? Did you tell her how you feel?"

He rubbed his hands over his face. "No. I did not tell her how I feel. It doesn't much matter how I feel. She doesn't feel the same. She doesn't want me to tell her anything at the moment and especially not how I feel about her. She could barely look me in the eye."

Gigi B chuckled. "I wonder, do boys ever get smarter?"

"Really? I've gone from Greek god to dumb as a box of rocks in the course of this conversation?"

"Now, don't go getting upset. It's not you. In my experience, men usually don't catch on to these things. I want you to think about something for a minute. When Katie's been mad at you, I mean mad, has she ever backed off?"

Nathan didn't try to stop his grin. He loved it when Kate stood toe to toe with him. Her chin would rise, and her shoulders would be straight and stiff. It didn't matter that he was bigger.

She would give him the fiercest looks and refuse to back down. "No, ma'am. She hasn't."

"So, what makes you think she's mad now? You're not dealing with mad, son. You're dealing with conflict. Katie's a smart girl most times, but in this, she can't see the truth. And the truth is she's as much in love with you as you are with her."

"I never said I was in love with Kate."

She threw her hands in the air, shaking them in front of her as she addressed the sky. "Do they think we're blind?" She leveled him with a single look. "You do not have to tell me you're in love with her. I can see perfectly well that you are. And I can see it with equal clarity that she's in love with you too. She wouldn't be wrestling with the past if her heart wasn't trying to look to the future. Besides, I think Katie's wrestling days are coming to an end. Now might be the perfect time to lay the future out in front of her one more time."

"And if she says no?"

One shoulder raised. "Then, I'm wrong. But at least you've put it out there plain and simple."

Wrong is what he was worried about. "I'll think about it. For now, I believe we were both heading in to volunteer."

Nathan took her arm and walked her up the sidewalk. He tried to push Gigi B's words to the back of his mind as he held the door for her. The time to talk with Kate might be approaching, but right now, he had some work to do for those who couldn't do for themselves anymore.

"I THINK it's time to sign them both up for swimming lessons."

Anna glanced over her shoulder at Gabe and Sammy in the back seat of the jeep. "I think you're right. I've never seen two boys more eager to get into the pool."

Katie thought about the tear-filled break-down at the end of their swim time. "Or more obstinate about getting out."

"Thank you for taking us. It was the perfect way to spend a sunny Saturday afternoon."

"You're welcome. I'm glad they enjoyed it as much as they did."

She didn't need to tell Anna part of the reason she'd been suggesting various activities the last few days was to keep her mind occupied. After seeing Nathan at the nursing home that Monday, her mind had been stuck in a "what if" rut. She couldn't let it go there. The only cure was keeping busy, but even that was temporary. The moment she slowed down, memories and wonderings flooded her mind. And since Sammy's cast had come off, it seemed a perfect time.

"Who's at the house?"

Katie looked where Anna pointed to a familiar truck. Her heart pounded as she pulled into her spot and put the jeep in park. What did he want? "It's Nathan."

Anna hopped out and turned to the boys in the back. "Okay, you two. Who's ready for ice cream and a movie?" She turned to Katie as she began unbuckling Gabe. "You go ahead and see what Nathan wants. I've got these two. Take all the time you need."

She wasn't sure if the offer was a favor or punishment for some wrong she'd forgotten. Anna's heart was in the right place. She couldn't hold it against her. "Thank you."

NATHAN WATCHED the exchange at the Jeep from his place on the front step. Before Anna even had the boys out of the Jeep, Kate was on her way to meet him.

"What are you doing here?"

He was less than wanted, but it was now or never. Gigi B's words had eaten at him all week. "I think we need to talk."

"I don't think there's anything to talk about."

If Gigi B was right, it was her defenses talking, not her heart. "And I believe we do. I don't suppose I could talk you into going someplace a little more private? I'd hate to have an audience, even one as cute as the one coming up the walk."

Nathan smiled past Kate to Sammy, tugging on Anna's hand to reach them. "Hi, Sammy. How're you doing, little partner?"

Sammy launched himself into Nathan's arms. "We went swimming!"

He inhaled the faint scent of chlorine and children's watermelon shampoo. "I can tell. And what's this? Where did your cast go?"

Sammy held up his arm. Nathan bit back a smile at the strange tan line it left as a reminder of his injury.

"I got it took off. My arm's all better."

Nathan hugged him tightly. "I'm so happy to hear that."

"Mr. Nathan, can I ride horses too?"

Nathan grinned at the little boy nestled against his mother's legs. "I think we can work something out, if your mama says it's okay."

"Can I, Mama? Please? Sammy got to!"

The young woman rolled her eyes. "We'll talk about it later. I thought you two were ready for ice cream and movies."

Sammy left Nathan's arms to take Anna's hand. "I'm ready."

Gabe puffed out his chest. "I'm ready first."

"Nuh-uh."

"Uh-huh."

Anna shook her head. "It doesn't matter. You're both ready. Now let's go get that ice cream."

Nathan vacated his place on the steps and held open the door for Anna and the boys to pass by. When he turned, Kate watched him with a guarded look in her eyes.

"No."

"No, what?"

"No. I'm not going to go somewhere with you. But we can take a walk in the woods if you want. I guarantee no one will come barging after us demanding to ride a horse."

Nathan waved a hand, palm up in front of him. "Lead the way."

KATIE PICKED a stick out of her sandal for what seemed like the millionth time. She wasn't dressed appropriately for a hike. The path was easy enough, but the sandals were never a good idea in the woods. There were too many uncontrollable variables, sticks being the least of her worries. What possessed her to bring Nathan into the woods? Sure, they would have their privacy. But these woods were her sanctuary. Did she want to discuss whatever they were about to discuss in the place where she usually found peace? They could turn back, but that would only delay the inevitable. It was better to keep moving forward.

In keeping with her overall lack of judgment, Katie led Nathan to the waterfall. She sat at the edge, folding her legs in front of her. There was no way she would strip off her sandals and dangle her feet in the water, no matter how refreshing it might be. That was way too comfortable. She had a feeling she knew where the conversation was headed, and she had to keep her wits about her.

Nathan sat beside her with his legs stretched out in front of him and leaned back on his forearms. He took in the view before speaking. "It's beautiful here." His chest rose and fell as he took in and released a deep breath. "And peaceful. Do you come here often?"

She picked at a blade of grass growing through the cracks in the rock. "Not as much as I used to. Growing up, I came here every chance I got. I could think here, and I could cool down after fighting with my mom."

"If I remember correctly, that happened a lot, didn't it?"

"More often than I care to admit. Mom was particular, and it often ran counter to her daughter's freer spirit. I don't know if you recall this, but I had a pretty hot temper back then."

His eyes widened, and his mouth dropped open. "No. You don't say. I could never imagine you with a temper. You're so sweet and reserved."

She smacked his arm. "You don't have to be a smart aleck. I admit it. I have my issues. My temper is one I've tried hard to overcome. Sometimes it still gets the best of me."

He looked honestly chagrined. "I'm sorry. You were open with me, and I shouldn't have poked fun at you. My mama taught me better than that, but the lesson must not have stuck."

"It's fine. Anyway, I'd come down here to cool off. Most times, my dad would give me some time and then follow me down here. He'd sit here with me and talk it out before leaving me to think and pray. That's actually how I met Austin."

His brow rose. "Really? He was out wandering your woods or something?"

"I'd just come home from Bloomington to care for my mom after a fall. I ran smack into him on the sidewalk. Barely said hi, I was so wrapped up in being furious with Mom. I came down here and started working through things. I heard someone approach and assumed it was Dad. I vented without even looking behind me. You can't imagine how embarrassed I was to find out I was airing all my dirty family laundry to a complete stranger."

"At least he was a pastor. He was probably used to hearing stuff like that."

"Only I didn't know that until later. I felt betrayed. Since someone I thought I loved had betrayed me right before coming home. I decided I wanted nothing to do with Austin and his friendship."

"But he won you over, and it was smooth sailing until his death."

She snorted. "Not hardly. He'd just started falling for me when my ex-fiancé came begging me to take him back. I did and left Austin without even a good-bye."

"Ouch."

"Yeah. The guy I went back to Bloomington with proved that saying about a leopard not changing his spots. I was devastated again. Even after God got hold of me and changed my heart, it took some time before Austin and I ended up together. But after that, yeah, it was good. We had disagreements, but we loved God first and then each other with everything we had."

Katie wiped tears from her eyes. "I miss him so much."

She felt Nathan's arm settle over her shoulders. "I know you do."

"Does it bother you to hear about him?"

The weight of his arm lifted from her shoulders. He cupped her chin with his hand and turned her face to his. "Kate, I need you to look at me when I tell you this. I know you've loved before. You and Austin had a blessed godly marriage for the short time you had it. Your life with Austin is part of who you are today. Sammy is here because of that love, and Sammy needs to know all about his father. You can't deny that part of yourself, and I would never want you to. I expect you'll always miss Austin, and you're right to do so."

She sniffed. "So, you understand why I can't have a future with you?"

The shadow of a sad smile crossed his lips. "That's where I think you're wrong, sweetheart. I don't think you loving Austin keeps you from a future with me. I think you're doing that all on your own. You're afraid if you make room to love me, you'll lose the love you had for him. But that isn't how love works."

"Why not?"

"Because you don't have a limited amount of love at your

disposal. You don't have to take from Austin to give it to me. I know you're an only child, but try to look at it from my perspective. My parents had Tonya and me. When Tonya came along, they didn't give her part of the love they'd given me before she was born. They loved both of us with everything they had. They loved her because she was Tonya. But they loved me because I was me. We didn't have to be the same, and we didn't have to compete for a limited amount of love from them. If you and Austin had another baby, you wouldn't love Sammy less, would you?"

"Never."

"And the new baby wouldn't be loved less than Sammy?"

"Of course not."

"You get what I'm saying. My question for you is, why are you treating love like it works any differently for a man and a woman than it does for a parent and child?"

"It's not the same kind of love."

"True. But being a different type of love doesn't mean it works any differently. You can and should continue to love Austin. That love isn't going to have the chance to grow and mature through shared experiences, but it's going to stay part of you forever. When special days come, and even on the ordinary ones, you're going to miss him. You can't lose that by letting yourself fall in love with me. What we have will be different, but it will be as real and full as what you and Austin shared. I'm not out to replace him. If that's all you want, then I'm wrong. I'm not the man for you. I have no interest in being a stand-in. But I know there's a place for both of us in your life if you'll only give it a chance."

She wound a curl through her fingers and watched him. What he said made sense, but did that make it true? Could she continue to love Austin while loving Nathan too? "How do you know?"

"I can't tell you from personal experience, because you're the only woman I've ever loved. But I've watched it happen."

"When?"

He watched her like he expected her to know the answer. When she kept still, he continued. "I've watched it happen with us. When our friendship grew into something more, I know neither of us said it, but it was there. I only waited because I knew you weren't ready to hear it. And you weren't ready to admit it to yourself, but I know you loved me too. And that's how I know there's room for both loves in your life. You never stopped loving Austin even though you'd started loving me."

He brushed a tear from her cheek with his thumb. She captured his hand against her cheek when he would have dropped it to his side. She closed her eyes. How could she know for certain? Was she allowing fear to keep her from love in one more area of her life? Could she keep her love for Austin and still find a future with Nathan? Did his reasoning even hold up? Did she already love him?

In reliving the beginnings of her love with Austin, Katie was reminded of what love looked like for them. What she had with Nathan was different. As teens, they were flirty and linked together through her friendship with his sister. As adults, their childhood friendship provided a solid base to grow from. She couldn't deny their friendship had deepened over time any more than she could deny her attraction to the man he'd become. But love? Yes. It was different than what she'd shared with Austin, but for all the differences, it was no less love. She loved Nathan. She loved him, and she had to decide if she was willing to put herself at risk for another chance to go through life with love at her side.

Katie's eyes flew open as Nathan's soft lips brushed hers. In one fluid motion, he stood and looked down at her.

"You know my heart. It's yours if you want it, but I'm not going to beg and plead for you to accept it. You have to want it for yourself. I'll go now and leave you to decide. But, before I go, I'm going to say something in case I don't have the chance to in the future. Kate, I love you."

With that, he headed for the trail leading home. Watching his retreating back, Katie imagined what it would mean for this to be his final goodbye. Could she let him walk out of her life forever? The thought alone made her throat tight. *Oh God, give me the strength to love without limits. I'm afraid, but fear is not from You, and it has nothing to do with love. Help me be brave.*

She scrambled up from where she sat and rushed across the rock to catch him on the path. "Nathan, wait!"

She huffed in frustration as another stick lodged between her sandal and toes making her pause in her pursuit. She bent to pick it out. She took off before she was fully standing again and ran head-first into Nathan's solid chest.

He caught her arms in his hands and helped steady her before letting go. Laughter showed in his eyes, though he almost successfully contained a grin. "You called."

"I don't want to go through life knowing I gave up the opportunity to have someone who loves me walking beside me through it all. I don't want to lose you. You're right about everything. I love you, Nathan Phillips."

He lifted her from the ground and swung her around before setting her feet back on the path. He pulled her to his chest with one arm around her waist. For the first time, she looked up at him without fear and without hiding the depth of what she felt for him. His free hand cradled her cheek as he lowered his lips to hers.

His forehead rested against hers as he broke the kiss, his voice thick with emotion. "Sweetheart, you don't ever have to worry about losing me. God willing, I'm yours as long as you want me."

Katie smiled. "How about we make that forever?"

Epilogue

Three Years Later

Katie sighed as Nathan's arms came around her expanding waist to rest on her protruding belly. The baby nestled safely inside kicked in response to his touch.

"I don't think I'll ever get over that."

She leaned back into him. "It's just for you. She doesn't put on a show like that for anyone else. I think we're getting ready to meet a real daddy's girl."

"You two want to stop with the googly eyes already and come help us set the table. We're supposed to be celebrating, you know."

Katie laughed at Anna's description and moved from her husband's arms. "We're coming. Keep your shirt on."

Nathan took a bowl of potato salad from the young woman's hands. "Let me help with that."

Erin rolled her eyes as she joined them at the table. "Oh yes, you're her hero now. You carried some potato salad."

Paul poked her in the ribs. "They didn't ask you to get involved."

Gigi B put in her two cents from the other end of the picnic table. "When did any woman in my family need to be asked to get involved?"

The laughter and banter continued as the group set out the fixings for their picnic. Katie sighed. It was a beautiful day to celebrate the opening of Cal's Haven of Hope with a family picnic. And looking around the table, that's exactly what each person was to her, even though there wasn't one blood relation.

"I'd like to say something before we round up the kids and start eating."

Everyone quieted for Katie's announcement. "When Nathan and I married two years ago, and I moved to the ranch, I wasn't sure what to do with Mom and Dad's house. God surprised me by letting me know. I was already using it the way He intended." She smiled at Anna. "Though it wasn't named at the time, you and Gabe will always be the first family helped through Cal's Haven of Hope. I know without a doubt, Dad would have loved you and this ministry. I'm so thankful God brought you to story time and placed you so firmly in my heart. He's brought you into His family and ours, and I look forward to the years ahead as you serve as the house parent for other girls who find themselves in the same situation you were when we met. With God's help, we can look forward to offering help and healing to young mothers and their children who have no one else to go to."

Nathan stood beside her. "Thank you all for your part in helping this ministry get started. You are truly our family. Now go ahead and fill your plates while Kate and I round up the kids."

Never needing encouragement to eat, plates began to fill while Nathan and Katie made their way to the playhouse. Their son's voice could be heard from the rock wall.

"No, Joy. You're too little."

Gabe's voice chimed in. "Yeah. Rock walls are for big kids like us."

Nathan and Katie rounded the structure in time to see the

three-year-old's lip puff out in a pout. They had approximately five seconds to divert Joy's attention and save them all from tears. Erin and Paul's daughter could turn them on in seconds, and when she did, Gabe and Sammy became putty in her toddler hands.

Nathan scooped her up. "Hey there, Miss Joy. Are you hungry?"

She nodded, still looking longingly at the rock wall.

"Lunch is ready, and I think your mama has some chicken nuggets for you. You, Gabe, and Sammy head on over there. Okay?"

Another nod, and Nathan placed her between the boys. Each one took a hand, and together they led her in the direction of the table.

Katie watched them go. "They're going to be great friends, aren't they?"

"The best."

"We better get over there ourselves, or we may miss out on the fried chicken."

Nathan grabbed her hand and pulled her back. She pulled, but he held tight. "I can think of something I'd like a little more than chicken. I want a kiss from my beautiful wife."

She pursed her lips. "Well, your beautiful wife would like some chicken. How about that?"

She smiled when one brow lifted over his eyes. She knew that glint well, along with the lopsided smile that came with it. She'd first seen it on her seventeenth birthday. "Nathan Phillips, we have guests."

"No, sweetheart, we have family over there who understand that I love my wife. But I see you're going to fight this. You leave me no choice. Kate Phillips, I dare you to kiss me."

Katie laughed. "You shouldn't dare a woman to kiss you. Didn't your mama teach you better than that?"

He pulled her into his arms. "Sure, she did. But some lessons didn't seem to take."

Any response she might have had fled as his lips covered hers.

Letter to the Reader

Dear Reader,

Thank you for joining me for Katie's story. It's not always been an easy one, but I hope this final installment brought Katie a satisfying conclusion for you to enjoy.

The inclusion of Cal's dementia in book two and the toll it takes on Katie in book three came at a time when my own family was dealing with the same issues, though they hadn't progressed to a completely life-changing stage when I introduced the possibility in Grasping Hope. While the events Katie faced in dealing with her father are not actual events that happened as we cared for my grandmother, they do accurately portray some of the more prevalent symptoms of dementia we struggled to cope with in daily life with my grandmother. His story also highlights some of the real choices caregivers are faced with every day.

For those who haven't dealt with dementia and Alzheimer's disease, I liken it to being on a roller coaster in complete darkness. Your mind and body can't prepare for what's around the next bend or drop because it never sees them coming. It's tiring in every way possible and on a deeper level than you imagine possible.

If you're a caregiver, I encourage you to find a support network. Whether it's an official support group or trusted friends, find people who will lift you up in prayer and help ease your load. Be good to yourself. The choices you have to make in dealing with this disease are not easy ones to make. Cover them in prayer, and then move in the direction God leads. Whether you care for them on your own, get daily in-home help, or have to make the tough choice to relinquish daily care to a nursing home, the love you show makes a difference to them and those who witness it.

For those who aren't dealing with these issues, I pray you never have to face them. But I'm sure most of you know or have known of someone who does. You can live out God's love to those facing these circumstances. Daily prayer support is invaluable. An offer to sit with their loved one for an hour can give a much needed break. Offering to do tasks like grocery shopping that become increasingly difficult as the disease progresses ease the load for a caregiver whose time and energy is already stretched thin.

Thank you again for joining in Katie's story with me. I pray it has entertained, encouraged, and challenged you. For more stories of faith, both mine and others, check out my blog at www. heathergreer.com. And remember to live out God's love every day.

Blessings,
Heather Greer

Also by Heather Greer

Katie McGowan left her parents and their faith behind years ago.
However, when faced with a devastating betrayal, Katie is ready to go
back to Carbondale, Illinois to help her elderly parents despite their
tempestuous relationship. Drained by the constant friction, Katie finds
emotional support and encouragement in Austin. His practical, simple
faith speaks to Katie, and she finds herself yearning for a new
connection to God. As their friendship grows, so does the attraction
between Katie and Austin. Before her fledgling faith and thoughts of
romance have a chance to take root, Katie's cheating fiancé returns,
remorseful and promising change. Can her tentative faith strengthen
their past love? And if her heart breaks again, will Katie's journey to
faith end before it has really begun?

Katie McGowan knows her fears are irrational. They're also beyond her control. Her mind says her fiancé is faithful, but the betrayal of her past love ignites a fear stronger than her trust. Attempts to overcome it are unsuccessful. Nothing banishes her panic attacks for good. Dreading Austin's response if he finds out about her struggle to trust, Katie hides the truth nearly destroying their relationship.

It takes a lesson in hope to start healing. Katie is released from the nightmare holding her captive to enjoy the blessings God has given. But when tragedies change her life forever, Katie's understanding of hope is challenged. Unresolved anger and disappointment leave Katie doubting the sincerity of her beliefs. Desperate to prove her faith and minimize her failure as a believer, Katie buries her feelings beneath all the right words.

When she's faced with losing everything, will Katie abandon her hope or cling to the lifeline God has given?

Also from Scrivenings Press

Hope needs more hope. Faith needs more faith. .

They both need a whole lot of love.

Two sisters. One summer. Multiple problems.

Younger sister Hope has lost her job, her car, and her boyfriend all in one day. Her well-laid plans for life have gone sideways, as has her hope in God.

Older sister Faith is finally getting her dream-come-true after years of struggles and prayers. But when her mom talks her into letting Hope move in for the summer, will the stress turn her dream into a nightmare? Is her faith in God strong enough to handle everything?

For two sisters who haven't gotten along in years, this summer together could be a disaster, or it could lead them to a closer relationship with each other and God. Can they overcome all life is throwing at them? Or is this going to destroy their relationship for good?

Faith and Hope by Amy Anguish.

A battered heart needs healing.

A community needs rescuing.

A chartered course needs redirecting.

College history instructor, Josie Daniels is good at mothering her three brothers, volunteering in her community, and getting over broken hearts, but meeting aloof, hotshot attorney Ches Windham challenges her nurturing, positive-thinking spirit.

Josie longs to help Ches find his true purpose, but as his hidden talents and true personality emerge. Will she be able to withstand his potent charms, or will she lose her heart in the process?

A rising star in his law firm, Ches Windham is good at keeping secrets.

He's always been the good son, following his father's will to become an attorney and playing the game for a fast track to partnering with a law firm. Lately, though his life's path has lost whatever luster it had—all because of his unlikely, and unacceptable, friendship with Josie. He struggles between the life he's prepared for and the one calling to him now. Opposing his father has never been an option, and spending time with Josie can't be one. The more he's with her, however, the more he wants to be.

When a crisis tarnishes his golden future and secrets are revealed, Ches is forced to reexamine the trajectory of his life. Will he choose the path his father hammered out for him or the path that speaks to his heart?

Forever Music by Hope Toler Dougherty.

Scrivenings
PRESS
Quench your thirst for story.
www.ScriveningsPress.com

Stay up-to-date on your favorite books and authors

with our free e-newsletters. Visit us at ScriveningsPress.com to sign up.

Made in the USA
Columbia, SC
28 September 2020